A
CAGE
SO
GILDED

Ingrid Seymour is a *USA Today* bestselling author of over fifty novels. She writes new adult fiction in a variety of genres, including fantasy romance, urban fantasy, paranormal romance, sci-fi, and high fantasy – all with badass heroines and irresistible heroes. She used to work as a software engineer at a Fortune 500 company, but now writes full-time and loves every minute of it. She lives in Birmingham, Alabama with her husband, two kids, and a cat named Ossie.

Instagram: **@ingrid_seymour**
X: **@Ingrid_Seymour**
TikTok: **@ ingridseymour**
Facebook: **/IngridSeymourAuthor**

A CAGE SO GILDED

II

INGRID SEYMOUR

HEADLINE
ETERNAL

First published in 2023 by PenDreams

First published in Great Britain in this paperback edition in 2024
by HEADLINE ETERNAL
An imprint of HEADLINE PUBLISHING GROUP

1

Cataloguing in Publication Data is available from the British Library

ISBN 978 1 0354 1701 8

Typeset in 12/15pt EB Garamond by Jouve (UK), Milton Keynes

Printed and bound in Great Britain by Clays Ltd, Elcograf S.p.A.

HEADLINE PUBLISHING GROUP
An Hachette UK Company
Carmelite House
50 Victoria Embankment
London EC4Y 0DZ

www.headlineeternal.com
www.headline.co.uk
www.hachette.co.uk

Sometimes, it's okay to let Mr. Hyde out.
Those who truly love you will understand.

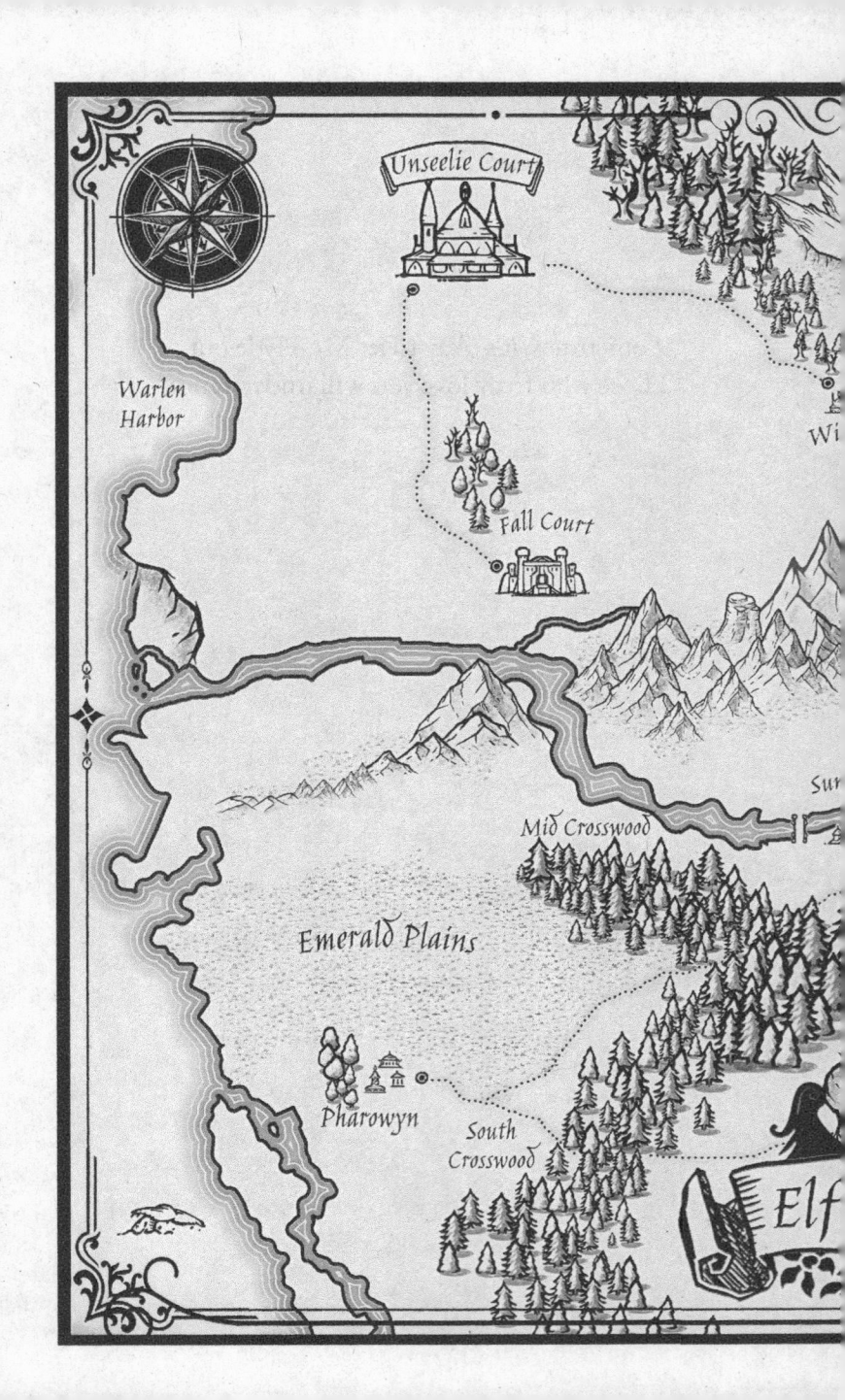

CHAPTER 1

WÖLFE

The fool would have let her go, would have sacrificed everything for nothing.

Not me.

She was mine.

Daniella Sunder belonged to me. I made her mine at dawn, and after a taste of her, there could be no one else. She now bore my mark, and she would bear it forever.

DANIELLA

Kalyll let me go home, but the beast came back for me.

When he took me, I had no chance to say anything, do anything. He rendered me unconscious and then . . .

Warmth bathed one side of my body as I slowly awoke. A spot in my neck hurt, the pressure point he'd used to make me lose consciousness.

Tender hands caressed my hair, pushed it away from my face. I was afraid to open my eyes, to discover where I was and why.

"Wake up," he said, his voice an octave lower than his already normal deep timbre.

Holding my breath in fear, I did as he asked.

He—not Kalyll—was kneeling next to me, his face sharp and angular with wildness. He smiled when our gazes met, pointed canines flashing his satisfaction.

I took a quick second to assess my surroundings. He had laid me atop a pile of furs in front of a wide fireplace brimming with crackling logs. The furniture's medieval look and the stone walls told me I was back in Elf-hame.

"You're safe, *melynthi*. You're with me." He kissed me, his possessive lips sending a jolt of desire through me.

I reined in the instant rush of passion he unleashed in me and pushed it down, down. It was a monumental effort, but I managed. Awkwardly, I got up from the floor, skirting around him.

"Why . . . why am I here?" I asked, casting my eyes around to better assess my situation.

He remained kneeling on the furs, his cobalt eyes shining with the warm fire as they roved over the length of my body. A salacious smile stretched his lips.

When he took me from my bed, I'd been wearing nothing but my bra and panties. Feeling self-conscious, I took several steps back and hid behind an armchair. Venturing another quick look at my surroundings, I saw the room was dominated by a massive canopy bed draped with gray curtains. All the simple but elegant décor suggested this was a rich male's chamber. I marked two sets of windows, both shuttered.

"Shy, are we? You weren't so bashful in the clearing as I recall." He chuckled, then rose to his full height and proceeded to remove his jacket, a mid-thigh velvet affair with a wide lapel and gold trim. He discarded it on the armchair in front of me, then took off his shirt and offered it to me.

I snatched it from his hand, doing my best to ignore his muscular torso and to shove aside the memories of how it had felt to touch all those perfect muscles, to trace his tattoos. I quickly pulled the shirt over my head and stuffed my arms in. The hem came to my knees, and I had to push back the sleeves to free my hands.

"Thank you," I said reluctantly, resisting the temptation to sniff the fabric and enjoy his masculine scent.

"Don't think I'll let you keep that on for too long." His face was full of sexual hunger as he said this, leaving me no doubt of what he intended to do.

He walked to a bureau, where he poured two amber drinks from a crystal bottle. He offered me one, then took a sip of his. I did the same, hoping to settle my nerves. It was the same expensive Scotch I'd tasted in Imbermore, Glenfiddich, or something like that. Peering over the rim of the glass, I watched him.

Two gold chains hung low on his chest, and rings adorned his fingers—two things I had never seen him wear. His midnight blue hair was unbound and wild, and there seemed to be something restless trapped in him, something that made him pace the length of an intricate rug in front of the bed.

"What am I doing here, Kalyll?" I asked.

He whirled. "No." He pointed a finger at me. "Not Kalyll. I'm not that weak male."

Oh, God.

What was going on? Some sort of Dr. Jekyll and Mr. Hyde situation? A rush of panic washed over me as I felt the truth of it. I'd already been thinking of him as something different, someone other than the Kalyll I knew. Before Mount Ruin, even when he'd been half wild, it had still been him when he was in his human shape. But this . . . I didn't recognize him.

The demon energy I'd used to save his life . . . I had to entwine it with his heart in order to bring him back from the dead. I'd hoped there would be no consequences. I'd hoped the prince would be strong enough to keep that evil force at bay, but my hopes had been in vain. Was Kalyll even in there anymore?

What if Kalyll was gone and some hell dweller now possessed his body? I nearly started sobbing at the thought. He couldn't be lost.

"Who are you then?" I asked, fearing the answer. "A demon?"

He shook his head and waved a hand in the air.

"Not a demon, though part of one is in here." He placed a hand on his bare chest and slid it across one of his pecs, causing my mouth to go dry. "It was always there, if dormant."

I tore my eyes away—the male was a walking temptation, and it didn't help that I'd had a taste of him and knew how good he felt. I tried to focus on his words: *not a demon.* That was a good thing. Maybe it meant there was still hope.

"I must thank you," he continued. "This feels wonderful, freeing. He has so many . . . principles. It's stifling."

"If you're not Kalyll, what should I call you?"

"I don't know. Whatever you want. It doesn't matter."

I frowned.

"How about . . . *More*? You'll be saying that a lot soon." He chuckled, a deep rumble in his chest and a lecherous look in his eyes that immediately had my desire rising like a tide.

"I don't like your sense of humor."

"Are you sure about that?" His nostrils flared as he sniffed the air. "I smell a hint of arousal."

"You're mistaken."

He didn't argue. He only raised an eyebrow, letting me know my denial was useless. I couldn't lie to him. Not about that. His senses were too sharp.

"Call me . . ." He thought for a moment. "Wölfe."

"Wölfe?"

"Yes. I liked being the wolf. Such wanton savagery. It's a shame he's gone."

Relief nearly drove me to my knees. He couldn't shift anymore. At least there was that. The beast had been completely irrational—not that I had any proof that he, Wölfe, was much better.

I set the glass down on a table behind me. "Okay, Wölfe, tell me why I'm here?"

"Isn't it obvious?" He looked at me as if I were stupid.

I played along. "No. I'm supposed to be back home. The deal was that I would help you, and then you would let me go."

"*I* never made a deal."

"I need to talk to Kalyll then. Where is he?"

"Not here, obviously." He gestured with a hand around the room.

"When can I see him?"

"Never."

I shook my head. Did that mean Wölfe had complete control and Kalyll couldn't fight his way back? Before, the darkness used to lose its hold as soon as the sun came out. Was that not the case anymore? Dawn couldn't come fast enough. I need to know.

"I can't stay here," I said. "My life is back in my realm."

Wölfe walked closer, came around the armchair, and set his glass next to mine. "You belong to me, and you will stay here."

I shook my head adamantly. "I don't belong to anyone."

"You're mistaken, Melynthi."

Melynthi? He had called me that before. What did it mean? I was about to ask, but he wrapped an arm around my waist and pulled me to him with such force that I nearly lost my breath.

"You are mine," he said. "Body and soul."

What? Had he gone crazy?

"We can't be together," I said. "You're engaged. You have to worry about the fate of your kingdom."

"Again, none of that has anything to do with me. Those are Kalyll's worries. He'll take care of them."

I paused, latching on to his words. Did he mean Kalyll would be in charge at some point? Or did he mean he would pretend to be Kalyll and take on his princely duties? And in either option, where did that leave me?

Voice trembling, I asked, "So Kalyll will marry Kryn's sister. Is that what you're saying?"

He shrugged and let me go. I stumbled backward and had to hold on to the chair. A million questions whirled inside my head. I did my best to wrangle them and ask the most important one.

"And what happens to me in that scenario? What am I supposed to do?"

"You can live here," he said. "Have everything you want."

"Here? In this room?"

"Everything you could possibly desire is here." He threw a pair of double doors open and gestured inside. "Clothes, jewelry, shoes, hats, anything." He marched to the other end of the room and opened another set of doors. "Thousands of books. You like to read, don't you?"

When I did nothing but stare at him, he swaggered in my direction, grabbed me by the arm, and shoved me into the second room. I extricated my arm from his tight grip and rubbed the spot, letting my eyes rove over a three-story room full of books, a library such as I'd never seen. There were shelves upon shelves, each at least twelve-feet high and equipped with sliding ladders. Several tables with ornate lamps and settees bedecked with blankets and pillows sat in the middle of the room. A massive chandelier hung from the ceiling, glowing with fairy lights that cast a perfect glow for relaxed reading. Three reading nooks sat under shuttered windows. The place was a librarian's dream.

"Best of all," Wölfe threw his arms open, "you'd have me." He raised an eyebrow and smiled as if he were offering me a slice of paradise.

I said nothing. Instead, I walked to a window and tried to open it, but the shutters were latched, securely locked. I ran around the massive space and checked several closed doors. They were also barred.

My blood running cold, I turned to face him. "It's a pretty cage you offer me," I said, my voice sounding as cold as I felt inside.

Wölfe's right eye twitched.

"You can't keep me prisoner." I turned around and pounded on the door. "Please, somebody help me. Let me out of here."

"No one can hear you, Daniella. Don't waste your time."

"You can't do this. You can't."

"I can do whatever I want."

"Kalyll would never. He's better than you."

He growled and rushed at me, his hands gripping my shoulders and shaking me. I screamed in pain as my skin broke under both my collarbones. Wölfe pulled back and let me go. He stared at the razor-sharp, black claws that had sprung from his fingertips. Blood seeped into his shirt, growing on the white cotton.

"I didn't mean to do that," he said, trembling, fangs flashing as he spoke. "Just . . . heal yourself," he added, offhand, as if it was no big deal, as if he could do anything to me because I could heal my own wounds.

Despite the pain, I didn't use my healing magic, and instead, allowed the blood to keep flowing, the stain a dark crimson rose that kept opening up, blooming wider and wider. When I didn't do anything to relieve my own pain, he grunted and pulled me out of the library.

He took me to a lavish washroom almost as big as the bedroom. There, he procured a washcloth which he wetted in a golden vessel sink. He pulled the oversized shirt out of the way and dabbed at one of the wounds. I stood stiffly as he cleaned it and then worked on the second one. He did so tenderly, a worried expression shaping his features.

Still, that same coldness ran through my veins.

When he was done, he threw the washcloth in the sink and planted a kiss on my neck. His mouth trailed a warm path along my jawline, then met with mine. My lips didn't move.

He pulled back, his eyes dark, angry. "You have to want me," he said.

I said nothing.

"You made me, Daniella. I am here because of you."

My heart ached at the truth of his words. "I only wanted to save Kalyll."

"And you did, but in the process, you also got me."

"I don't want you." There was no emotion in my words, but despite that, the weight of their truth was undeniable.

Wölfe growled and whirled away from me. "Ah, but you will. You will. You have no choice, Melynthi."

Stomping and cursing, he left the washroom. I stood there, gathering the shirt around my shoulders and wrapping trembling arms around my torso, lonely tears streaking down my cheeks. I didn't know how long I stood there, but when I walked out into the bedroom, he wasn't there. Padding silently on bare feet, I checked the library, but he wasn't there either. Gone.

I hadn't heard any doors open and close, so I didn't feel at ease until I checked every square foot of the large space and convinced myself that he had truly left. With that knowledge in mind, I checked every locked door and window, tugging on them and calling out for help.

Exhaustion weighed on me, and hunger gnawed at my stomach. I still hadn't fully recovered from healing Kalyll. Feeling numb, I lay in the middle of the enormous bed and stared off into space.

My cage was gilded, but it was still a cage.

CHAPTER 2
DANIELLA

The *clink* of silverware woke me up. I sat up straight. The smell of food tickled my nose. There was a slight whirring sound somewhere in the room that was vaguely familiar. I pulled closer to the edge of the bed and peeked around the heavy curtain tied around one of the bedposts.

A tiny blue figure flew back and forth in front of the fireplace, leaving gold dust floating in the air, and setting a table with a luxurious breakfast.

"Larina!" I jumped out of bed, startling the pixie so hard that she nearly smacked into the ceiling as she flew upward.

"Oh, dear." She held a miniature hand to her chest. "You scared me half to the grave. Good morning, Lady Sunder." She inclined her head as she flew back down. "I have brought you breakfast." She smiled pleasantly.

Larina was here. Valeriana's pixie playmate when we were in Imbermore. Was that where Kalyll—Wölfe—had brought me?

"Larina, where is . . . the prince?"

"I don't know, Lady Sunder."

Had Wölfe gone back to being Kalyll? It felt like my only hope, except I had no idea if things worked as they had before.

What if Wölfe was in charge *all* the time? If that was the case, I was screwed. Or was I?

"What about Jeondar? Please, can you get him for me?"

Her smile disappeared, and she fluttered down to the mantle above the wide fireplace. She stood next to a clock that ticked away the seconds. There, she shifted from foot to foot, looking uncomfortable.

"Prince Jeondar is not here, Lady Sunder. He is in Imbermore."

"Wait, what? Then . . . where are we?"

"Elyndell, Lady Sunder."

"The Seelie Court capital."

"Yes. At the palace."

The palace? I was at the Vine Tower? I'd only ever seen it in paintings. It lay at the center of the city, a tall white tower with vines crawling up its sides and getting lost in its many windows. It was where the royal family lived.

"But how?" I asked.

Just last night, we'd been on the outskirts of Mount Ruin, which was about two weeks from Imbermore, the Summer Court capital, which in turn was that far from Elyndell.

Witchlights! Did the demon power in Wölfe allow him to open portals to travel anywhere? Because demons were the only ones who could do that. No one else—not even the most powerful Skews—had the ability to instantly travel from one point to another within the same realm.

"How did the prince get here so fast?" I pressed.

Larina pulled on her gossamer dress, a skimpy shift that hung on her small, blue-skinned frame. She was no taller than a pencil. "Um, I don't know if I'm supposed to say."

"Did he order you not to?"

She shook her head.

"Then." I put my hands up and shrugged.

"Um, he's using veil magic."

"Oh."

I should've thought of that option. He was utilizing a transfer token to go to my realm, then wish himself back to Elf-hame to whatever location he wanted.

"He appeared in Imbermore last night," Larina continued. "Took me to your realm, then brought me here and told me to make sure you had everything you needed."

"Where is he now? Here?"

The pixie shook her head. "Like I said, I don't know."

I thought for a moment and decided he must be back with his party—Kryn, Jeondar, Cylea, Arabis, and Silver (his traitor friend and prisoner)—still on his way back from Mount Ruin. Did that mean he was keeping up appearances? When would he be back?

After sundown, my logic told me.

"So . . . I got your breakfast," the pixie said, snapping me back to the moment. She pointed at the food on the low table that sat between the two armchairs by the fireplace. "And I filled the wardrobe with garments that will fit you."

"I don't need any of these things, Larina. I need to go back home. Can you please let me out of this room?"

Larina picked at her dress. "I can't, Lady Sunder."

"Yes, you can. You have to."

She shook her head. "My prince gave me an order, and I must obey him."

"That was *not* your prince."

13

"What do you mean? Of course that was him."

"I can tell from your expression that you're not so sure about that."

She bit her lower lip but said nothing.

I took a step closer and craned my neck to look at her better, wishing she would come down from the mantle.

"He needs help," I said. "Something, a dark force, has taken over him." I was careful with my words. The future of Kalyll's realm depended on keeping his affliction secret from everyone. He had inherited a shadowdrifter curse from his father, a father who was not the Seelie King. If anyone found out he wasn't the king's legitimate son, it could spell war.

"He said you might try to lie to me." Larina looked hurt, as if I owed her nothing but sincerity.

"The way you lied to me about Queen Belasha's necklace?" I demanded.

"I hated to do it, but it was an order from her."

"Do you have no mind of your own? Would you kill your mother if either Prince Kalyll or Queen Belasha ordered you to do it?"

She bristled, her wings fluttering harshly, a clear sign of her anger. "Of course I have a mind of my own, and right now, it's telling me that you're a human I cannot trust."

I drew in a breath to let her have it, but I bit my tongue in time. It wouldn't be to my advantage to make her angry.

"I'm sorry, Larina. I didn't mean to yell at you. I'm just very upset. I'm sure you can tell I'm here against my will. The prince—who is definitely not himself—locked me up and won't let me go back home."

"I'm sure he has his reasons."

What could I tell her to make her understand? I thought for a moment and realized I had to make this about her beloved prince, not me.

"All I want to do is help Prince Adanorin. At night, he changes. Those dark forces . . . they take over him and make him act in ways the prince would never act. Don't you think all of this is strange?"

I could see the conflict in her expression. She knew exactly what I was talking about. She'd noticed a difference, and how could she not?

Kalyll and Wölfe were like oil and water.

She flew off the mantle, slowly floating away.

"Where are you going?"

"I must leave, Lady Sunder. Enjoy your breakfast."

"Please, don't go. Hear me out."

She shook her head and floated toward what looked like a tiny door close to the ceiling.

"At least do one thing for me," I urged, just as she was about to slip through the hole.

She paused and glanced back.

"Pay attention to him," I begged. "You'll see the signs. He's your prince, and if you want to do what's best for him, there would be no better service than to alert Jeondar or Kryn of what's happening to him."

Larina disappeared through the hole, leaving me alone. I stomped my foot in frustration. I had to find a way out of here. If I didn't, I would go stir-crazy. But first things first, I needed to get some food in my stomach.

The breakfast was lavish, and to my surprise and delight, it included coffee. Kalyll had once told me that he enjoyed the brew and made a point to keep it at hand. It seemed he'd given the pixie some instructions on how to take care of me. I felt touched by the knowledge, even though I didn't want to be.

Because of him, I was a prisoner once more, and this time, the cage was more real than ever before. The first time, at least, his motivations had been noble. He'd wanted to keep his kingdom safe, wanted to prevent a war. Now, he was just being a selfish dick.

He'd implied that Kalyll would marry Kryn's sister in order to create an alliance that would prevent war, and yet, he wanted me here. Like what? His mistress? His sexual toy?

The damn jerk wanted to have his cake and eat it too.

After a breakfast of eggs, pastries, and fruit, I took a quick bath in the luxurious tub, trying not to enjoy the continually perfect water temperature and delicious-smelling soaps. The soft towel was also a treat, something from a five-star hotel, but its gentle touch against my skin was accompanied by the bitter taste of my captivity.

Once I was dressed in leggings, a matching tunic, and supple boots, I set to exploring with more care. Sunlight came in through narrow slits near the ceiling, giving me a better view of the rich rooms. There was no denying it . . . Wölfe had deposited me in the lap of luxury.

But even if the bindings were made of silken ribbons, they were still bindings.

I cleared my head and shook myself, getting my thoughts in order. I was in Elyndell, the Seelie Court capital, which was Kalyll's home. That meant I was likely in a castle of some sort, and castles always had secret passages, didn't they? Time to find one.

For the next hour, I poked anything that looked like a button, pulled anything that looked like a lever, inspected every wall, peered behind every painting and tapestry, and found nothing. The closest thing to a secret compartment was a cubbyhole next to the fireplace that held tongs, a sooty broom, a shovel, and a poker.

I held up the poker and glanced between it and the door. Wasting no time, I rushed to the door, shoved the tip between the door and the jamb, and leaned into it. I managed to get a bit of the metal tip into the gap, though not enough to get any leverage, and all I accomplished was to rip small pieces of wood that splintered and dropped to the floor.

Since that didn't work, I attacked the metal handle next, beating it with the blunt end of the poker. My bones shuddered with every blow. The sound of metal against metal reverberated through the room, but no matter how hard I hit the thing, it didn't budge in the least, which made me think it was probably reinforced with magic. I took to the hinges next, but it was the same. The window shutters followed. Same result. Wölfe had planned this well.

Angry and losing all my composure, I hurled the poker across the room. It hit a wall and clattered to the wooden floor, chipping a piece off, then sliding under the bed.

I nearly tore my hair out as angry tears streamed down my face. If no one helped me, I might end up trapped here for the rest of my life. I had to figure out a way to escape. Everything I'd attempted had yielded no effects except for one thing. I got on my hands and knees and retrieved the poker from under the bed. Even if it took me all day, I would chip away at the door one bit at a time. Jaw clenched with determination, I set to work, whittling pieces off by digging the metal point into that gap and leaning all my weight into it.

When my arms started hurting, I examined my progress. The wood was hard, but I'd managed to dig a hole about an inch deep. The problem was, it barely seemed like a dent.

"How thick is this fucking door?"

I worked for another long while, resting my achy arms every so often and healing the blisters that quickly formed on my fingers. A pile of wooden splinters lay on the floor, and yet I hadn't broken through. I was still at it when Larina came in through the hole by the ceiling.

"Lady Sunder, what are you doing?" she asked in a panic, peering at the indentation I'd carved and the debris at my feet.

"What do you think I'm doing?"

I jabbed the poker's tip into the hole over and over to illustrate my point, each blow as hard as I could manage.

"Please, stop. You're going to hurt yourself." She fluttered around me, fretting.

"What? Is your prince going to roast you alive if something happens to me?"

She didn't answer and simply continued to fly around in erratic patterns.

I whirled, holding the poker like a baseball bat. Anger took over me, and I swung, trying to knock her out of the air. I missed her by a mere inch. She quickly flew out of reach and looked at me with wide eyes.

"Oh, my God." I dropped the poker with a clatter and walked away from it. "I'm sorry. I'm sorry. I don't know what took over me. I don't do things like that. I heal people. I don't hurt them."

Larina watched me closely with a frown, as if she didn't believe a word I was saying. I collapsed in an armchair and buried my face in my hands.

"It's . . . time for your noon meal," the pixie said tentatively.

I glanced up and, for the first time, realized that the morning dishes were gone. They had magically disappeared at some point, and I hadn't noticed. I was still staring at the table when more dishes appeared, these loaded with a few different meat entrées, and a variety of vegetables and bread rolls.

"I'm not hungry," I said, sounding like a pouty child.

"You can eat when you are. The food will remain warm." She floated out through her tiny hole without another word.

I didn't eat. Instead, I continued chipping away at the door. I hammered and pried and carved until the light coming through the high windows dwindled. I'd labored with barely a thought in mind—my way of coping and staying sane—but as I noticed the hour on the mantle clock, I panicked. Quickly, I put away the poker and swept the debris under a rug, as if that would hide anything given the damage I inflicted on the door.

Cursing, I went into the bathroom and splashed my face with cold water, washing away the sweat. I also changed my tunic and rearranged my hair. After that, I stopped in front of the fireplace and ate some beef stew, dipping bread into the

INGRID SEYMOUR

delicious sauce. I had worked up quite the appetite while attacking the door and constantly using healing magic to remove the blisters. I needed to replenish my energy.

When I was done, I sat back, watching as the light retreated and shadows elongated. A few sconces came to life on their own. I wrung my hands, my heart pounding with a mixture of nerves and excitement. I hated myself for the latter.

Wölfe didn't come that night.

CHAPTER 3
DANIELLA

The next day passed in very much the same fashion as the last one. I doubled my progress on the door, but I still couldn't see through to the other side.

Every time Larina visited to bring food or ask if I needed something, she frowned at the door and shook her head. At some point, it occurred to me that she might use her magic to nullify my progress and set the door right, so I started glaring at her suspiciously. But she let me be as if her duties were only confined to keeping me fed and dressed.

As evening approached, I worked harder, feeling as if I was getting close. It wasn't as if I would be able to climb through the tiny hole or anything, but I was desperate, and maybe that desperation was causing me to lose my mind.

I was frantically digging the tip of the poker into the hole when the tool broke through, embedding itself halfway. With an eager gasp, I pulled the poker out, cast it aside, and peered through the hole. All I saw was a stone wall a distance away.

Pressing my mouth to the orifice and cupping my hands around it, I screamed. "Help! Somebody help me. I'm trapped in here. Prince Kalyll is possessed."

I pulled away from the door and peered through the hole once more. The same stone wall greeted me. Then suddenly, a yellow eye peered back. I jumped, screaming, then remembered this was exactly what I wanted.

"Help! Get me out of here."

The handle rattled and there was the sound of a key sliding into the lock.

"Oh, thank God!"

I waited, my heart in my throat. The door inched open, and an enormous male appeared at the threshold, obscuring it. He was nearly seven foot tall, his shoulders as wide as an armoire. His legs looked like small tree trunks. His head was nearly bald, making his pointed ears really stick out. His nose was flat and wide, and two small tusks protruded upward from his lower jaw. A scar cut across his cheek, a lighter shade of green than the rest of his skin. I didn't know much about Fae races, but if I had to bet, I would say he had ogre in him.

"Um, hello, I need help. I'm a prisoner," I said, unsure of whether or not he could understand me.

He said nothing. He just looked at me impassively with those yellow eyes.

"I'm so glad you're here to let me out. I . . . . I need to talk to Queen Eithne Adanorin." This was a stretch, but I couldn't think of what else to say. Kalyll's mother was the only one who knew about the shadowdrifter curse.

"Wölfe can take you when he returns," the large male said in a gentle, educated voice that would've seemed more proper in a college professor. Maybe he would be reasonable. Maybe there was hope, but he said Wölfe. I nearly started crying.

"He will not let me out of here, you know that."

"I don't know much. Only that you should perhaps get some rest before he gets back. You have been . . . busy."

He heard me banging at the door for two days, the same as Larina. They let me exhaust myself even though, all along, Wölfe had left a guard.

Assholes!

Well, if they thought I was going to sit here and wait for the third asshole to arrive, they were highly mistaken.

Lunging forward, I ran at the male. His eyes went wide in surprise, as if he'd been expecting nothing but docility from me. Still, he reacted quickly, thrusting a hand out to stop me, except I dropped one knee to the floor and used my momentum to slide between his legs.

Once on the other side, I scrambled to my feet and ran past the threshold, arms pumping, legs kicking . . . but kicking at nothing but air.

The guard had taken hold of the back of my tunic and had lifted me off the ground as if I were nothing but a petulant child. In a couple of beats, he had me back in the room while I screamed at him to let me go.

"Get your hands off me, you bastard. Let me go. You have no right."

He narrowed his eyes.

I should have been scared of his massive strength and those pointed tusks, but I was beyond fear. All I felt was fury. Blind and unadulterated. Twisting, I took hold of his arm and dug my nails into it at the same time that I tried to kick him in the stomach.

"Let me go!" I growled between clenched teeth.

23

He only looked at me with pity in his eyes, as if he were some sort of merciful cat playing with a dumb mouse.

My anger redoubled.

Fueled by my ire, something stirred in my chest, something I'd never felt before. It was familiar somehow, similar to my healing magic, except I knew that was not it. My rising anger stoked the strange force, ushering it in. It flowed through me, cold and smooth, like mist. Oddly, I enjoyed the feel of it, the surety it gave me, the way it seemed to recognize and condone my anger.

They can't do this to you, it seemed to say. *You're not a bird to be caged.*

No, I'm not, I responded, then dug my nails more deeply into my attacker's arm.

"Just calm down," he said gently. "If you—" He stopped and glanced at his arm, blinking.

"You can't do this to me," I growled, my voice nearly unrecognizable to my own ears.

That energy in my chest unfurled fully, slicing its way through every cell of my body, making even my bones go cold. It settled in place and made itself comfortable, sidling next to my anger and feeding it, magnifying it, corrupting me until I could feel myself becoming someone else, someone I didn't recognize. The Daniella who derived fulfillment from healing innocent children flipped like a coin, and what lay on the other side destroyed all the assumptions she'd ever made about herself.

As the switch tripped somewhere deep inside me, my healing abilities also flipped to show me an unknown dark side. A part of me tried to fight back, but it was weak. What was once a force that knew nothing but to give and flow outward morphed into something that drew and drew and drew.

And drew.

The male made a choking sound as his head fell back. His skin turned gray, and his veins popped to the surface. Strength filled me, stretching my ribs, and I felt fully refreshed and awake, as if I hadn't toiled at the door all day.

Suddenly, my feet hit the floor, and I landed in a crouch. I stared at the male as he teetered for a moment, then collapsed with a *thud*, making a horrible wheezing sound.

CHAPTER 4
DANIELLA

I stood confused for a moment, looking between my hands and the fallen male, an awful pressure in my chest. It took me a moment to make the connection, to realize that *I* had done that to him, that somehow my healing powers had gone in reverse and I'd—

"Oh, no." I fell to my knees next to him. "I'm sorry. I'm sorry. I didn't mean to. I didn't know what . . ."

Desperately, I pushed the darkness away, shoved it in a corner, and closed it behind a mental cage. Turning away, I focused on the male.

My hands hovered over his chest. I had to fix this. I had to make him better. My fingers trembled as I lowered them. He was still alive, but what if I touched him and ended up killing him, sapping away what little life he had left in him? But if I didn't do anything, he would die for sure. He was on the brink of taking his last breath. I could feel it.

I pressed my hands to his chest. My healing powers sputtered, refusing to work. The switch was slow to flip, even as I urged all the goodness back in.

"C'mon, c'mon!"

A jolt went through me. Light and warmth replaced the

dark energy that had taken over me. I pushed good energy forward, carefully watching the male's face.

Nothing happened. He had gone completely silent. I'd been too late. Too late.

"No." I shook my head over and over. "No, no, no."

I pushed away from him, kicking with my feet and scooting back on my bottom. Horror washed over me at the sight of what I'd done. A dull ache expanded under my ribcage.

Where I'd always ushered in life, I had now wrought death.

"No."

Sobs racked my body and threatened to choke me. I could hardly breathe. Desperation and incredulity pressed down on me as if an entire world had collapsed on my chest. I buried my face in my knees and wailed, torn apart by the barbarity of my actions.

I barely felt it when strong arms slid behind my back and under my legs and picked me up. I buried my face into the warmth that enveloped me, and inhaled the scent of leather and rosewood, searching for comfort that wouldn't come no matter how hard I tried.

I don't know how long it took, but I finally gathered the strength to pull away. I found that I was in the library, sitting on Wölfe's lap, while he, in turn, sat on a velvet settee. I knew it was Wölfe and not Kalyll because his eyes were dark, and, at this distance, I could see tiny black veins spidering from the corners of his eyes.

"Everything is fine, melynthi." He drew me against his chest, offering reassurance.

Disgust washed over me. I pushed him away and climbed off his lap. "This is your fault. I killed him. I killed him."

"Yes, it is my fault," he said with no more emotion than a snake discussing the mouse it would eat for dinner that night. He didn't care if he took the blame, not as long as it made me feel better. It was nothing to him, even if he'd known the male and should feel *something*.

His admission gave me no satisfaction, especially because I understood none of this was Kalyll's fault or even Wölfe's. I was the only one to blame. I was the one who made the decision to save his life when I should've let nature take its course.

And something else had happened that night. As I'd labored to heal the prince, my healing energy had also tangled with the demon energy, and it seemed I hadn't come out unscathed. Some of Kalyll's darkness now lived in me. I'd tried to fight it back, but it was much stronger than me, and I was left to its mercy.

My anger toward Wölfe suddenly fizzled out. Whatever remnant of darkness had seeped inside of me was only a fraction of what he was dealing with. How could I expect him to resist? Yes, he was a strong male, but maybe more than brawn and muscle were needed to push away the evil. Maybe there was no real way to control it. I had no idea.

"Stay here," Wölfe instructed, then left the library.

He was gone for several minutes. I sat back down on the settee, turned sideways, curled my legs up, and hugged them. Emotions swirled inside me in a sea of confusion. There was something dark in all of us, something capable of horrible things if we were driven to the edge. The force that infected us knew how to latch on to that. Like called to like and joined forces. Of course, it would be hard to fight back. Still, I had to. I couldn't get angry again, not when the consequences could be devastating for anyone who got in my way.

Most important of all, I had to figure out a way to get this malevolent force out of me and out of Kalyll. For now, I shut the door and tried to forget what I had done.

Wölfe returned, and I could only assume he'd taken care of the guard's body.

"I didn't know you were capable of that," he said, looking strangely proud.

"I shouldn't be. I'm sick. It's a sickness. The same one you have."

"I'm not sick. I am liberated. You should embrace this. You have a way to defend yourself now. You won't be so useless in a fight anymore."

I narrowed my eyes at him. Was that what Kalyll had been thinking all along during our quest to Mount Ruin? That I was useless?

"Asshole," I said. The insult was meant for both of them.

He shrugged it off. "Are you hungry? We should eat dinner together."

"Eat dinner? After what I just did?"

"I can get Larina to serve us here in the library instead."

I shook my head in disgust. "Pig out if you want, but I'm not eating."

"He is dead. No amount of self-loathing will change that." He waited for a response, and when I said nothing, he rolled his eyes and left the library again. When he came back, Larina was with him, and she quickly set up a big spread on one of the tables, her tiny body weaving through the air as she used her magic to conjure the food.

"Before you leave, repair the damage she made to the door and take the poker away," Wölfe instructed.

Larina nodded and left with an apologetic glance in my direction.

Wölfe sat down to eat. He seemed to have a huge appetite and demolished half the food in no time, guzzling wine, wiping his mouth with his sleeve, and displaying the table manners of a lout. His etiquette teachers would be horrified.

He kicked back, patting his stomach. "I was starving. Kalyll takes no time to enjoy himself, the idiot. Are you sure you don't want anything? The ribs are delicious."

I stared fixedly at a spot on the rug, my mind bustling with ideas and questions that had to do with removing the evil that infected us. Would we have to stab ourselves in the chest and ask Caorthannach to take it out of us? When I was healing Kalyll, I'd known how to usher the darkness out of him because it had already been at the surface and it had reacted to my healing light. But now that the force was intertwined with the very fibers of our body, would it work the same way?

"What are you thinking about?" Wölfe asked, standing from the table and sitting in front of me.

"Nothing." The last thing I needed was for him to suspect I was trying to figure out a way to cure us. I glanced around, surveying the three stories of books. Good thing I was in a library.

Wölfe scooted a little closer, his thigh touching the points of my boots.

"Why don't you get comfortable?" He wrapped a hand around my ankle, stretched my leg, rested it across his thighs, and proceeded to remove my boot.

"Please, don't." I tried to pull out of his grip, but he held me firmly, and in no time, had removed both of them and discarded them on the rug.

"Isn't that better?" He began massaging my foot over the comfortable wool socks I'd found in the closet.

"I don't want you to do that." I extricated my legs from his lap and stood. In the next instant, he was standing behind me, one arm wrapped around my waist as he pressed my back against his hard torso.

"You need to learn to relax," he said, his whispered words brushing my neck as he leaned down to nuzzle it.

I tried to get free of him, but he held me fast, and my strength was no match for his.

"So what are you going to do now? Force yourself on me?"

"Force? Who said anything about force?" He pressed his nose to the back of my ear and inhaled deeply. "You want me just as much as I want you."

"Don't flatter yourself. It is Kalyll I want, not you."

His arms tensed around me. He didn't like hearing that at all.

"Except he doesn't want you." He pulled away as he bit out the words. "He let you go. He chose that insipid woman over you."

I took several steps back, putting some distance between us. "Because he's not a selfish bastard like you, because he puts his people and his kingdom ahead of his own needs."

"And ahead of yours. He is a coward. If he wasn't, he would choose you and defy everyone. He would forsake that treaty and face war if it meant being with the female he loves."

The female he loves? Did that mean . . .?

"Oh, yes, he loves you," Wölfe said, bitterness in his voice.

I shook my head with incredulity. The prince of the Seelie Fae couldn't be in love with me, with a human.

"If he wasn't a coward, he wouldn't care about some tradition that says a Seelie Prince can only marry one of pure blood."

Pure blood? That wasn't how Kalyll had put it, but it was, undoubtedly, what it boiled down to. Pure blood meant a Fae female preferably of royal descent, which probably disqualified 99.9 percent of all the females in all the realms, including me. But love, and definitely marriage, wasn't something I ever thought was a possibility with Kalyll. I spent one month in Elf-hame and during that time I got to know the prince a little, enough to discover there was a fierce physical attraction between the two of us, but certainly not enough to fall in love, and most definitely not enough to talk about marriage.

"So what is this?" I asked. "Put down Kalyll so you can prop yourself up?"

He chuckled, not the least insulted by my comment. "Whatever it takes, darling."

I crossed my arms. "Don't call me that."

"What would you prefer? Babe? Sweetheart? Princess?"

That last one was uncalled for.

"Call me Dani."

He scanned my face, frowning.

Only my friends called me Dani, and he knew that, but I wasn't about to allow him to call me anything else, especially Daniella, when it was what Kalyll preferred to do, when he made my full name sound like poetry on his lips. For a moment, I thought Wölfe would refuse, but in the end, he nodded.

"Dani suits me. He calls you Daniella, and I know you like it, but I don't want you to confuse me with him, not even a little."

"Oh, don't worry, I've already told you. He's better than you. You're not worthy of shining his shoes."

"He is the kind that likes to service others, not me. Unless . . ." He looked me up and down. "You're the one in need of said services. May I oblige?"

"Don't flatter yourself. Nothing is going to happen between you and me. That is, unless you're a rapist." I threw the word at him with all the venom I could muster. I would be lying if I said I wasn't afraid of the possibility of Wölfe forcing himself on me. I knew he didn't bring me here for conversation, especially when all we did was argue.

Looking amused, he hummed in the back of his throat, a deep sound like a cat purring. "I won't have to force you. You will beg me for it."

I burst out laughing. "You really are deluded."

"Am I?" One moment he was there, and the next he vanished into ribbons of darkness that flowed through the air at baffling speed. The next thing I knew, he was in front of me, his nose nearly touching mine.

Shadowdrifter!

He still possessed the ability. I thought it was gone, but—

"I won't even be touching you when you ask me to fuck you," he purred.

The words felt like a slap, the kind that makes your skin tight with arousal.

"Do you know how I know that, Dani?"

I wanted to step back, but I knew that would prove to him that he had an effect on me, and dammit, I wasn't going to give him that satisfaction.

"I know because it wasn't only Kalyll who made love to you in that patch of woods. I was there too. I was the wildness you liked. I was the abandon. It was I who licked your cunt and loved it."

I gasped at the word. No one had ever talked to me like this, and it was mortifying.

"You taste delicious." He licked his lips while looking down at mine. "You are nectar. Ambrosia."

The hell with not letting him know he got to me. I made to step back. He captured me, his large hands wrapping around my waist.

"I thought you said you wouldn't touch me."

"I never said that. I said that when you beg me to fuck you, I won't be touching you." He chuckled, amused. "Let me kiss you."

"No!"

"Let me brush my tongue against yours."

"Definitely not."

He kissed me anyway, his lips crashing against mine with desperate hunger.

I tried to push him, but his arms were locked around me, like the bars of a cage that lived within a larger one, the bars of a cage that not only stole my freedom but also my will. Unbidden, desire washed over me as his tongue swiped along the seam of my bottom lip. He tasted of wine and of . . .

Kalyll. The same wildness he had unleashed in me that fateful dawn was there. Of its own accord, my mouth opened, letting him in. His tongue lapped over mine, warm and demanding. One of his hands wrapped around my neck, gripping me hard, while the other one slid down my back and cupped my ass.

He deepened the kiss, making it nearly impossible to breathe, impossible to form a thought. My hands were on his pecs before I realized it. They splayed over them, my thumbs brushing his nipples, making him groan.

He bit my lower lip, pushing me against a bookshelf.

It was like a battle of one body against another, a desperate, hungry dance of hands and lips, and lapping tongues. He pulled my hair, and I dug my nails into his back, pulling him closer. He squeezed one of my breasts, and I moaned in his ear, my teeth closing around his earlobe. He pulled harder, throwing my head back, and let his fangs pierce my skin while I stuck my thigh between his legs and roughly rubbed it against his crotch.

I was gasping for breath when Wölfe pulled back and left me like a scarecrow reclining against a bookshelf, completely unhinged and bereft.

His entire body was trembling, and blackness filled his eyes. He took deep breaths, his large chest rising and falling with effort.

"Beg me, and I'll pound my cock into you until you scream my name in pleasure."

I grabbed a book from the shelf and threw it straight at his head. "You insufferable bastard."

He ducked easily and laughed, the darkness around his eyes clearing. "I would love nothing more than to stay with you, but I must go."

"No!"

He raised an eyebrow, looking pleased.

"It's nothing like what you think."

"It isn't?"

"I hate being here alone." It was true, but there was another reason why I didn't want him to leave. I had a lot of questions, and I hadn't had a chance to ask any of them.

"That's why I brought you Larina. Someone you know. You can talk to her."

"She won't talk to me. She only brings the food and leaves."

"I'll take care of that."

"But I . . . I want to talk to you."

He twisted his mouth to one side. "You want to interrogate me about Kalyll is more like it."

That was exactly like it. "Does he . . . does he know about you?" I asked, going on something I'd started to suspect. Wölfe had only visited me after dark, which must mean Kalyll was in control during the daylight hours.

Wölfe grunted, his face twisting with condescension. "He has no clue."

So I was right. The darkness hadn't fully overpowered the prince. *Thank the witchlights!*

Now, I wanted to know more: where he was, what he was doing, what he was thinking. Did he believe he was sleeping soundly at night while Wölfe was here? Did he think of me? How were his efforts to prevent the war going? Would the marriage to Kryn's sister be enough to stop it? But more importantly, I wanted to know if he was planning to come to Elyndell. And if so, when?

Wölfe walked away from me, rearranging the front of his pants as if something there had shifted to a not-so-comfortable position. He thought for a moment, then said, "Ask away. I'll tell you everything you want to know. But when that is out of the way, I don't want you to ever, ever mention Kalyll again. Is that understood?"

The last bit was a demand, and if I didn't agree, I knew he would tell me nothing. So I composed myself, smoothing the front of my tunic, pulled a chair from under a table, and sat.

"I understand," I said.

"Good. What do you want to know? You get three questions."

"That's not what—"

"Take it or leave it."

Three questions were nothing when I needed to know everything. I had to be careful and not waste a single one of them.

"When is Kalyll coming to Elyndell?" I said after careful consideration.

Wölfe paced in front of a bookshelf, absently reading the titles. "You didn't ask *if* he was coming because that would have been a *yes* or *no* answer. Instead, you asked *when*." He chuckled. "You're clever, but of course, I already knew that. The answer to your double-edged question is that he should be here tomorrow."

"What?"

"Yes, he will be here tomorrow. That counts as your second question, by the way."

"That's not fair. That wasn't a question."

"Yes, it was."

I clenched my teeth, seething with anger. What an asshole. But of course, it was my fault for not being careful.

Tomorrow. Kalyll would be here tomorrow. That meant that, like Wölfe, he'd also thought of using veil magic to travel.

For the first time, I wondered why Kalyll hadn't used it to travel to Mount Ruin. It would have saved us a lot of time and trouble. The thought left me feeling uncomfortable, though. As easy as that would've been and as much as I was hurting now, I couldn't stand the idea of never sharing that time with the Seelie Prince. So whatever reasons he'd had for not using veil magic to begin with, I didn't care.

But why use it now? Why the hurry? Did he know I was here? He used to remember everything he did, even when he was in beast form. Did he still?

"What is your last question?" Wölfe asked impatiently.

I opened and closed my mouth, trying to figure it out but failing. This was a job for my younger sister. She would have definitely been able to come up with something Machiavellian that would help her escape. But I was the sweet sister, the caring sister. If only Lucia was here to help me. Except . . . There was a little darkness in me now, wasn't there? Couldn't *it* help me come up with something?

"Well?" Wölfe insisted.

I put a finger up. "Give me a moment."

Carefully, I peeked into the corner where I'd shoved that evil invader. It was there, waiting to pounce if invited. I rocked back and forth on the chair, unsure of whether or not I should tempt my fate. But what choice did I have? I couldn't fight Wölfe's vileness with a goody-two-shoes attitude.

So, despite what the darkness had made me do just moments ago, I opened the cage door.

CHAPTER 5
DANIELLA

"C'mon, do you have a question? Or not?" Wölfe let out a growl.

"I do." I stood from the chair, an alien force driving me.

As I walked, my hips swayed from side to side in a way that was sumptuous and entirely not me. One of Wölfe's perfect eyebrows went up, and he watched me with hungry eyes. I stopped right in front of him and played with one of the shirt strings. I batted my eyelashes like some sort of butterfly on steroids. In the back of my mind, the real me was throwing her hands up in the air, demanding what the hell was going on. What kind of femme fatale bullshit was this?

But whatever it was, it seemed to be working on Wölfe, which was the only thing that mattered.

"I was thinking . . . I don't want to be a prisoner here."

Wölfe blew air through his nose, annoyed. He already knew this, of course.

"And I don't think it's fair to either of us. I mean, think about it, Kalyll will get to parade Kryn's sister around. Mylendra, that's her name, right?"

He nodded.

"He gets to act like the perfect Seelie Prince," I went on,

"making an alliance to save his people. While you and I have to hide in here."

The dark veins around Wölfe's eyes made an appearance, which let me know I was getting to him.

"Is there a point to any of this?" he asked. "An actual question?"

"I'm getting to that." I caressed his jaw, my fingers so light he shuddered. "If you're going to keep me here in Elf-hame, I want to make the most of it and enjoy everything the realm has to offer. I can't do that in here, trapped between these walls. You can't disagree with that."

He grunted. "I'm not letting you go, Dani."

"I know that, but . . ." I paused, thinking about my next words carefully. "You're smart, so much smarter than Kalyll. Can't you figure out a way to bring me out, to show me off, to rub it in the prince's face?"

His upper lip twitched, and his darkest-blue eyes acquired a faraway quality, as if he were already thinking how he could cause distress to his worst enemy.

I lowered my chin and smiled. It had worked. Time to push the darkness back into its corner. I grappled with the slippery energy, but it slipped away, and the next thing I knew, my hand was on Wölfe's crotch, stroking his cock up and down.

"Umm, that didn't take long," he said, going immediately hard and thrusting his hips forward to give me better access. "How about you do that with your tongue?"

The thought of going down on him and pleasuring him sent a spiraling jolt to my core.

"You would like it. Wouldn't you, my little caged bird?"

Well, that was the entirely wrong thing to say. Neither the light side of me, nor the dark, liked the idea of being anyone's caged bird.

I jerked away from him, putting a safe distance between us. "I think you will be the one begging," I said as I scrambled to force the darkness down. The irony didn't escape me. I was also a jailer. Wrangling the foreign invader was harder than the first time. After much clenching of teeth, I managed to shut the cell door, regaining full control of myself.

"I like this side of you," he said with a crooked smile, and looked down at his bulging erection. "Don't fight it, embrace it. It feels good, doesn't it? You can't deny it. Let the darkness free and be mine. Together, you and I can figure out a way to overpower Kalyll. I would make you my princess. I would worship you."

I held my breath and quivered, using no small amount of strength to keep my dark desires at bay. What he proposed was tempting. I hadn't known how much I wanted what he offered until this moment. Why shouldn't I have the man I loved? Because I did. I loved him.

You love Kalyll, not Wölfe. You love his generous heart, his loyalty, his kindness, his conviction to do the right thing.

Wölfe didn't possess any of those qualities. He was raw desire and lust. He was wanton sexual hunger and abandon, and though I also wanted all of that, eventually, it would not be enough. Worse yet, it might, in the end, obliterate his goodness as well as mine, leaving behind only our worst selves and condemning us to a somber future.

And that was not what I wanted.

The next morning, I was up and ready when Larina showed up with breakfast. I was already sitting in front of the fireplace as she laid everything down. I even had a pleasant smile on my face.

"All the sunshine to you," I said.

She returned the greeting.

When she finished setting everything up, she sat at the edge of the armchair across from me, her tiny legs and slippered feet hanging off the edge.

Humming, I buttered a piece of bread and dropped a cube of sugar in my coffee. Thoughts of what I'd done last time threatened to surface, but I shoved them deep inside the same cell with the darkness.

I started nibbling, focusing on the pixie, knowing that now she had no other choice but to talk to me.

"Have you eaten?" I asked.

She shook her head.

"There is plenty of food here." I swept a hand over the wide array of food.

"No, thank you, Lady Sunder." Her cheeks turned violet, and she stared at her lap.

"Please, no more of that Lady Sunder mess, okay? Just Dani. It's what my friends call me. And you don't have to be embarrassed. You can eat whatever you want."

She looked so surprised I figured none of the people she'd ever served had invited her to share a meal with them.

I set my bread and coffee down and cut the tip of a small strawberry, creating a tiny piece that should fit in her hands. Then I speared it with a fork and offered it to her.

She stared at it with wide, blinking eyes.

"It's all right. Take it."

It took her a long moment to grab it and venture a nibble.

I smiled, and to my relief, she smiled back. I hated that she felt this way. No one should have to feel *less than* anyone else, especially no one as amazing as Larina. Her iridescent wings were a work of art, her skin was the most beautiful shade of aquamarine, and from what I'd seen, she had amazing magic that allowed her to do all kinds of things.

"Strawberries are my favorite," she said, taking another dainty bite.

"They're pretty good. My favorite is mango."

"Mango?"

"It's a tropical fruit. It's yellowish-orange inside, very meaty and juicy. They're about this big." I gestured with my hands.

"I'd love to try it."

"Maybe one day I'll get one for you."

We were quiet for a moment, then I decided it was time to talk about important things.

"Wölfe, I mean Kalyll, said that he'll be in Elyndell today."

She frowned, probably wondering why I thought that was such a big deal.

"I mean that he'll be here during the day."

She frowned more deeply, probably realizing for the first time that, so far, the prince had only been here at night.

I went on. "I guess he decided a long journey on horseback was a waste of time. So . . . you haven't seen him, have you?"

She shook her head, her cheek puffy with strawberry.

"Can you let me know when he gets here? He's probably finalizing things in Imbermore. Maybe, when you see him, if you have a chance, you can ask him to come see me."

She shook her head. "I'm sorry. I can't do that."

"Why not?"

"The prince forbade me to talk to him. I can only address him if he addresses me first. Besides, I'm not one of Prince Kalyll's attendants. There is no situation in which I would encounter him. Unless he calls on me, of course."

Damn! So Wölfe had thought of everything. What now?

"Too bad," I said. "Though, don't you think that request is kind of strange."

"Not at all. Really, he didn't even need to make it. I would never dare speak out of turn."

Witchlights! The medieval treatment some people received here was infuriating.

Would it be the same with Jeondar, Cylea, or Arabis? Probably. Still, I had to try.

"What about the prince's friends? Could you talk to them, if they come with him?"

"I know what you're trying to do, Lady Sunder, and I won't fall for it."

I slumped in my chair. "Can you blame me? He's got me locked up." I abandoned all pretense of being a manipulative mastermind and reverted to my run-of-the-mill self. "It's not right, Larina. I need to go back home to my family. There's no life for me here."

The pixie's eyebrows drew together as she looked up at me.

I could see sympathy in her expression, but I knew it would never be enough to overrule her loyalty to her prince.

"Where is your family?" I asked.

"My brother lives in Imbermore. My parents are still in our village."

"Is that where you grew up?"

She nodded.

"Do you ever see them?"

"Once a year they visit, during the Summer Solstice. My brother and I send them coin for the trip."

"Oh, so you saw them just recently then?"

"I did."

"They must be very grateful and proud of you and your brother."

She shrugged her tiny shoulders. Her feet swung from side to side, no bigger than a Barbie doll's.

"I have two sisters and one brother." It was only fair for me to share as well. "My mother's still alive, but my father passed away."

"I'm sorry to hear that, Lady Sunder."

"Dani."

She stared at the ceiling, avoiding eye contact. I would break her out of that habit. Eventually.

"I'm a healer, and I could do nothing to save him." Every time I thought about Dad, and the way he died, a wave of sadness crashed into me, threatening to drown me in sorrow.

He died of pancreatic cancer. There were no signs that he was sick until it was too late. I tried my best to save him, as did other healers and doctors, but cancer is a tricky disease.

How do you heal someone from their own body attacking them? If only I'd had more time.

"I didn't mean to make you sad," Larina said.

"You didn't make me sad." I shook my head at how silly it was for her to blame herself.

"The prince said you were bored." She fluttered upward, her beautiful wings whirring. "What if we play Knock?"

"Knock?"

"Yes, it's a board game. It helps pass the time. It's not hard. I can teach you."

In no time, she had cleared the table and replaced it with the game. She quickly explained the rules, and I realized it seemed suspiciously like Sorry!

Soon, we were knocking each other's pieces back to the beginning and fretting every time we rolled the dice. By the time we were on our third match, Larina seemed more at ease, laughing and even taunting me when she got close to one of my pieces.

Her company made the time pass and lightened my heart a great deal.

We'd been playing for a couple of hours when she startled. "By Erilena! I have to go. I need to help in the kitchen and make sure your midday meal is prepared to satisfaction."

"Don't worry about that. I can eat whatever. Promise."

She looked incensed at that.

Waving my hands in the air, I said, "All right, all right, you can bring a banquet as long as you agree to eat with me." I thought she would refuse, but it seemed the fun time we'd spent together had gone a long way to make her less stiff and proper.

While the pixie was gone, I decided it was time to explore the library. I was always curious to find new books on healing techniques and herbs, but I also had an additional motivation. I had to find out everything I could on demons, shadowdrifters, possessions, anything that could help me figure out how to get rid of the darkness that had taken hold of Kalyll and me.

I thought it might take a long time to locate what I needed, but the library had a logical, well-organized system, and in a matter of minutes, I found the sections on healing magic, medicinal plants, and demons. I thought of taking down the books and bringing them to a table, so I could read at ease, but I couldn't have Wölfe suspecting my plans. It was a wonder he hadn't already realized that holding me prisoner amongst all this information was a bad idea. Unless, of course, he already knew I would be unable to find anything useful.

The thought nearly discouraged me, but I rallied up and began reading.

I didn't get far because, within an hour, Larina was back with lunch. I'd barely touched my breakfast, so I was hungry, and she served me a nice amount of roasted quail and something that looked like Brussels sprouts. Except they were blue.

"The fig sauce is delicious with the quail," Larina instructed.

I drizzled some over my tiny roasted bird and had to agree with her.

This time, the pixie brought with her a set of utensils that looked like they belonged in a miniature toy kitchen and ate with me without needing encouragement and cajoling.

"The prince is here," she announced when we were half-way through our meal.

My fork clattered as it hit my plate. Kalyll—Kalyll, not Wölfe, was here.

"Did . . . did you see him?" I asked.

She shook her head. "No, but the kitchen was in a flurry, with everyone cooking different dishes that would please the prince and his friends." She looked up at me with a tiny smile, which let me know she was sharing the information because I needed it, because I'd asked earlier.

"Thank you for letting me know, Larina. I know you have to follow your own code, but I promise you I don't mean Prince Kalyll any harm. On the contrary, I want what's best for him and your realm. I know you want the same too. So, once more, all I ask is that you pay attention to the prince and that you help him if you decide he's in need."

The pixie's expression grew forlorn, and I could tell my words had the intended effect. Deciding to go against Wölfe's orders would be difficult for her, but I had a feeling she would do the right thing if it came to it.

After lunch, Larina left, and I went back to reading, thumbing through tome after tome, looking for anything of import. I ran into some interesting material on the use of poisonous mushrooms to treat a disease that sounded suspiciously like viral meningitis. I wrote the details on a piece of paper I'd found on a desk on the second level. If I ever went back home, I could run some tests and help my patients.

Knowing that Kalyll was in the palace had me restless at first, looking to the door every few minutes, hoping he would come in and set me free. But no such luck and further proof that he had no memory of Wölfe. Eventually, I settled down, resigned to wait until sundown for another go at my captor. Maybe if I kept pestering him, he would get tired of me and bring me home. One could hope.

When the light seeping through the high windows started to dwindle and the sconces came on all around, I rubbed my eyes and blinked in surprise. I'd been reading for hours, sitting on the floor, legs crossed, two bookshelves flanking me, and I'd lost track of time. Wölfe would be here at any moment, and it would be best if he didn't find me perusing books on demons and their evil forces.

Making note of their location, I re-shelved the books and hid my notes. After that, I found an adventure novel, took it with me and placed it between a couple of cushions in one of the sitting nooks on the first level, a mere afterthought.

I was still in the library when the door in the bedroom area opened. I hated the way my heart sped up, anticipating the threat of seeing that handsome face and hearing that rumbling voice. That presence charged with masculinity and self-assurance was a delicious sucker punch every time.

I resisted the urge to go into the next room, and instead waited, listening to his firm steps as he came looking for me. My back was to him as he entered the room, and I didn't need to turn around to know it was him. I felt him like a gentle caress down my back, like some celestial body radiating its warmth solely for me.

"I've waited all day to see you," he said, causing a shiver to run down my spine. "Have you waited for me?"

"I have," I said, unable to find the strength to lie to him.

As I turned to face him, I did a double take. He was wearing a jacket without a shirt, his smooth, golden chest in full display. Long jeweled necklaces that draped over his abs hung from his neck again, rings adorned his fingers, and a small crown sat on his head. He smirked, enjoying my surprise.

He extended a hand in my direction, crooking a finger in a *come here* motion. I wanted to resist, but who was I kidding? I approached him and lifted my hand to his.

"I have someone I want you to meet," he said.

That really, really surprised me.

He led me into the bedroom area, and I was shocked to find a regal female sitting in one of the armchairs by the fireplace.

"Dani, this is Naesala Roka," he said. "She's a good *friend* of mine, and she's here to set you free."

CHAPTER 6
DANIELLA

I didn't like the way he said the word *friend*. His tone suggested there was a history there, and it made me jealous.

Naesala didn't leave her seat and simply waved with a couple of red-tipped fingers. She had jet-black hair and pale eyes the color of stardust. Her skin was as smooth as cream, not a blemish in sight. Her mouth was painted bright red to match her fingernails, and if not for the pointed ears sticking out through her silken hair, I would have figured she was a vampire—one of those that like the Morticia Addams look.

"I was expecting more, *Wölfe*," she said, the name sounding forced on her lips, like she knew it was fake, which meant this wasn't a recent friendship. She knew Kalyll.

There was a deeper rumble in Wölfe's chest that clearly expressed his dissatisfaction with her comment.

Naesala waved a hand in the air. "I'm sorry. I didn't know you had become so sensitive." The comment was loaded with disapproval that she didn't try to hide, not even one bit.

Friend, pshaw! She was no friend of Kalyll. If she were, she would know to tell someone that the prince needed help. Instead, she was here, doing who knew what, but I had a feeling it couldn't be good.

"Let me look at her, then." She stood and came close. She was tall and thin like a runway model and wore a black dress that hung from her spindly frame. The front dipped low, two swaths of fabric covering her small breasts, a "V" revealing a bony sternum. Her arms were long and slender, covered in alabaster smooth skin.

She stopped in front of me and looked me up and down, tilting her head from side to side as if judging a racehorse she was planning to buy.

She finished her perusal with a shrug. "Good bone structure. She appears strong. Passable."

What the hell? Was she going to ask me to show her my teeth next?

"What's going on, Wölfe?" I demanded.

He smiled, looking satisfied. "You'll see."

"I think that I—" I started, but was unable to finish when Naesala lifted a hand in my direction, and a lightning bolt of pain shot from the top of my head down to the base of my neck.

I screamed and fell backward. Wölfe caught me, and as I convulsed in agony, he scooped me in his arms and laid me on the bed.

Naesala approached, and hovered over me, her hands weaving with some sort of spell that seemed to turn my bones to molten lava. I twisted, my spine arching. My hand reached out in an effort to take hold of my tormentor. I wanted to desiccate her, turn her into a brittle fossil, but the pain was too much, and I couldn't reach her.

The agony went on for an eternity while Wölfe did nothing but watch with interest. Kalyll would have never allowed me to suffer, but Wölfe only seemed to care about his endgame, whatever it was.

I passed out and was lost in darkness.

At some point, I resurfaced and fought to regain my consciousness. Drowsily, my eyes opened and closed, catching glimpses of Wölfe sitting by my side.

There was something cool and damp on his hand. He dabbed my forehead with it, my neck, my naked breasts. He did so tenderly, his darkened eyes showing more hunger than concern. It seemed I lay in that state for days, but when I awoke, Wölfe was standing in front of the fireplace, staring at the burning logs and wearing the same clothes.

Naesala was gone, and the effects of what she'd done to me were mostly gone, except for a dull ache in my skull and an itchy warmth all over my skin. I sat up, the sheets rustling. I now wore a nightgown instead of my tunic and leggings. I flushed with embarrassment and hugged myself, pushing up and resting my back against the headboard.

Wölfe turned to face me and approached, one hand casually stuffed in his jacket pocket.

"How do you feel?"

I didn't answer. I couldn't, not as my breaths came hard and fast, anger building inside of me. "What did she do to me?"

"Find out for yourself." He offered me a hand.

I glared at it.

He rolled his eyes and shrugged. "Just look in the mirror." He pointed toward the closet, where a full-length, gilded mirror stood in one corner.

Trembling with anger and apprehension, I slid off the bed and padded into the closet. The image that reflected back at me in the luxurious mirror nearly drove me to my knees.

A tear slid down my cheek as I peered at my face. "What have you done?"

The person looking back wasn't me. My jaw was slightly elevated with a chin that ended in a delicate curve. My cheekbones were higher and my brown eyes were lighter and somewhat slanted, sparkling with flakes of gold. My hair was also a lighter shade of brown, and it now had red and golden highlights enhancing its color. But what shocked me the most were the pointed ears slicing through the silky hair. I raised a hand to touch one of them, then stopped, horrified.

"Don't be shy." Wölfe stood behind me, placing both hands on my shoulders.

My breaths were so fast, I was nearly hyperventilating and on the edge of a panic attack.

Wölfe traced the length of my pointed ear with the pad of his index finger. "What do you think? Beautiful, huh?"

In an instant, panic was replaced with fury. I whirled, my hand coming up, then cutting across his cheek, delivering a slap that jerked his head to one side.

"You fucking bastard. I will end you for this."

He glanced back in surprise, the red imprint of my hand on his cheek. His fists opened and closed.

"Go ahead. Hit me. Break something." I stuck my chin out defiantly. "Undo this nightmare."

"Nightmare? It is what you wanted."

"No, it's not. I never asked for this." I gestured at my face as if it were a pile of garbage.

"How else do you think you would be able to leave this place and be with me?"

I shoved past him, exiting the closet. Out in the bedroom, my eyes roved all around, as if looking for a solution.

"Bring that bitch back," I demanded. "Make her undo this." I would endure the excruciating pain ten times over to take it all away.

"You're not thinking clearly," Wölfe said behind me.

"Yes, I am. Bring her back immediately."

"Give it time. You'll get used to it."

I faced him, barely containing the urge to slap him again. "Tell me this can be undone."

He looked doubtful for a moment, and I nearly went for his eyes with clawed hands. "Sure. It can be undone," he said finally. "But we won't do such a thing."

"Yes, we will." I got right in his face. "And we will do it now."

"You are being irrational. You should sleep on it." He started to walk away.

"Irrational? You have destroyed my identity and turned me into . . . into someone I am not. If this is what you want," I swept my hands down my torso, "you could have your pick from your damn court."

"You know it's not like that." His eyes darkened further, that evil force inside of him rearing its head. "It is you I want.

No one else. Besides, it is your heart I care for, not your appearance."

"And yet, you think this is beautiful." I pointed at my ears.

"*You* are beautiful, Dani, regardless of the shape of your ears. Don't you understand? No one has to know who you are. You and I can take over the realm without worrying about stale statutes about pure blood."

"I don't care about your stupid realm. I don't care about any of this. I just want you to set me free."

Wölfe turned his head toward the shuttered window and inhaled. "It's nearly dawn. I need to go. Tomorrow night, you'll change your mind."

He walked toward the door. I grabbed his arm. If I could keep him here until the sun came up, then Kalyll would see what was happening and free me.

"This can't wait until tomorrow. You can't leave me like this," I said, stalling for time.

"Get some rest. You had a rough night. You will feel better later." He extricated his arm from my grip, and with a few quick steps, made it to the door.

I rushed forward and slid between him and the exit, my back against the wood. "Please, Wölfe, I'm begging you." I stared up at him with pleading eyes. If anger hadn't worked, maybe this would.

He seemed moved for an instant, then his expression hardened. "I know what you're trying to do." Roughly, he grabbed me by the elbows, pushed me out of the way, and before I could do anything, he was out the door, the lock clicking into place.

Standing alone in the middle of that large room, I felt insignificant. Had Kalyll been lying when he said he didn't care I was human? Had he felt ashamed about his feelings for me? Had he wished for a Fae version of me all along?

No matter how much he changed my appearance, I was not Fae. So what did that make me in his eyes?

Trivial?

My heart aching, my ribs fit to burst with pressure, I succumbed to despair.

CHAPTER 7
DANIELLA

A couple of hours later, Larina found me sitting on what had become my favorite armchair by the fireplace. I hadn't gone back to bed and seemed unable to do anything other than stare blankly at the floor. She came in through the tiny door by the ceiling, cheerfully wishing "all the sunshine" to me.

When she fluttered down, she froze in midair and gasped.

I looked up, my expression rigid and cold. I was done falling apart. I was done crying. I'd emptied my soul after Wölfe left, but no more.

"Do you see what he has turned me into?" I asked. "Do you still believe your prince is all right?"

None of this was Larina's fault, but my harsh tone made no attempt to spare her feelings. Finally, shaking herself from the shock, she flew down to the coffee table where she normally set up the breakfast. She examined my face, my pointed ears.

"If I'd had wings," I said. "He would've plucked them to make me look like this."

The pixie's entire body shivered with horror. Her iridescent wings had to be precious to her, and the idea of losing them would likely inspire nightmares of the worst kind.

"How?" she asked in a whisper. "How is this possible?"

"He brought someone with him last night. A female called Naesala Roka."

Another gasp from the pixie.

"I take it you know who that is."

She nodded. "She's a wealthy . . . *trader*."

"Let me guess, she doesn't trade in physical goods."

Her silence was answer enough.

"I wondered what Wölfe offered in return if this was a trade," I said almost absently, my level of *giving a shit* almost on empty.

"I am so sorry, Dani," she said, using my name for the first time. "I can only try to imagine how this must feel."

I nearly cried again, but I bit my tongue and held the tears back. "Thank you."

"I will leave your breakfast and be right back."

Food materialized on the table, and she was gone too fast for me to tell her I wasn't hungry. I did pour myself a cup of coffee and let the bitter taste enhance the one I already felt.

I was still sitting on the armchair, staring into space, when the door handle rattled. I stood and stared intently at the door, wishing against all odds that it was Kalyll, though I knew better than that. Wölfe was being careful to the extreme. He seemed to have thought of everything.

But that left me with the question . . . who was it? A guard?

When the door swung open, shock froze me for an instant, then relief spurred me forward.

"Jeondar!" I crashed into him and wrapped my arms around his neck. He stood stiffly, his arms hanging at his sides. I was hugging the prince of the Summer Court as if he were my brother, but I didn't care. Someone who could help me was here. Someone who cared about Kalyll and had always been good to me.

I eventually came to my senses and let him go. His amber eyes roved over my face, shock brimming in his expression. His locks were unbound, framing his handsome face.

"Dani?" The tone of his voice told me he wasn't at all certain it was me. Maybe he thought I was a doppelgänger, a Fae lookalike, but no such luck.

I nodded as he looked at my pointed ears and altered face with something close to horror, which was all I needed to let me know he understood the wrongness of what Wölfe had done to me.

Larina came into the room—hands interlaced in front of her, head lowered—the perfect picture of contrition. She exchanged a glance with Jeondar, who seemed to say, *I'm sorry I didn't believe you.*

"What is happening?" he asked, looking miserably confused.

"It's a nightmare."

If Jeondar had been here yesterday, everything would've been so different. I could've gone back home. I could have started rebuilding my life, the life that was stolen from me for the sake of saving a realm that wasn't my own. But I couldn't go back now. Not like this. My life was forfeited again, this time for wicked, selfish reasons.

"Maybe . . . we should sit, and you can tell me everything from the beginning." Jeondar pointed at the armchairs.

Larina hurried forward and quickly cleared the untouched

food with a wave of her hand. We sat, and she bowed and started toward the door.

"No. Stay, Larina. Please," I said.

She had gone against her prince's orders, and whether her motivation was to help Kalyll or me, I believed we could trust her not to divulge any secrets that would hurt the future of the Seelie Court.

She shook her head. "It's not my place, Lady Sunder." Her eyes darted toward Jeondar.

The pixie had been a servant at the Summer Court when I'd met her, so we were back to *Lady Sunder* in front of Jeondar.

He seemed okay to let her go, likely out of habit. As a prince, he'd grown up with servants slipping away unnoticed and without a second thought from him. I gave him a raised eyebrow. He blinked in surprise and paused to examine the pixie. A series of considerations flashed through his face. Then he seemed to decide, like me, that Larina could be trusted.

The pixie fluttered about nervously, clearly stressed by this turn of events. She spun this way and that, unsure of where to settle herself. With a smile of sympathy, I flicked my eyes toward the mantle. She nodded gratefully and sat on the edge.

Gathering my thoughts, I told them everything that had happened since the night Wölfe took me from my bed up to what he'd done last night.

"I never suspected anything was wrong." Jeondar rubbed his forehead, looking mad at himself. "Kryn and I have been watching him closely. Kalyll asked us to do it, told us about what you had to do to save his life, the darkness you left in him. We noticed nothing amiss. Except for his sudden desire to get back to Elyndell. We were supposed to visit the Fall Court."

He gave me an apologetic look that made it clear that the trip's purpose had everything to do with visiting Kalyll's betrothed. I did my best to ignore the awkwardness. Jeondar owed me no consideration in this regard. Kalyll and I were a one-night stand, and nothing else.

My only relationship with him now was through Wölfe, who felt so detached from the prince that I didn't even think of them as the same person.

Up on the mantle, Larina wore a deep frown. I knew she was trying to understand what had taken us to Mount Ruin and how we'd ended up in a situation where the Seelie Prince needed to be healed using demon energy. I would have to catch her up later.

"How do we get that out of him?" Jeondar asked.

It didn't surprise me that his first concern was for Kalyll, though that didn't mean it didn't bother me.

"I'm sorry," he said abruptly, probably noticing something in my expression. "What he's done to you . . . We need to fix that too. He had no right, but that wasn't Kalyll. You know that, right? He would never do something like that. Never."

"I know."

"By Erilena!" He stood abruptly, pulling out his hair. "This is bad. Almost as bad as the beast. Or worse. He's been lying so artfully. We have noticed no difference in him after twilight. He continues to act exactly the same. He has been broody and makes excuses to go to bed early, but we thought that was because . . ." He trailed off, his eyes once more connecting with mine, leaving things unsaid.

He paced, his eyes darting from side to side as he thought at a million miles per hour.

"I can't fathom what deal he made with Naesala Roka, but whatever it is, it can't be good. She doesn't deal in trivialities. More than that, she's friends with Cardian."

"Can you find someone to undo this?" I asked, desperation filling my chest.

His expression darkened. "I'm afraid she's a very powerful sorceress whose spells can only be undone by her. It is the reason she has become and remains powerful among the court folk. The fools don't know who they're trifling with. Or maybe they do, but their greed far exceeds their common sense."

I wondered briefly if a mage or witch in my realm could help me set things right, but I quickly dismissed the idea. Fae magic was different. Not more powerful exactly, just a different brand. And if she'd developed her own variation of spells . . .

"I'm stuck here," I spat.

"I'm sorry, Dani," Jeondar said.

"You, your prince, and your fucking realm have destroyed my life."

Maybe it wasn't fair to unleash all my anger on him, but who else was there? He, along with Kryn and Silver, kidnapped me from Pharowyn, and for all his goodness, Jeondar had certainly been all right with doing morally gray shit for his own gain.

"No apology is enough. I know," he said. "But I promise I

will do everything in my power to ensure you get your life back."

I pressed the heel of my hands to my forehead, trying to stave off a migraine. "This is unproductive. I need to think." It was my turn to stand up and pace. After a moment, I started talking out loud, letting my ideas evolve as I went. "So I'm stuck here. I can't go back home this way. My family would freak out. At work, they'd probably think I'm some sort of impostor. Also, to be honest, I don't think Wölfe will leave me alone. If I go, he'll find me, even if I try to hide. I know it. The damn male is obsessed."

"I think you're right," Jeondar said, sounding certain, which made me wonder why he would agree with me so readily. What had he seen in Kalyll? Did Jeondar think the broodiness he'd witnessed from the prince meant he missed me?

I shot the question away. None of that mattered. Pining over Kalyll was as futile as expecting niceness from Wölfe.

"It seems the only way out of this is to heal Kalyll once more," I said.

"Do you have any idea how?"

Jeondar took a seat again, his nerves immediately at ease. I had saved his friend once. Clearly, he thought the odds were that I would do it again. Bitterness felt like a pill in my mouth, one I had no other choice but to swallow. Of course, Kalyll came first. If I saved him, everything else, everyone else, could go to hell, including me.

I whirled away, dealing with the negative feelings. I felt that darkness inside of me trying to push its way out, influencing the way I felt. Logically, I knew that the fate of an entire realm, the avoidance of a war that would end thousands of lives, was more important than my freedom and my appearance. Still, it wasn't my logic that the darkness was trying to manipulate. It was my emotions.

"Are you all right?" Jeondar asked.

"I'm fine," I said too quickly, embarrassed to admit that Kalyll wasn't the only one fighting against his demons.

"So, how do we cure him? Take him back to Mount Ruin?"

"I don't think so. This is different. I've been trying to figure out a way. I found some books that may shed light on the matter, but it's slow progress." I pointed at the door that led to the library.

"Books? Do you mean you have access to his library?" Jeondar walked through the threshold and I followed. His amber eyes roved over the many shelves as he shook his head.

"What is it?" I asked.

"It's clear that . . . Wölfe has some level of control over Kalyll."

I'd already explained that, but he was making a connection of his own. "What makes you say that?" I asked.

"This is one of Kalyll's favorite places in the entire palace. His chamber is beyond that wall. Wölfe must be preventing him from coming in here even during the day."

Larina, who was fluttering by the threshold, cleared her throat tentatively, as if afraid she would be rebuked. "That . . . that sounds like more than just a small level of control."

But there was no rebuke, which had the pixie blinking in surprise. Instead, Jeondar considered her words.

"Maybe." Suddenly, he gasped. "What if . . . what if we're assuming? What if Wölfe is always in control and he's just pretending?"

I shook my head. "I don't think so. Wölfe keeps complaining about Kalyll. He hates him. He thinks he's weak and stupid."

"You talk as if they were two different people."

"It feels that way, worse than before when his mood used to change. Then, it seemed to be mostly anger. Now, it runs much deeper. It's as if every negative trait is center stage, as if the worst of Kalyll is in charge."

Jeondar sighed. "At least Kalyll's still in control half the time. That has to mean there is hope."

I walked deeper into the library. The thought that this room was sandwiched between Kalyll's chamber and mine made me wonder about all kinds of things. Why would Wölfe take a risk like that?

"Thinking about how this all works is giving me a head-ache," Jeondar said. "If Wölfe can influence Kalyll not to come in here, what about the other way? Can Kalyll influence Wölfe?"

Foolishly, I suddenly wondered if that was the reason I was sleeping so close to the prince. Had he somehow swayed Wölfe in that decision? If that was how things work, neither one seemed aware of the other's influence.

"So . . . what will you do?" Larina asked. "Prince Wölfe can't know I brought you here."

"Prince Wölfe?" Jeondar and I said in unison.

She put her hands up and shrugged.

"I don't think you have to worry about using the honor-ific, Larina." Jeondar gave her a warm smile. "But yes, I agree with you. I think we should keep this secret from him. Obviously, I'll have to tell Kryn, Arabis, and Cylea, but—"

"Not Kryn!" I nearly stomped my foot. "You can't tell him."

"He *has* to know."

"He hates me, Jeondar."

"That's not true."

"C'mon."

"He doesn't hate you. He's grateful for what you did. He's a bastard, but not that big of a bastard. He's just . . . loyal to the realm. And his sister. Can you blame him?"

That dark side in me definitely blamed him, though Logical Dani said otherwise.

"Either way," I said. "I don't know if it's such a good idea to tell them. What if they slip up while Wölfe is pretending to be Kalyll?"

"I don't think we have a choice, Dani. Are you forgetting this?" He gestured with one hand from the top of my head to the tip of my toes. "He changed you in order to take you out of this chamber, to bring you places. Others will not recognize you, but Kryn, Arabis and Cylea will."

I rubbed the back of my neck. "You're right. You're right. This really is boggling my mind." Without even thinking, I found myself asking something completely unrelated. "What happened to Silver?"

It was strange hearing everybody else's names and not his. The five of them had been friends since childhood. I still couldn't imagine how hard it must be on them to find out Silver was a traitor.

A veil of sadness fell over Jeondar's face, though the

sadness quickly morphed into concern. He blew air through his nose as he suddenly seemed to realize something. "*Wölfe* put him in a dungeon, and Kalyll has forgotten about him."

"Oh." I didn't know what else to say to that.

"Under normal circumstances, he should get a fair hearing, but we can't let everyone know why we went to Mount Ruin. Not that the hearing would help Silver's case. He's not talking, hasn't said a word to defend himself. Maybe he deserves to be in a dungeon for what he did, but . . ." All Jeondar could do was rub a hand down his face.

I tried not to feel sorry for Silver. He *had* stabbed Kalyll in the back. Literally. He was the vilest of traitors. He deserved no sympathy. Still, I couldn't help but wonder about his well-being.

After a moment, Jeondar brought the conversation back to the prince. "Kalyll's library is extensive. I must trust you can find something to help you here."

"I just got started, so I don't know, but I did find several books that look promising."

"Good. Now, I should go. I need to find the others and tell them what's happening. I'm sorry you are locked in here." He turned to Larina. "Please, make sure Dani gets everything she needs, and thank you for letting me know what was happening. I know it must have been hard for you to go against Prince Kalyll's orders."

The pixie bowed lightly, relief evident in her expression.

"She's already taking good care of me, Jeondar. Larina is a wonderful friend."

At this, her gaze snapped to mine. Her reaction gave me a pang in my chest. She was so used to always being the servant that being called a friend came as a shock to her. That made me all kinds of mad. The Fae were not better than humans, and humans were not better than pixies. There wasn't a race in this realm or any other that was superior.

At the core, we were all the same, and only those who didn't value life and dignity didn't deserve it.

CHAPTER 8
DANIELLA

I spent the rest of the day studying some of the books I'd found. Since I was afraid to take them to the sitting area, I brought cushions and a blanket with me to make myself comfortable. Kalyll had a very exacting system for his books, but I quickly devised my own, separating the books I'd already searched from the ones I hadn't, then separating the former category into books with potential and books without.

So far, the relevant information I'd found didn't seem promising. All I'd read was definitely informative, and it strengthened my knowledge of demon energy. Still, I was far from finding anything that would lead to any sort of cure, be it medicine, a spell, or anything else.

Too soon it was near twilight, and I carried the cushions and blanket downstairs, threw them on a settee, and placed another adventure novel haphazardly on top of them.

When Wölfe came, he found me sitting by the fire, sipping a cup of tea. He waltzed in through the door, carrying a large box that he deposited on the bed. He turned his head to look at me, clearly trying to judge my mood.

"Not hysterical anymore, I see," he said at last.

"Hysterical? That's what you're opening with after what you did to me?"

"Get over it. It's not a tragedy. You're still the same person."

"How about you give me a knife and I round off those stupid ears of yours?"

I expected him to flinch, but he only looked amused. He made a dismissive gesture with one hand, then turned to the box and opened it.

"I have something for you," he said. "We're going out tonight."

I stood up slowly, curiosity getting the best of me, and approached the bed. Inside the box, there was a sparkling evening gown made of silk and chiffon. It was a deep shade of blue, with a high and round neckline, and fitted sleeves ending in flared cuffs adorned with intricate silver embroidery. The bodice was fitted, with the same silver embroidery running down the center and around the waist, and a gold ribbon lacing up the front. The skirt was full and flowing, made of layers of sheer fabric cascading down to the floor.

"Where are we going exactly?" I asked, fingering the soft fabric.

"There's a party tonight. It's the little prince's birthday. You're coming with me."

"What little prince are you talking about?"

"My useless brother, of course."

I shook my head. "You can't take me to that. I thought we would go out on the town or something like that, but a party in the palace? That's crazy."

He took a step closer and snarled. "You say that because you're thinking of *him*, not me."

"You don't want to start a war. Kalyll is engaged. Any slight toward Mylendra Goren might break the alliance."

"I don't care about any of that. How many times do I have to tell you?"

I clenched my teeth, trying not to show pain on my face. "So if a war breaks out, what are you going to do? Hide here, bring me dresses, and harass me every night? How long do you think that will last before your enemies come banging at your door? How long do you think you will get to enjoy me?"

He narrowed his eyes as he breathed down on me, his lips inches from mine. He didn't say anything, but I could tell I'd stumbled onto something, so I pressed my advantage.

"Don't rock the boat so soon," I said. "Think about it. It will seem strange to everyone if you show up with someone no one knows. Besides, there are Kryn and the others to consider. They will recognize me the moment they see me."

"How do you know they're here?" he growled.

"Aren't they attached at Kalyll's hip?"

He grunted and stepped back.

"They won't recognize you," he said, digging in the box and pulling something from under the dress. He handed over a jewel-decorated swath of fabric.

"What is this?"

"A veil."

"A veil?"

"Yes, to cover your face."

"What? Won't that be strange?"

"Not if you are a Jovinian."

"And what is that, exactly?"

73

"Someone from Jovinia, a region where single females wear veils."

He had to be kidding me. I had to wear a veil? Women had gone to war not to have to put up with this kind of shit. Worse yet, if he was planning on me wearing a veil, why did he have to change my face? I was about to go off on him until I realized the veil was the sort that belly dancers wear, which didn't cover your hair or ears. They only covered half of your face from the nose down.

"But I'm not from Jovinia," I said, "and when somebody asks me about it, which will inevitably happen, it will become obvious."

"Just keep things vague." He acted as if it was no big deal.

"And what about my accent, won't that give me away?"

"Try to sound a bit like Arabis. She had a Jovinian tutor when she was growing up."

I shook my head. "I don't think this will work."

"The gentry will have things to say no matter what, especially because you're with me. Even if you portray a perfect Jovinian female, they would speculate about . . ." He waved a hand in the air. "About the quality of your jewels, the color of your dress, the way you walk. They'll say you have a pig's nose under the veil or a harpy's mouth."

"Witchlights, you make everyone sound awful."

"That's because they are."

"So you will be throwing me into a viper pit?"

"You wanted to be free, didn't you?"

This *was* my fault, but when I asked, it had been my only path to freedom. Now, there was Jeondar, and he was a better alternative. But who was I kidding? I didn't want to be locked up in this chamber like some sort of criminal.

"You'll learn to play the game," Wölfe said, sliding the back of his hand tenderly down my cheek and giving me an electric jolt right to my core. "You're smart, melynthi."

I took a step back, escaping from his touch. "You keep calling me that. What does it mean?"

He only gave me a crooked smile. I would have to ask Jeondar about that damn word.

Wölfe quickly covered the small distance I'd placed between us and locked an arm around my waist, pulling me close. I pressed my hands against his chest, which was a mistake because the feel of him was simply decadent.

"Here you go, forcing me again," I spat.

"I won't have to, after tonight."

Why did he keep saying that? Was he planning to get me drunk or roofied?

"You're delirious." I tried to push him away, but I might as well have been trying to push on Mount Ruin.

"I *am* delirious . . . with want. You have no idea the effort it takes not to rip your clothes off and make you mine again. But I'm not a monster, regardless of what you may think. I simply know what I want, and I'm not afraid to go after it. You will be mine, willingly. And that will be the reward for my patience."

Despite his words about waiting for my acquiescence, he leaned down and kissed me, his lips warm, his tongue trying to pry my mouth open. The feel of him was intoxicating, and it took all of my willpower not to respond.

When I gave him little more than a dead fish, he pulled

away. I thought he would be angry, but he only appeared amused.

"You're either lying to yourself or trying to lie to me," he said. "Either way, it's a waste of time, especially the latter." He tapped his nose. "Your arousal never goes unnoticed." He released me and walked toward the fireplace.

Dammit!

Without thinking, I allowed my dark side to come out and play.

"Well, you do have an advantage," I said. "You are wearing Kalyll's body."

I practically felt his growl of anger reverberating through the air and was glad to be a distance away from him. His eyes darkened, and those spidery veins around his eyes spread toward his temples and cheekbones. It took him a moment to rein in his fury, but he did.

After a deep breath, he said, "Have you stopped to consider that it may be the other way around?"

"Don't be ridiculous. You didn't even exist a few days ago."

"Are you sure?"

He sounded so confident that I hesitated.

"Who might have the Seelie Prince been without all his tutors and lessons about right and wrong? Without the shackles of duty and responsibility? Well, I'll tell you who. You're looking at him. I'm all his secret wants and desires. I am his selfish needs, the one who will never put anybody else's happiness above his own."

"Not even mine," I bit back.

"Not even yours, melynthi." He held my gaze unapologetically. "But don't forget this . . . you have a choice in the matter. A righteous male who always does the honorable thing but puts you last, or a scoundrel who raises you on a pedestal and worships you above all else."

His words hit me like arrows to the chest. I was no princess, no heroine from an epic tale. I never dreamed of star-crossed love affairs with males who could lead legions and defeat evil for the good of the many. I was only a simple girl who wanted to find someone who would love her unconditionally and would choose her over anything and anybody else.

I turned away from him, faced the bed, and buried my hands in the dress's soft layers, feigning interest. Silence reigned over us for a moment, then Wölfe walked toward the door.

"I will send the pixie to help you get dressed and will be back in half an hour."

CHAPTER 9
DANIELLA

The makeup around my eyes was a work of art. With half of my face covered, Larina made sure that my one visible feature was flawless and striking. She also weaved my hair in an intricate style that nothing but her agile, magic fingers could have accomplished. Lastly, she adorned my new pointed ears with jeweled cuffs that sparkled, complementing the shimmering eyeshadow.

The dress was also an art piece to complement everything else.

When Wölfe returned, there was no gawking, no compliments, no startled expression necessary. It was his hooded eyes and unapologetic erection that said it all. The heat of a blush warmed my cheeks as he took my hand in his, locked his gaze with mine, and traced a circle in the palm of my hand, as if he were suggesting the way he'd like to caress my most tender spot.

He tucked my arm under his elbow and guided me toward the door.

My heart thudded out of control for many reasons, the least of them managing to fool the locals that I was Fae *and* Jovinian. Honestly, I didn't think that even the best Hollywood actress could pull this off.

You'll learn to play the game, Wölfe had said. But I wasn't so sure.

I wasn't raised to scheme or use my tongue like a weapon. I was only a healer in a quiet corner of my realm, a person with no other ambition than to live a happy life helping others, spend time with my family, and maybe, one day, raise a family of my own. What did I know about kingdoms and the powerful people who ruled them?

He guided me out of the room and down a narrow hall with walls made of stone. The air was cool despite it being summer. Shivers slipped down my spine like foreboding warnings, urging me to turn tail and run away. I clenched my teeth and kept walking. Our steps echoed as we began descending a winding staircase, not a soul around to hear them. It seemed this was a private passage, reserved for the prince.

"Is this a tower?" I asked as we kept going down in a spiral.

"Mm-hmm."

How Rapunzel of me and Dame Gothel of him.

Tapestries and paintings decorated the walls, depicting breathtaking scenes of the Fae countryside. Fairy light sconces along the walls and beams of moonlight streaming through circular windows illuminated our path.

I was almost dizzy from going round and round when we reached the bottom and faced an arched metal door.

As Wölfe went to turn the handle, it didn't budge. He tried again, to no avail. For a moment, he seemed frustrated, then took several deep breaths and tried once more. This time, the door unlocked magically, a metallic click reverberating with finality.

Curious.

It seemed the lock was coded to the prince.

I was familiar with this kind of thing. Securities spells were my mother's specialty. Back home, her door remained locked, but it always allowed access to her kids, even after we moved out. She could "program" whoever she wanted, and her spells could also raise an alarm if they detected an intruder.

In this case, it appeared this particular magic hadn't detected Wölfe as a rightful user—at least not until he calmed down and tapped into a different version of himself.

We exited into a manicured garden, bathed by moonlight. Wölfe closed his eyes, lifted his face to the sky, and inhaled deeply.

Silver light delineated his sculpted features. He was so handsome that my knees wobbled. The column of his neck was strong, and I longed to run my tongue along its length, longed to feel him squirm under me, his length thrusting deep inside of me.

Without opening his eyes, he spoke with a rumble in his chest, "I can almost hear your dirty thoughts, Dani."

What the hell? What was he? Psychic?

"No, not psychic. There is a slight scent of pheromones in the air. That's how I know."

Clever asshole. Unable to help myself, I jabbed my elbow into his ribs. He shrank back a little, more to chuckle than to express any sort of pain.

"Next time, I will knee you in the balls," I shot back.

"Try it, and I'll punish you."

The threat should have scared me. Instead, it sent a thrill of excitement straight to my middle.

"Let's run along," he said. "We don't want to be late."

We walked around the circumference of the massive tower we'd just exited. I glanced up and found that, beyond my prison, the top of a white, vine-covered spire scratched the underside of the clouds above.

The Vine Tower.

This was the Seelie palace, and it was worthy to be called that.

It turned out the chamber where I'd been confined was in one of the smallest towers that rose alongside the big spire. Still, if I'd managed to open one of the windows, it would have been for naught. Unless I was feeling suicidal.

It was a fifteen-minute walk to make it to the front of the palace, where a majestic staircase led to a crystal door, resplendent with fairy lights glowing from within. We stayed out of sight. Just a few people dressed in high Fae fashion climbed the steps on their way in.

"You go first," Wölfe instructed. "Don't talk to Kryn and the others. Understood?"

I narrowed my eyes in answer.

"If you do, I won't be able to let you leave the tower again. Please, don't try anything stupid."

I crossed my arms and rolled my eyes. "Okay, fine."

"Walk to the page and announce yourself as Ylannea Fenmenor."

"What? I'm going to forget that. You should have told me all of that beforehand."

He took my hands in his and made me face him. "Repeat with me. Yla-nnea."

"I'm not a child."

"You just said you would forget, so I'm trying to help.

Don't be unreasonable, wench." His face looked pinched, as if he were forcing back a smile.

"Don't call me wench, you . . ." I fought to find a mean word to call him. "You troglodyte."

"I'm a troglodyte?"

"Indeed."

"Fine. What is your Jovinian name, then?"

"Um . . . Elana something."

"Wrong."

"Okay. What was it?"

"Ylannea Fenmenor."

I repeated the name carefully a few times until he approved.

"Now go up there." He whirled me around and spanked me on the butt.

I glanced over my shoulder, pointing a finger straight at his nose. "Don't you dare do that again."

"Oh, I will dare, and you will like it more than you did just now."

I was about to let out a string of curses that would bring his mother into the conversation when he pressed a finger to his lips, then dissolved into a cloud of black mist. I held back a gasp and stared.

The darkness settled on the ground and crawled in my direction. My heart picked up its pulse, and I hurried forward. I tried not to look, but it was impossible not to let my eyes wander after the puddle of shadows that moved unnoticed by everyone else. It slithered carefully among other shadows, taking inconspicuous shapes.

I finished climbing the slick marble steps and made it to the top. That pressure in my chest that seemed to never leave grew tighter with nerves. A Fae page bowed and asked for my name.

"Da—" I bit my tongue. Wölfe's shadow had me so distracted that I nearly messed up. I cleared my throat, "Ylannea Fenmenor."

He quickly checked the list, then inclined his head, and gestured in invitation, urging me into the Seelie Palace, the place where Kalyll had grown up.

I stepped into a grand ballroom and gawked. Shimmering walls shifted, as if made of sparkling water. Twinkling fairy lights hung everywhere, casting a warm and magical glow over the massive room. Gauzy streamers and sparkling crystals adorned the ceiling, casting rainbows all around. Music flowed from second-floor balconies flanked by stained-glass windows.

The diverse guests drew my attention. There were the slender, elegant types with stately noses and mesmerizing good looks, stout dwarfs with braided beards and more gold necklaces than height, green-skinned dryads with gossamer dresses and tinkling laughter, horned males with thick manes, and more.

As for the food . . . there were tables laden with every imaginable delicacy, from sweet fruit tarts and creamy pastries to savory hors d'oeuvres and spiced meats. The guests feasted on the food and drink, while lively music enchanted the senses. Others danced and twirled, their outfits shimmering with the light.

Tangled up in my awe, I lost track of Wölfe's shadows. For a moment, I searched for it, until I noticed a few people looking at me strangely. I paused, my back pressed against a wide column, and looked around the room, trying to spot a familiar face: Jeondar, Arabis, Cylea, or even Kryn. I saw none of them and only noticed a buzz of curiosity travel around the room.

Whispers were exchanged and charged glances were directed at me.

No one knew me. Naturally, they would wonder who I was.

Panic was setting in when I noticed Jeondar near one of the food tables. He was reaching for one of the many glasses filled with what appeared to be red wine. I made my way in his direction, not caring about Wölfe's instructions. I was nearly there when the jerk materialized behind Jeondar and shook his head at me, his expression saying, *didn't I tell you not to try anything stupid?*

I veered slightly to the left, pretending Jeondar hadn't been my intended target, and instead focused my attention on a platter of small pastries. As I picked up a tiny pink cake, Wölfe slapped a hand on Jeondar's shoulder, startling him.

"What?!" His head jerked to one side. "Oh, it's you. You scared me."

Wölfe came around Jeondar and picked up a glass of wine for himself. He pretended to notice me for the first time.

"My apologies," he inclined his head, his expression pleasant, unencumbered by darkness. My heart ached as, for the first time since Mount Ruin, I caught a glimpse of Kalyll. "I didn't mean to get in front of you. Here." He offered me the glass of wine he'd picked up.

I met Jeondar's gaze for a brief moment, too afraid we would give each other away.

"Um, thank you," I said in a slightly deeper voice, affected by an accent that I hoped resembled Arabis's. I felt ridiculous acting this way, especially since the subterfuge wasn't necessary. Jeondar knew exactly who I was. Not to mention the fact that I felt as if Wölfe could see right through my act.

"I haven't seen you before," Wölfe said. "Are you one of my brother's friends?"

Witchlights! What was he doing putting me on the spot like this? I nearly panicked, but, of its own accord, that other side of me interjected and came to the rescue.

"A friend of a friend," I said smoothly.

"I'm Kalyll Adanorin." He pressed a fist to his chest and bowed slightly. "And this is my friend Jeondar Lywynn."

"I know. The Seelie Prince and the Summer Court Prince. Your reputations and ranks precede you. I'm Ylannea Fenmenor."

Wölfe gave me a quick wink, as if approving of my work. Little did he know he was the one being fooled, not Jeondar.

"Am I right in assuming you come from Jovinia?" Jeondar asked, playing his part flawlessly.

Wölfe's eyes slid in his friend's direction for a quick assessment of his reaction, and the tint of satisfaction in his expression told me he was buying the performance within the performance.

"I am," I said, "but I've been enjoying Elyndell for the past few months."

"And what do you think so far?" The wolf in Kalyll's skin asked.

"Honestly, I haven't had the chance to see very much of it. I've had to remain indoors due to my seasonal allergies." I was laying it on a bit thick, but the hell with it. This situation was already fucked up beyond recognition.

Wölfe cleared his throat, and Jeondar hid his reaction by taking a swig of his wine.

"It's a pity," Wölfe said. "Perhaps I should take it upon myself to show you around."

"That sounds like a magnificent idea."

Jeondar shook his head slightly. I ignored him, hoping he didn't make a habit of expressing disapproval like this. Too much of that, and Wölfe would notice sooner or later.

Wölfe opened his mouth to say something, but before he had a chance, Kryn, Arabis, and Cylea joined us.

"There you two are," Cylea said with her usual liveliness. She flipped her blue hair to one side.

I smiled under my veil, glad to see them, even Kryn. The time we spent with a common quest in mind undoubtedly created a link between us, even if it was a tenuous one.

Cylea went on. "We've been looking for you. This is such a vexingly boring party. The word is the real celebration is happening in Cardian's quarters." She reached for a glass of wine, then appeared to notice me for the first time. "Who's your friend?" she asked, tipping the glass in my direction.

"Her name is Ylannea," Wölfe responded. "We just met."

Cylea looked me up and down, her clear eyes as cool as a winter morning. She twisted her mouth to one side, appearing unimpressed by what she saw. Her assessment confused me.

Had Jeondar not had a chance to tell them about me? And if he *had* told them, were they angry at me? Blamed me for creating Wölfe? It wouldn't be the first time they acted like assholes because they feared I would drive a wedge between Kalyll and his betrothed, ultimately becoming the reason for a war everyone was desperate to avoid.

The appraisal I got from Kryn was no better, but of course, I wasn't expecting anything else from him. Arabis, as usual, was the only one that held a modicum of sympathy for me when she politely introduced herself and bowed, her blue eyes intent on mine.

After a quiet moment, Wölfe's gaze roved over the crowd. "I must agree with you, Cylea. This party leaves a lot to be desired. No one is even dancing anymore."

With a slight bow, he turned to me and extended his hand. "Will you dance with me, Lady Fenmenor?"

"Oh, no," I objected. "I'm not familiar with any of the steps."

"Something else I can take upon myself to remedy."

"Kalyll," Jeondar said in a pinched voice, "I don't think that's advisable."

"Would you have me be rude to one of Cardian's guests?"

Undeterred, Jeondar leaned forward and hissed something I couldn't hear in his friend's ear.

"Nonsense." Wölfe dismissed him, blowing air through his nose.

He snatched my hand and pulled me toward the center of the now-empty dance floor.

Intricate marble patterns inlaid with other beautiful materials created a design at our feet. I stared at them as if trying to decipher the shape they created—something that could only be discerned from high above, I suspected. Still, I made a show of trying even as Wölfe wrapped an arm around my waist, even as every pair of eyes turned in our direction.

Wölfe nodded toward the musicians, and on his command, the tune changed to something slower.

"I don't think this is such a good idea," I whispered. "Kalyll will know something is wrong when he hears about it tomorrow morning."

"No. He will have a vague recollection of dancing with a beautiful Jovinian female and think he did it while intoxicated with wine."

"You can make him believe that?"

He nodded, smiling. "Every day, I seem to have more control. Soon, I'll drive him out."

The thought was terrifying, and I had to armor my spine not to slump with dejection.

He guided me forward, keeping eye contact the entire time. His hands were gentle as he twirled me this way and that, making sure I didn't falter. He was an excellent partner, and in his arms, it wasn't hard to pretend I knew what I was doing, despite my nerves.

"Ignore them," Wölfe said as I glanced around the room and saw several people whispering in each other's ears, all the while throwing daggers at me.

"It's not easy," I said. "It's like I'm a freak show. I'm the center of attention."

"They're only wondering who the unknown beautiful female is. The veil makes the secret more alluring. And you are no *freak show*, though you definitely are the center of attention, especially mine," he added the last two words in a low, husky tone that immediately brought my awareness back to the circle of his arms.

Our gazes locked, we danced, my movements becoming more adept.

"Much better," Wölfe said, crushing me against his toned body.

Looking up at him, somehow forgetting everything else, I felt like the heroine of an unlikely fairytale. I was dancing with the Seelie Prince, secure in his strong arms, while he looked at me as if I was the only thing that mattered.

I lost track of the ballroom, lost track of everyone around us, lost track of myself as I fell into his beautiful eyes and felt the truth of his feelings for me. For all the wrongness of his approach, Wölfe wanted me and wasn't afraid to let the entire realm know it.

It would have been beautiful if it wasn't so terrifying, if it might not lead us down a path of destruction that would hold nothing but regret for both of us.

As images of war-torn cities exploded inside my mind, three things happened at the same time. I pushed away from him, repelled by the possibilities of what we could bring about. The music stopped, and someone started clapping.

CHAPTER 10
DANIELLA

A Fae male of about my height and build approached, a crooked smile twisting his thin lips, his perfectly manicured hands held high as he clapped. There was something slightly familiar about him that I couldn't place.

A small retinue of people hung behind him, one that included the last person I wanted to see there.

Naesala Roka.

"Thank you for getting things going, brother," he said, gesturing around to indicate a few others who had joined in the dance. "Who is your lovely companion? She is quite good at The Faerie Mystic."

Brother!

That was why he seemed familiar. There were minor similarities between the two, such as the shape of their eyes and nose, though Cardian's features were weak, boyish, and ill-proportioned. He definitely got the short-end of the genetic pool, though since they didn't really share a father, it was no surprise.

"Cardian," Wölfe said in greeting, not a hint of annoyance in his attitude, though it was clear that causing annoyance was Cardian's aim. "Best wishes on your special day. One hundred is a great number."

One hundred? He didn't look any older than me—on the contrary, he looked like he belonged in high school, though he must have found a great remedy for acne because his skin was baby-smooth.

"My lovely companion's name is Ylannea Fenmenor. We just met. She's a fairly new arrival in Elyndell."

"Enchanted, Lady Fenmenor." Cardian peered at me with curious eyes that were much lighter than Wölfe's deep cobalt shade.

"The pleasure is mine, Prince Cardian. My best wishes on this day."

He smiled condescendingly and offered no thanks. There was an oily quality about him that made me dislike him immediately. The sorceress bitch's presence at his back didn't help his case. Naesala would pay for the pain she'd put me through.

"I haven't seen you in some time," Cardian said. "How was your journey to Imbermore and *beyond*?" The way he pronounced the last word immediately brought to mind Mount Ruin.

Wölfe narrowed his eyes, probably wondering the same thing I was. What did Cardian know about our quest?

Wölfe smiled pleasantly. "My journey was excellent. King Lywynn and Queen Belasha send their regards."

Cardian rolled his eyes as if he thought nothing of the considerate tidings from ally monarchs. "I'm wondering . . . should you be dancing with beautiful females who are *not* your betrothed, brother? People will talk, especially since you didn't visit your bride-to-be during your trip as you were supposed to," Cardian said a bit too loudly as he watched closely for my reaction.

I offered none, but the same couldn't be said about those within earshot. The din of their gossip increased immediately. What Cardian suggested seemed to cause enough panic. Hell, *I* was panicking, but the comment slid off Wölfe like butter in a hot skillet.

He chuckled. "I'm far from married, my dear brother." He patted the top of Cardian's head as he would a dog's.

Cardian jerked away, his face blushing with anger. I had siblings. I knew what it was to tease and be teased. I knew what it was to send and receive annoyed looks, but this was quite different. Cardian was beyond all of that. He was full of wrath and hatred. He held no sympathy for his brother. Not one bit.

The younger prince composed himself with some effort. "You're right, as always. We should enjoy ourselves while we're single."

Smoothly, he stepped in front of me. "May I?"

Without waiting for an answer, he wrapped an arm around my waist and twirled me. I blinked, disoriented, a feeling of repugnance washing over me at the sensation of his clammy hand as he grabbed mine. I wanted to push him away, to make it clear I had no desire to dance with him, but I was paralyzed by indecision. For Kalyll's sake, I didn't want to make a scene.

The problem was . . . Wölfe didn't share the same concern.

With one large hand, he pulled Cardian away by the

back of his jacket. The collar tightened around Cardian's neck, nearly choking him. His arms windmilled as Wölfe let him go.

Eyes as large as saucers, Cardian stared at his older brother. Wölfe started to raise a fist as if to deck him, but I stepped in front of him.

"Thank you for protecting my virtue, but your brother meant no disrespect," I said, making up shit as I went and staring daggers at Wölfe, trying to convey a message: *This is not normal behavior. Supposedly, you just met me, remember?*

"Nobody touches you but me," he said, low enough that no one else could hear him, thank goodness.

My eyes begged him. *Please.*

He controlled his anger, though not easily, then donned the nonchalance he'd been wearing earlier. "Have you forgotten your manners, Cardian? You're supposed to ask a lady's permission before you touch her. Mother would be disappointed. Lady Fenmenor." Wölfe crooked his elbow in invitation.

I slipped my hand through it and walked away as he led me out of the dancing floor. Everyone's stares felt like invisible whips, flogging away my dignity. I felt humiliated and completely out of place. I didn't belong here. Even though they believed I was Fae, they still hated me. I didn't want to find out how much worse it would be if they knew I was human. They would probably lynch me and put me on display as a warning to any of my kind who'd dare to tangle with their royals, no less.

When we made it back to the others, and I noticed their expressions, my knees wobbled. I felt as if I would die of mortification, and at that moment, I wouldn't have cared if the entire city of Elyndell cracked in two in order to swallow me.

This is a disaster, Jeondar's face said.

The others' expressions weren't much better.

Arabis: *What now?*

Cylea: *Not the kind of excitement I was hoping for.*

Kryn: *I will kill you.*

Maybe I deserved to die at Kryn's hands. I had brought this upon myself, thinking it was a great idea to force Wölfe into giving me freedom. I should have stayed locked up in my tower, safe from the sharp edge of all the tongues that wouldn't stop wagging.

We'd barely stepped out of the dance floor when a young page approached Wölfe and leaned in to deliver a message. "The king wishes to see you, Your Highness."

Wölfe looked annoyed, though not worried. He patted my hand, which was still resting at the crook of his elbow, and said, "I will be right back. Don't go anywhere, Lady Fenmenor."

I would've said something smart-aleck if I'd had the presence of mind, but I was addled, thrown off base.

He moved to leave, but on second thought, leaned close and whispered, "Don't think that revealing yourself to Jeondar and the others will help you. They'll only be angry at you after what just happened."

Oh, they were angry all right. Maybe they would decide to kidnap me again. Though this time, they would do it right after digging a grave for my miserable bones, over which they would dance a jig in celebration of being rid of me and all their troubles.

Kryn stepped to my right and looked straight ahead at the dancing couples in the crowd, who were slowly returning to normal.

"You mean to ruin us all," he said between clenched teeth.

So Jeondar *had* told them about me.

"You were the one who begged me to save him when fate spelled his death," I retorted.

He had no answer to that, and though I was right, his animosity still seemed to wrap his hands around my throat, intent on choking me.

"Say something productive for once, Kryn," Arabis said. "Otherwise, keep your mouth shut."

Kryn opened his mouth, but Jeondar preempted him. "This is no time or place to argue about this."

"The one person out of the bunch who has any sense," I put in.

"Incoming," Cylea warned.

I glanced around to find Naesala Roka walking in our direction. She moved as if floating, her black, shimmering dress and red, red lipstick accentuating her femme fatale look.

Surreptitiously, the others moved away from me.

"Greetings, *Ylannea*," the sorceress said, as if I were her long-lost friend.

I would be lying if I said I didn't have the urge to strangle her right then and there, but somehow, my common sense prevailed, probably because Logical Dani seemed to be in full control at the moment. I had the sense that the dark side of me was amicable to necessary evils such as involuntary magical plastic surgeries.

"Fantastic performance," she said.

I bit my tongue. If I hadn't, I was sure the word *bitch* would have slipped out.

"You are certainly rocking the boat," she added.

I glanced at her sidelong, pondering her use of the phrase *rocking the boat*. It seemed she had spent some time in my realm or had studied some of our phrases. I wondered if she also *exchanged favors* with Hollywood types and filthy-rich oligarchs.

She shook her head, causing her silky black hair to sway from side to side. "You need tough skin in court, my dear. I could tell they got to you. You have to do better."

Tough skin. There was another phrase that I didn't think the Fae used. She either was trying to butter me up or rub my *humanness* in. I didn't like either option.

"What do you want?" I demanded, losing my patience.

"Oh, I don't want anything. I already have everything I could ever desire." She smiled, stretching those painted lips to the max.

"What did Wölfe offer you in exchange for my disfigurement?"

"Disfigurement," she repeated, sounding amused, though not insulted, which I found interesting.

"Well?" I pressed when she didn't answer.

"That's between him and me. But I wouldn't worry if I were you. I just wanted to greet you and say that sometimes you need to bite back. Enjoy." She walked away, waving at me over her shoulder.

"I want to strangle that bitch," I hissed through clenched teeth.

"You and me both." Cylea stepped up to occupy the space Naesala had just vacated.

"She hates King Beathan," Kryn said, appearing next to her.

Jeondar and Arabis joined my other side until we were all standing in a row with me in the middle. For a moment, I worried about what everyone would think about the new-comer standing among the prince's friends. Then I realized it didn't matter—not after the show Wölfe had put on.

"Any progress with those books?" Jeondar asked, smiling and nodding pleasantly at anyone who passed by.

I shook my head. "I suggest all of you get your hands on as much reading material as you can. We should hurry this up."

"Wiser words have never been spoken." Kryn shot me more darts from his emerald eyes. At this rate, he was going to run out before the night was over.

When Wölfe returned, he seemed slightly annoyed but generally unperturbed. Whatever his father had wanted to talk to him about didn't seem to be of much consequence.

"Lady Fenmenor," he addressed me, inclining his head, "I would love to show you the Eastside gardens. They are lovely at night."

A million blaring horns went off inside my head, and from the startled looks of the others, it seemed I wasn't the only one with that cacophony pounding between their temples.

"I would rather—" I started, but Wölfe didn't let me finish.

My words were cut short when he grabbed me by the elbow and practically dragged me out of the ballroom.

Jeondar tried to intervene by offering Wölfe a glass of wine, but it didn't help, and in a matter of minutes, we'd left the party behind and stood alone under a moonlit garden, the same one we'd traversed on our way in.

Wölfe guided me to a bench where he made me sit while he paced in front of me, wearing a rut in the lush grass.

I said nothing and instead stared at my hands in my lap. I'd had enough of words and people for one night. All I wanted to do was lie in bed and hide under the covers. I'd never been particularly fond of social situations, but what I'd endured in the past was nothing compared to the pressures of performing for a bunch of royal dicks.

"Mylendra is coming to Elyndell," Wölfe said after several minutes of pacing.

"What?"

"You heard," he barked.

I stood in one fluid motion. "Take me back to the tower."

He stopped his pacing and faced me. "You don't give me orders, melynthi."

Damn! That word again, and I forgot to ask Jeondar about it.

"Take me back to the tower," I demanded, more forcefully this time.

He barreled in my direction and stopped just short of crashing into me. "You really want to go back to the tower?" he growled.

"Yes, and you'll take me right now," I growled back, even though my bones felt like putty under the intensity of his stare and powerful presence.

"Fine, then."

Before I even knew what was happening, Wölfe scooped

me up in his arms and moved across the garden like a dark tide. In a matter of seconds, we were at his private entrance, up the stairs, and into my chamber.

There, he threw me on the bed as if I were nothing but a sack of potatoes, then climbed on top of me, his strong arms and legs caging me in.

CHAPTER 11
DANIELLA

I held his gaze, trying to appear unfazed, even as I berated myself. How else did I think demanding to be brought back to the tower would end? *Shit*.

"Are you happy now?" he demanded.

"I will be happy when you get off me."

"Oh, I doubt that."

"I know very well what will make me happy. I assure you."

"Is that so?"

I set my jaw in response.

He kissed me, his tongue forcefully slipping into my mouth. I jerked my head to one side to break the kiss, trying to deny the heat that immediately began to simmer in my belly.

"You pretend you don't want me, but I know this makes you *very* happy." He spoke against my throat, his breath hot, his lips wet.

"Get off me, Wölfe," I repeated, though without as much conviction as before.

He kissed the column of my neck, trailing a scorching path from my collarbone to the hollow under my earlobe.

I moaned despite myself.

"Do you still want me to leave?" he asked.

"Yes?"

"You don't sound so sure."

He covered my mouth with his to stifle any answer I might have come up with if I'd been able to, but I was too busy trying not to pull him down so I could jump on top of him instead.

"I know you want me. How could you not, melynthi?"

Arrogant bastard!

Not that he was wrong. The male was delectable and knew how to pleasure a female.

He kissed along the seam of the dress, along the top of my breasts.

Deftly, he started undoing the golden ribbon in the bodice, pulling one strand out at a time, like unlacing a pair of shoes. As he did so, he continued kissing me, his tongue flicking and making circles, promising mischief in other parts of my body, while my blood temperature continued surging.

After a moment, he growled and pulled away. "Damn ribbons!" He reached toward his boot and came up with a dagger.

I flinched, suddenly aware of the darkness around his eyes. He made no attempt to reassure me. Instead, he brought the dagger to the bottom of the bodice, slipped its tip under the ribbons, and yanked it up, slicing the delicate fabric as if it were air.

He discarded the dagger. It thudded to the floor, while his hungry eyes focused on the swath of skin he had liberated. Grabbing each side of the bodice, he opened it to reveal his present. My breasts fell loose. He bared his teeth, a savage grin spreading over his lips. Slowly, he lowered his mouth to my right breast and paused a mere inch from the hardened bud.

"Do you want me to take it into my mouth?" he asked.

The question wasn't fair—not when his hot breath already felt like a caress, not when he'd destroyed all my defenses.

"I do," I answered breathlessly.

The bastard pulled away.

"Beg."

My anger flared. "I will not beg."

"Oh, but you will."

I made to get up, but he met me halfway, his mouth taking mine once more. Dexterously, he relieved me of the torn bodice as well as the rest of the dress until I was left in nothing but my panties. It wasn't until I felt the rough scrape of his pants against my inner thighs that I came to. His kisses were that good and hypnotic.

How had I ended up at such a disadvantage so quickly? I had to remedy that. I reached for the clasp of his pants. He slapped my hand away.

"No, my princess," he chided.

He continued kissing me, but soon he abandoned my mouth. His lips walked a gentle path between my breasts, down to my belly button, and further south. I thrust my hips forward, eager for much more, the heat of my desire for him building, building, building.

He caught my panties in his teeth and pulled them down to my knees. He turned his attention to the aching mound between my legs.

"I like this shape," he said, speaking so closely to my sex

that I felt his hot breath the same way I'd felt it on my nipple. "How do you accomplish this perfection?"

"Mar-tini w-wax."

"Most excellent," he spoke those words hotly right between my legs. "Beg," he added.

"Goddamn you!"

"Is it so hard?" One of his fingers followed the seam of my leg as it attached to other important places. "Just say please. One little word."

Oh, what the hell. Let my pride suffer.

"Please," I begged.

He chuckled deep in his throat and reared up to kiss my mouth. "There's no shame in it, my princess. Pride is useless between the sheets. First things first."

I sucked in a breath as his mouth landed on the breast he'd abandoned just moments ago. His tongue whirled and flicked my nipple as if savoring it. His large hands traveled up and down both sides of my body. He switched to my other nipple, giving it equal attention.

I moaned as his hand traveled down and traced the small triangle of hairs. I was on the verge of screaming for him to forget about my breasts when he completely removed my panties, tossed them to the side, and settled himself between my legs, forcing them wide open.

Licking his lips, he dove in. He slipped his tongue between my wet folds, separating them, then lapping upward to where I needed him most. He inhaled my scent as his tongue flicked and swirled. He used the very tip of his tongue to tease the tender nub, then lapped with more force, then sucked. He alternated several times, driving me crazy, leaving me unsure of which motion I liked most.

After he thoroughly explored with his tongue, one of his fingers inched up my inner thigh and tenderly explored the swollen folds. Moaning, he slipped inside. Curling his finger deep inside my warmth, he stroked that place he discovered the first time, the one no one else had found.

As I let out a sharp moan, he pumped his hand, causing my back to arch and my hips to buck forward. Still working his finger, he clamped his lips around my clit and began sucking at the same time that the tip of his tongue flicked.

Oh, what sorcery is this?

My eyes flew open in surprise, and I met his gaze to ask for more, more!

He obliged.

Sliding another finger into me, he kept the sorcery on my clit. My hips thrust hard against his hand and mouth. He increased the intensity of his plunging fingers. I tightened my fists, taking handfuls of the sheet.

Expertly, seeming to enjoy what he was doing to me as much as I was, he brought me to the edge, where I teetered until I fell over the side and screamed in rapture, my body assaulted by tremors as I found my release. He didn't stop and carried me all the way through the very last of my rocking climax.

As the last waves of pleasure rippled through me, he sat with his back against the headboard, picked me up, and cradled me in his arms, a defenseless, trembling bird in the cage of his arms.

He smoothed my hair, whispering words I didn't understand in my ear, making me feel loved and appreciated.

"You make me understand why in your realm *honey* is used as a term of endearment," he said in a husky voice. "You certainly taste like it."

Awkwardly, he reached for the covers and wrapped them around us, making me more comfortable than I already was. He kissed the top of my head and breathed me in.

I started drifting off to sleep, my ear pressed against the thump of his heart. I was nearly lost in dreams when he stood abruptly, dropping me as if I'd burned him.

Confused, I blinked up at him, gathering the sheets around my chest. Hatred burned in his eyes.

"It is not he who seeks your heart and your pleasure," he bellowed.

I shook my head, my mind reeling, trying to . . . then it hit me. I'd spoken a name as I'd been drifting off to sleep.

"I am not Kalyll, and you should know he's never sought you out. It has always been me." He hit his chest. "Wölfe. Remember that the next time you beg me to fuck you."

He stomped out of the room and slammed the door shut, leaving me trembling in the middle of the bed. Confusion and a million questions morphed into a pounding migraine as I scrambled to answer them truthfully.

Was he telling the truth? And if he was, did it mean I loved Wölfe and not Kalyll?

CHAPTER 12
DANIELLA

I didn't cry myself to sleep, though I wanted to. Except, I had no right to cry. I brought this on myself. I even begged for it.

Despite the lack of tears, the next morning I woke up puffy-eyed and wrapped up in the sheets that still smelled of him. I was still there when Larina arrived. She fluttered in and stopped in midair when she caught sight of the torn dress and dagger on the floor.

Her cheeks lit up to a bright lilac, and she proceeded to serve our breakfast in an effort to hide her embarrassment—not that she needed to, since *I* was already pretty well hidden under the sheets and behind the curtains of the canopy bed.

But I had work to do, and I couldn't lie in bed all day, so I walked to the washroom wrapped in a sheet. After a quick bath, I emerged, wearing a robe and running a jewel-encrusted comb through my wet hair.

Larina was fluttering by the mantle, staring at an envelope that rested against the clock.

"What is that?" I asked.

She shook her head, then used her magic to lower the

envelope to my hands. I opened it to find a letter written in a beautiful script.

You're free to do as you please. Go back to your realm. Stay. It's your decision. Maybe you can find your prince, profess your love to him, and live happily ever after. Destroy me, if you will. What is the point of a half-life?

Wölfe

With the letter trembling in my hand, I walked to the door and tested the handle. It turned. It wasn't locked anymore. I released the knob and took several steps back. Wölfe must've come back last night to leave the letter while I slept.

"He went back to the party last night," Larina said. "He fought with Kryn Goren and beat him pretty badly."

"Oh, no." I pressed a hand to my mouth, knowing it was my fault. "Did someone tend to him? Is he healed now?"

"I suppose so."

I crumpled the letter in my hand. "This is all my fault. I shouldn't have . . ." I paced, my eyes constantly going to the unlocked door. I could go talk to Kalyll, tell him what was happening. He would know what to do. He would move heaven and earth to find the information we needed to devise a cure. Then we would be rid of . . .

"Are you all right, Dani? Is there anything I can do to help?"

I shook my head.

"At least drink some of your coffee. You might feel better."

"I do have a migraine." I had healed it a few minutes ago, and it came back with a vengeance. I collapsed in the armchair and picked up the cup that magically appeared in front of me. I took a couple of sips, cradling the brew with both hands.

"I'm in love with him," I blurted out, needing to confide in someone. I met her gaze, expecting to find surprise in her expression, but there was none. "That obvious, huh?"

She nodded.

"The problem is . . . after last night, I don't know which version of him I love."

Now surprise did shape her features. "There should only be one version," she said tentatively.

"I'm not so sure. You don't know the entire story. You see, Prince Kalyll was, is, a . . . shadowdrifter."

Larina shook her head in confusion. "That's impossible." Despite her words, I could see the cogwheels working inside her mind.

I let her think, let her make her own deductions.

"That night in Imbermore," she started, "at the Summer Solstice Ball, a beast attacked and injured King Elladan. It was him."

"Yes."

"But that makes no sense. There has never been any indication that either the king or the queen are . . ." she trailed off, again making her own deductions. "He's not the king's son! Oh, dear!" She pressed the tiny hand to her chest as she floated down to the armchair across from mine. Her wings beat weakly, as if the shock had driven all the strength out of her.

I explained. "That was the reason we had to go to Mount Ruin. He confronted Caorthannach, demanding she take the demon energy out of him. There was a terrible battle against her spawn, but in the end, she lost and agreed to it. But in the last instant, Silver betrayed him. He stabbed him in the back, pierced his heart. I . . . the only way to save him was to use the demon energy to heal the wound. He would have died otherwise."

"Oh, dear. Oh, dear." Larina jumped to her feet, aided by her wings, then started fluttering up and down, up and down, her slippered feet barely brushing the chair before she was up again. "This is bad. So bad. If anyone finds out. Oh, Prince Cardian can't become king. It would be a disaster. Sure war." She kept ranting, switching to a low mumble that I couldn't understand.

I thought confiding in her would be helpful, but she was stressing me out. I abandoned my coffee and stood.

"I have to change." I hurried into the closet and got dressed, unsure of what to do. The more I turned things over in my head, the more I despaired.

When I came out, Larina was again sitting at the edge of the armchair, looking reasonably calm. Maybe she'd fluttered enough and had spent her nervous energy.

"You don't need books on demons and their dark forces," she announced.

I blinked, confused. "I don't?"

She wagged her index finger at me. "In fact, you don't need

any books. What you need to do is talk to Queen Eithne to find out the identity of Prince Kalyll's father."

"We need to do what?" Jeondar demanded, as I ran a finger along the spines of the books on one of the cases on the second floor.

"Shadowdrifter. Shadowdrifter," I mumbled as I skimmed the titles.

"Dani! I'm talking to you."

"Ask *her*. She seems to know what she's talking about." I pointed backward without looking in the general direction of the sound of whirring wings.

From what Larina had told me in the last hour, pixies were also affected by the shadowdrifter curse. It was a source of embarrassment to her kind, an ailment they didn't readily admit to. Not only that, the ailment was particularly prevalent in her village. According to her, it was actually more common between pixies than among any other Fae kind. A shadowdrifter in someone of Kalyll's kind was extremely rare, even rarer in a royal. She quickly explained all of this to Jeondar, then proceeded to the juicier details.

"Shadowdrifters share energy from a common demon," Larina said. "If we can find Prince Kalyll's father, he can help draw the energy out. Like calls to like," she added, reminding me of the thought I'd had the other night, the way the energy inside me seemed to call on my darker emotions.

"And how do you do that?" Jeondar asked.

Larina shrugged. That was as far as her knowledge went. Hence, my need to find some reference material.

I found a book that looked promising. It had been on my list to inspect, but I hadn't made it a priority because I'd been focused on being more specific and learning more about demon energy. I plopped down on the floor, crossed my legs, and started leafing through the book.

"But how could his father help do something like that?" Jeondar asked.

"He should have been helping the prince all along," Larina said, "if he knows how, that is. I'm assuming he does. With proper instruction, a shadowdrifter need not be wild. They can learn to control their instincts. It's not easy, but there's plenty of time to practice since the ailment doesn't present itself until late in life."

"You're saying that if Kalyll had grown up with his father, he wouldn't have turned into that . . . beast?"

"I'm saying he would have been able to do it in a controlled way."

"By Erilena, this is mad."

"Tell me about it," I piped in from the floor. "If Queen Eithne had owned up to her indiscretion, I would be happily oblivious back home." Not that this thought was exactly comforting, since it meant I would've never met the prince.

Jeondar scratched his chin. "And what exactly makes you think Kalyll's father knows how to control his instincts?"

"It's logical," Larina said.

I chuckled. This conversation was following exactly the same path that my earlier conversation with the pixie had. Jeondar was asking the exact same questions I had, and I was glad not to be the one explaining things. I was too overwhelmed to even make sense of the book's glossary.

"Logical how?"

"I doubt Queen Eithne would have . . . tangled with someone who would turn into a wild beast."

"Why not? *Others* have." Jeondar's amber eyes darted in my direction.

"Hey!" I slapped his leg without thinking, then pulled my hand back, reminding myself not to get so chummy with the royalty.

"There are simply too many safety fail-safes around the queen. It seems unlikely that an uncontrolled shadowdrifter would reach her circles."

"One came into the Summer Court," Jeondar said, more to himself than anyone else.

"Only because he was in the guise of the Seelie Prince," Larina said.

"True. So true." Jeondar put a hand on his forehead, as if he also had a migraine. "So, why didn't you mention any of this before?"

"I didn't know we were dealing with a shadowdrifter," the pixie said. "You mentioned demon energy."

"It's the same thing."

"Not necessarily."

"She's right, Jeondar," I interrupted. "Let's stop arguing and figure out what to do." I stood up and set the book down on a nearby table.

"Did you find whatever you were looking for?" Jeondar asked.

"No. I can't look at the words straight, but it doesn't

matter. What Larina is saying makes sense, so we should do as she suggests. We find Kalyll's father. His father does whatever it is he needs to do, then the prince gets Naesala to undo my disfigurement, and I go home." It all sounded very rational, so why didn't a big part of me like the sound of it?

Jeondar placed his hands on his hips and looked up at the ceiling, appearing frustrated. "We can't just march into the queen's waiting room and ask, *Your Majesty, could you please tell us who was that male you slept with one hundred and twenty-six years ago?*"

"I'll do it," I burst out. "Queen *schqueem!* I once walked into my boss's office and demanded a raise. How different can this be?"

Jeondar exchanged a glance with the pixie. "You obviously have never met Kalyll's mother."

CHAPTER 13
DANIELLA

I wanted to wear comfortable leggings and a tunic, but since I was supposed to be Jovinian, Larina said it was out of the question. Apparently, females from that part of the realm only wore dresses, so I was stuck with another silk and chiffon mess. *Witchlights*, I missed my scrubs. They really had spoiled me. At least I could be grateful for Fae shoes. High heels were not a thing—smart people—and the slippers Larina provided were as comfortable as walking on bare feet through spring grass.

I set the veil in place, glaring at my pointed ears in the mirror and thinking I would never get used to the sight of them, nor forgive Wölfe for altering me,

Yeah, right, Logical Dani piped in. *You're so angry at him that you let him* cuddle *with you last night.*

Cuddle? The darker side of me said. *He worshiped you with his tongue. Yes, a small contribution to the huge debt he had built, but I'll make sure he pays. Fully and thoroughly.*

Logical Dani rolled her eyes. *Of course, keep telling yourself that.*

"Are you ready?" Jeondar called from outside the large closet.

"Coming." I shrugged the insistent darkness away and joined Jeondar.

He examined me from head to toe and gave a grunt of approval. "It's not smart to make the queen wait."

It was nearly impossible to get an audience with Queen Eithne, but Jeondar had managed. He sent a private note, a cryptic message he was afraid she wouldn't understand, but that—considering how quickly her attendant returned—she seemed to have fully grasped.

"We will take a longer route through the western corridors," he said. "It would be best if no one sees us, especially you. *Especially* after last night. Gossip is already running rampant."

I had no objection to scurrying about the Seelie Palace. I much more enjoyed anonymity. Being the center of attention had never been my thing. My youngest sister, on the other hand . . . Lucia seemed to thrive in the limelight. Besides, I had the feeling that the court would eat me alive if given the chance. My skin wasn't tough enough for the likes of well-trained hyenas.

Jeondar took huge pains to lead us through empty halls. He even sent Larina to scout ahead and had us backtrack a couple of times in order to avoid being seen. Despite the stressful situation, I enjoyed walking through the palace, seeing the exquisite décor, a stately and whimsical interior design that only the Fae could pull off.

Vines were everywhere on this side of the palace. They seemed to make up the very structure of the building, coming in through the windows, twisting and turning, curling around pillars and frames. Some had shimmering flowers that caught the light and sparkled like jewels.

But it wasn't only vines. The abundance of greenery was a marvel. Everywhere I looked, there were plants of all shapes and sizes, from tall, flowering trees to tiny, intricate ferns. Some glowed with an otherworldly light, while others pulsed and moved of their own accord. A hum of enchantment seemed to ride the air, evidence of the Fae's innate magic. I could do nothing but gawk.

"I wish we could avoid the guards," Jeondar said as we made a turn into a long corridor. At the end, a huge door flanked by two Fae royal guards awaited. They wore purple livery, indicating they were the queen's guard. They stood like those British dudes by Buckingham Palace, staring straight ahead and looking like statues.

"I don't think you need to worry about them," I whispered, leaning toward Jeondar. "They are as dead as door knobs. Maybe I should check their pulse."

Jeondar snickered despite himself. "Honestly, I shouldn't worry. They're sworn to secrecy. They are highly trained and are the most loyal subjects you can imagine."

I shrugged. "Dead people tell no tales."

We stopped several yards from the majestic door they guarded. Several gold-trimmed benches were lined up against the wall, a place for visitors to sit and wait.

Two almost identical large paintings flanked the door. I was immediately struck by the scene: dark, enchanted forests with twisted and gnarled trees, their leaves outlined with a soft, ethereal light. Glowing eyes seemed to watch me from behind large, leathery leaves in the foliage. I tore my attention away from the canvases, denying the foreboding feeling they brought on.

Instead, I glanced surreptitiously toward the guards, but they stared straight ahead into the distance, acting as if we weren't there. I was tempted to walk up to one of them and stick my tongue out to see if they'd react. I suddenly wished for my cell phone, since it was the sort of silly, touristy shenanigans perfect for social media.

"You know," I whispered, "a video-conference would have saved us all this trouble. What do you people have against technology? You have access to it. You've seen everything that can be accomplished with it."

"Can you honestly say you would spoil the beauty you've seen in our realm with your technology?"

"I know there are a lot of bad things that can come from it, but you could pick and choose, I suppose."

"I don't think that's possible. It's not like you could introduce cell phones without the need to build towers everywhere, or without risking our minds."

"There's nothing wrong with my mind and I have a cell phone."

He scrunched up his nose. "That's debatable."

I mock-punched him in the shoulder. He smirked. I was about to tell him about the joy of cat gifs when the ornate door opened and a sprite dressed all in black and carrying a tiny spear came out. She fluttered on iridescent wings like Larina's, but that was where the similarities stopped. Her face was unlike any other creature I'd ever encountered. Her skin was gray and her eyes narrow slits with all-black orbs. Her nose was flat, almost non-existent, and her thin-lipped mouth gave way to rows and rows of curved teeth. Jeondar seemed to shudder in her presence, which made me instantly fearful of the creature.

"The queen is ready to see you," she announced with a slight bow and an extended hand, her demeanor at odds with her appearance.

My heart started pounding, which took me by surprise. The pressure in my chest grew tighter with anxiety. Being a little nervous had seemed okay, but this was major. My heart was suddenly in my throat, and I had the urge to run away.

Settle down. This is not like you.

You're about to meet your mother-in-law, my dark side quipped.

Shut up!

Reigning over my nerves, I matched Jeondar's measured steps and ramrod-straight posture. As I focused on placing one foot in front of the other, I stared at the floor, trying to convince myself the marble pattern was more interesting than the one in the ballroom.

A pungent smell had my nose twitching. Forgetting I was trying to memorize the floor, I glanced up to find something completely unexpected: a large room in complete disarray, filled with a myriad of canvases of different sizes, all set up on tripods.

I blinked, unable to focus on one thing. There were paintings in all stages of production, some mere sketches, others blotted-out shapes with no definition or depth, while others brimmed with detail and seemed to come to life with realistic lighting and shadows.

"Queen Eithne, your next appointment is here," the sprite announced, then quickly left the room.

A hum of acknowledgment came from behind a massive canvas. We waited for several minutes. Silence, except for the slight scratching of a brush against canvas, filled the air. The scratching stopped. I waited with bated breath, suspecting she was making us wait on purpose.

A moment later, she finally appeared, weaving through the many canvases and making her way to us. I exchanged a glance with Jeondar, trying to convey my surprise. This was nothing like what I'd been expecting. I'd been imagining a stately woman sitting on a throne set atop a dais from which she could look down on us. I'd even imagined a crown and a huge dress that made her look like a birthday cake. But I should've known better. It was Kalyll's mother, after all.

She was cleaning her fingers with a paint-stained rag and wearing the type of leggings and tunic I myself preferred. Her midnight blue hair—the exact shade of Kalyll's—was arranged in a messy bun atop her head. She had a few smudges of yellow paint under her cobalt eyes, also the same color as Kalyll's. She was tall and graceful, and there was no denying who her son took after. I imagined that after her illegitimate baby was born, it was a great relief to find that he favored her and not her shadowdrifter lover.

"Prince Lywynn," she said in a deep voice, addressing Jeondar.

"Your Majesty." He pressed a fist to his chest and bowed deeply.

She smiled graciously at him, then her eyes flicked to me as if she expected a bow or a curtsy from me, either of which she was not going to get. I wasn't her subject, and the fact that I was here entangled in this mess was indirectly her fault. She'd get no kowtowing from me. She had fooled around, made a shadowdrifter, then left everyone else to pick up her mess, which I imagined wasn't uncommon for the likes of her. She narrowed her eyes as if that would get that curtsy out of me. I narrowed my eyes back.

"Your Majesty," Jeondar glanced at me sideways, looking like he wanted to elbow me into compliance, "this is Daniella Sunder. Kalyll has told you about her already."

I lowered my veil.

"It's a pleasure to meet you, Lady Sunder. I am grateful for the help you offered my son." She inclined her head, her expression pained. I imagined she didn't like the fact that a human was aware of her adulterous business. She had kept a prodigious secret for over a century, and it hadn't been by sharing it with people she considered beneath her. I wondered if she feared I might blackmail her for the crown jewels in order to keep her secret.

That's a plan, dark me piped in.

She narrowed her eyes at my ears but said nothing about them.

"As nice as it is to meet my son's . . . benefactor, it was quite unnecessary, Prince Lywynn."

The bitch.

"I know," I interjected as Jeondar opened his mouth to answer, "I didn't want to meet *you* either. You can blame your precious son for the inconvenience."

Jeondar gulped, giving me a sidelong glance of disapproval.

The queen looked taken aback, surely unaccustomed to anyone being real with her. Well, I didn't know any other way to be. Where I came from, you weren't raised to kiss royalty butt, or any other type.

She sneered, then turned her attention to Jeondar, acting

as if I'd become invisible. "What is this about? Your note was rather cryptic, worrisome even. Don't tell me it was a subterfuge to gain an audience."

"No, Your Majesty. Nothing like that. We really need to talk to you about—"

"Kalyll is still *sick*," I said, cutting to the chase and making air quotes.

Her darkest-blue eyes flicked in my direction. She opened her mouth to say something, then shut it. Remembering I was supposed to be invisible, she addressed Jeondar.

"My son isn't sick. I saw him this morning *and* last night. He looked as strong as ever."

I sighed and preempted Jeondar again. "Very well. He's still possessed by demon energy, then. Better?"

"Get this person to stop talking to me," the queen ordered Jeondar.

"Seriously?" I said. "What are you? Three years old?"

"Dani, please," Jeondar appeared flustered, "maybe leave this to me."

I considered it. I really did. I preferred avoiding confrontation, always had, but I wasn't exactly the same person I'd been a month ago anymore, was I? Especially after what I'd done to save Kalyll's life in that cave and after killing an innocent guard.

"Listen, I'm going to tell it to you short and sweet," I said, "so you'd better pay attention."

The queen's eyes were practically blasting lasers in my direction, but I didn't care. She could sentence me to die by the sword of one of her many Fae royal guards for all I cared. She owed me and listening to me was the least she could do.

"There is a sliver of demon energy left in Kalyll. He doesn't turn into a beast every night like he used to, at least not entirely. But he stops being himself at nightfall, all the same. He calls himself Wölfe and hates Kalyll. In fact, he plans to take over him, to erase him. And from what I've seen, I think he can do it. I assume you don't want that to happen, and there's only one way to stop it. That darkness must be driven out of him, and at this point, there is only one way to accomplish this. So the faster you tell us who Kalyll's real father is, the faster we'll get out of your pretty blue hair."

Jeondar buried his face in his hands and scrubbed downward, looking as if everything was lost, but honestly, he had to realize that they blew so much air up this female's butt she was over-inflated.

Fit to burst, I would say.

The queen's mouth opened and closed several times before she found her voice. "You two, get out of here!"

"Your Majesty, please forgive Lady Sunder. She doesn't understand court etiquette and—"

"Get out of here. Now!"

"Yes, Your Majesty." Jeondar bowed and started walking backward.

When I didn't move, he put my veil back in place, grabbed my wrist, and pulled me along with him.

"Fine, it's your funeral," I called to the queen, waving with two fingers and grinning.

Once outside of the room, Jeondar pulled me down the hall, and when we were a safe distance away from the guards, he stopped and whirled on me.

"What is wrong with you? Have you lost your mind?"

I shrugged. Maybe I had. Who could tell? I'd lost a number of other things already.

"You're acting nothing like yourself, Dani. If I had known you were going to do that, I would have never brought you with me." He paced in front of me, pulling at his locks.

"That woman has a stick up her butt."

"Maybe she does, but she's the queen, and we needed her help."

"Excuse me, but I think she needs *our* help, wouldn't you say? We've already been doing her dirty laundry for her as it is."

"You've lost your mind. You have definitely lost your mind."

"If I have, it's thanks to you and your beloved prince. I had to tangle with demon energy, Jeondar. You didn't think I would come out unscathed, did you?"

"What are you saying?"

I rolled my eyes, batted a hand at him, and started walking away.

"Wait a minute," he grabbed my arm, spun me around, and looked me straight in the eye. His amber gaze scrutinized me for a long minute. "Oh, shit."

"Yeah, shit."

"Why didn't you tell me?"

"It doesn't matter. I have it under control."

"The events of moments ago say otherwise."

"Look, I think that—"

"Jeondar?" a familiar voice called from a corridor we'd just passed.

The way Jeondar's face turned into a mask of panic, I

thought he would grab me and take off running down the hall, but somehow, he managed to compose himself, and pressing a finger to his lips, he narrowed his eyes in warning.

He put on a smile that was almost convincing. "Kalyll," he said as the prince rounded the corner.

CHAPTER 14
DANIELLA

Kalyll came to a halt, the smile on his face slowly dying as he took me in. A frown cut across his forehead. He blinked several times, looking as if he were trying to grasp something slippery, something that didn't want to be caught.

"Lady Fen-Fenmenor." He swallowed thickly, looking mortified.

Wölfe said Kalyll would remember what happened last night, and it seemed he hadn't been lying.

Now, the prince stood there, looking like he wished it'd all been a bad dream. His head swiveled from side to side as if the words he needed to say were written on the walls.

I would've laughed if my heart hadn't been beating so fast. Kalyll was here.

Kalyll, not Wölfe.

I had the urge to throw my arms around his neck and tell him everything. He needed to know. He could help us, except Jeondar and I had discussed the possibility earlier and decided it was a bad idea. We needed to keep what we were doing a secret. We couldn't risk Wölfe getting a whiff of our plans. He seemed to have more control than Kalyll and was too unpredictable to trust.

You would betray Wölfe just like that? my dark side—Dark Dani—asked.

Betray Wölfe? For real? He was the one who turned *us* into a mutant Fae.

Us?

Witchlights! Maybe Jeondar was right, and I'd lost my mind and had multiple personality disorder. Only a fraction of what Kalyll was experiencing, and still extremely disorienting. What he must be going through . . . I couldn't imagine how he felt.

At last, Kalyll seemed to find his composure. "I must apologize for my behavior last night, Lady Fenmenor. It is no excuse, but I believe I had too much to drink and got carried away."

"I have no complaints about your behavior, Prince Adanorin," I found myself saying, while Jeondar threw another disapproving glance in my direction.

Kalyll smiled, his sculpted lips quirking to one side, and for the first time, he seemed to really look at me. He scanned my face, my ears. His eyebrows pinched slightly, and his nose twitched. For an instant, a spark of recognition shaped his features, then was gone, chased away by reason and plausibility. Once on the side of logic, his mind turned to practical matters.

"Jeondar, how come you're here and with Lady Fenmenor?" he asked, glancing around the hall, eyes full of suspicion. He could find no reason for the random Jovinian he barely recalled and one of his friends to be hanging out in his palace.

Jeondar didn't miss a beat. "I was showing her around. We

just visited the queen's second reception room. Lady Fenmenor really enjoyed your mother's paintings."

"Lovely work. Amazing talent," I said, building on the lie. "Though I was hoping to have a different tour guide. Don't get me wrong, Prince Lywynn, you're an excellent host, but . . ." I let the words hang, allowing my suggestive tone to do the work.

Oh, God! What am I doing?

I was totally unhinged.

"I did promise to show you around, didn't I?" Kalyll said, looking both eager to do as he'd promised and miffed by his own enthusiasm. He had his reserves about hanging out with another female, no doubt, and I would have loved to know why. Did they have to do with Daniella Sunder or Mylendra Goren?

Next to me, Jeondar was practically turning purple with frustration. He looked as if he wanted to wring my neck, but I didn't care. I had missed Kalyll, and the idea of spending some time with him and not Wölfe was enticing.

You really are a cheating whore, aren't you? Dark Dani's voice said inside my head.

This isn't cheating, my other side protested.

Kalyll and Wölfe were the same person.

You know that's a lie, Dark Dani again.

"It would be my pleasure to show you around, Lady Fenmenor." Kalyll offered me his hand.

I took it. "Please, call me Ylannea."

As I glanced back at Jeondar, he shook his head, his eyes practically screaming for me not to go anywhere with the prince. I gave him a sly smile. Did he really think I would miss this chance?

"Have you seen much of the palace?" Kalyll asked as we made our way down the hall, leaving a frustrated Jeondar behind.

"Not much. Just the ballroom, the wing with your mother's paintings. Oh, and the Eastside gardens you showed me last night."

He frowned, appearing confused, probably scrambling for the slippery memories Wölfe had left behind for him to glimpse. Slightly shaking his head, he rearranged his confused expression into one of self-assurance. His gaze hardened, and his large chest expanded as he inhaled and stretched to his full height, becoming the picture of that strong legendary prince I'd read about before I even met him. He cut an impressive figure dressed in a dark blue coat that perfectly matched his hair and eyes. A sword hung at his side, practically humming with lethal potential. The skin around his eyes was clear, no dark veins to obscure their striking quality.

"And what do you think of the palace thus far?" he asked.

"It's a beautiful place, certainly, but I tire of being indoors. I'd like to see the city. Maybe your favorite place."

He smiled at that, a twinkle in his eyes, as if he knew exactly where to take me. "Regrettably, my favorite place is also indoors."

"Is that so?" I asked, immediately curious. "Here in the palace, I assume?"

He nodded.

"Well, before we go anywhere else, I would love to see it."

I was surprised when I found myself back on the private staircase that led to my tower.

"Where are you taking me?" I asked, suddenly nervous.

Kalyll looked around, blinking as if he'd just realized where he was. "My apologies. I should've probably considered the . . . privacy of this route, but fret not, we're almost there."

When we reached the top of the stairs, we continued down the hall, and passed a door I assumed led to his chamber. We stopped at the next door, a very wide one that I knew belonged to the library. I swallowed thickly, wondering if this meant Kalyll was gaining strength. Up to now, Wölfe had kept him from coming here. Did I dare hope?

"Here we are." He turned the doorknob, which immediately responded to his touch and gave way, allowing us entry. Walking a few paces past the threshold, he spread his arms wide. "What do you think?"

I did my best to appear as surprised as the first time I'd seen the beautiful library. Despite its undeniable splendor, however, I couldn't deny I was underwhelmed. Out of all the enchanting places in Elf-hame, this was it?

"Your favorite place in the *entire* realm?" I said, my voice betraying a bit of my disappointment.

"Not exactly."

He marched across the library toward one of the sitting nooks, pointed at the window, and flicked both hands in opposite directions. The wooden shutters opened with a slight creak, and bright morning sunlight spilled in. He had no magic to do that, but it seemed the shutters were enchanted for his benefit.

"This right here." He patted the cushion. "This is my favorite place in Elf-hame."

I approached, my slippered feet padding softly. Stopping by his side, I glanced through the window and marveled at the breathtaking view. The city of Elyndell spread before us like an artfully weaved tapestry, dutifully put together by mother nature herself. The Seelie capital was a perfect blend of Fae-made buildings that seamlessly blended with the natural beauty of the land. Majestic trees turned into dwellings, thick branches served as bridges, vines held lanterns that likely glowed with fairy lights at night. A sparkling turquoise river wound its way across the city, running alongside cobbled paths, disappearing under buildings, reappearing on the other side, then climbing away to disappear in what looked like a painted horizon.

"It's . . . spellbinding," I breathed.

Kalyll smiled, satisfied, then proceeded to open the other two windows. When he got to the last nook, he paused and picked up the book I'd carelessly tossed there for Wölfe's benefit. He turned it this way and that in his hand, looking puzzled.

I watched warily from the corner of my eye and was relieved when he tossed the book aside, dismissing it. He came back to stand by my side and admire the view.

He sighed, "I've spent some of my most enjoyable evenings sitting here with a book, reading and pausing to contemplate between pages while letting my gaze wander over the city."

"It sounds lovely," I said, finally understanding why this was his favorite place in the entire realm. Despite being a warrior, he enjoyed peace.

We were quiet for a moment, and I got lost in my thoughts as I attempted to follow the river's path. It took me a moment to realize the prince was staring at my profile.

Feeling self-conscious, I met his gaze for a moment, then, as the heat of a blush assaulted my cheeks, I glanced away, thankful for the veil that covered my embarrassment.

"You remind me of someone," he said.

I let out a shaky breath. "Someone nice, I hope."

"She . . . saved my life."

"Oh."

"I owe her everything." He lowered his head, looking miserable. A muscle jumped in his jaw as he clenched his teeth.

I struggled against the lump that formed in my throat and turned to face him. "Where is she now?"

He said nothing. Instead, he raised a hand and pressed it to his chest.

Tears pooled in my eyes, my heart breaking. This wasn't fair. Kalyll deserved to know what was happening.

"Kalyll," I said, abandoning the stupid accent and tone of voice I'd been using.

His head jerked as he turned to look at me, frowning deeply.

Giving myself no time to think about the consequences, I tore the veil off my face.

Shock disfigured Kalyll's face. His mouth hung open. His eyes went wide, all as a sharp intake of breath seemed to paralyze him.

"It's me, Daniella."

He shook his head, his attention going back and forth between my pointed ears and the rest of my face.

"It can't . . . What tri-ckery . . . is . . . this?" His words came out chopped, stuttering. He wrapped a hand around his throat as if he were fighting a choking sensation.

"What is it?" I placed a hand on his biceps. It went taut and trembled.

He pushed my hand away and stepped back, his back hunching over as he racked stiff fingers into his hair and grabbed his head.

I took several steps back, my heart pounding. I barely had time to register his movement when he barreled into me, pushing me into the reading nook and holding me down.

"You really prefer him?!" Wölfe's dark eyes bored into mine as he growled in anger, bending me backward until I felt I might break. "Even when you tremble in my arms when I fuck you? Is he your choice?" He shook me and dug stiff fingers into my shoulders, making me whine in pain.

"You're hurting me," I spat.

"Answer me. Do you really choose him over me?" he repeated, unrelenting. "And don't lie to me."

He wasn't going to let me go until I gave him an answer, but didn't he know it was impossible for me to decide?

"I don't know," I burst out, tears spilling down the corners of my eyes.

"I said don't lie to me."

"I'm not lying. I don't know. He's tender, and you hurt me. He chooses duty, but you choose me. I don't know. I don't know. I don't know," I repeated over and over again, my voice growing louder each time.

He pushed away and whirled, turning his back on me and grabbing at his head again, struggling with his demons. His chest was rising and falling visibly as he panted. Slowly, he calmed down, his spine straightening.

On autopilot, I pushed away from the nook, smoothed my dress, wiped away my tears, and put the veil back on.

Kalyll glanced around, looking disoriented. When he spotted me, he blinked several times, looking lost. Then he seemed to remember himself.

"I'm boring you," he said. "You didn't come to Elyndell to see my library and hear me ramble on about . . ." He waved a hand in the air as if it didn't matter what we'd been talking about.

"I'm not bored. I can assure you," I said, affecting a fake tone again and swallowing my tears.

"How would you like to see The Stonepoint Fields? Have you visited them yet?"

I shook my head.

"Then let's go." He offered me his hand, his expression calm and placid once more.

We left the library, and this time, we left the tower through a different route. We encountered more people—servants mostly—who bowed and stood out of the way to let us pass. We were on our way out when one of the many page boys, who seemed to be everywhere, came after us.

"Your Majesty." He stopped, looking breathless as he inclined his head. "Your father requires your presence."

Kalyll looked annoyed. "Tell him I'll be back in a couple of hours."

"He said it couldn't wait," the boy added, staring at Kalyll's boots.

The prince smoothed one of his eyebrows as if to dispel a headache. "I'll be there shortly." When the boy disappeared around a bend, Kalyll offered his apologies. "I'm sorry, Ylannea. I'm afraid we'll have to do this another time."

"I understand. Your duty must always come first."

His face pinched slightly at the words, then he smiled, nodded politely, and walked away. I stood in front of the massive crystal door that led outside. Vines and roses created a frame around the edge, a detail I hadn't noticed last night. There was no doubt the exquisite door had been created through magical means. There was no other way to accomplish such splendor and functional beauty. I was taking a step forward to leave the palace and find my way back to the tower through the garden exit Wölfe had shown me, when the same messenger boy who delivered the king's message appeared at my side.

"My lady," he said, "the queen wishes to see you."

CHAPTER 15
DANIELLA

T en minutes later, I found myself back with Queen Eithne. I was sitting on an armchair across from her in the back of her workshop area, surrounded by canvases that seemed to stand and watch my every move, just like the queen.

Tea and pastries were set up in front of us, along with a jar of cube sugar and one of golden honey. She meticulously prepared her tea, drizzling honey into her steaming cup. I was too nervous and confused to partake, so I sat with my hands in my lap, worrying at a hangnail. Why was I here? And more importantly, why wasn't Jeondar?

When the queen dismissed us, she'd appeared rabid, ready to bite my head off, but now she was smiling, looking as pleasant as could be. What a psycho.

"Now," she said, after daintily sipping her tea, "explain everything from the beginning."

I pondered for several moments, unsure of how much to tell her. What would she think of her son kidnapping me for a second time and keeping me prisoner in their very home?

Are you truly asking yourself that? You know exactly what she'd think, Dani.

Both of my warring personalities could agree on that. Queen Eithne would not like what was happening between her son and an *altered* human right under her nose. Like everyone else, she would worry about their arranged alliance with the Fall Court, the possibility of war if Kalyll didn't marry Mylendra.

Either way, what was the point of lying? If she didn't already know I was staying here, she would soon find out, one way or the other. There was no point in hiding that fact, at least. The best thing was to tell her what she wanted to know, so I could get the identity of Kalyll's father out of her. The sooner I found that out, the sooner I could go back home.

Will you so easily give up? Dark Dani asked.

I don't belong here, fake ears or not. Trying to find a place where I'm not wanted will only cause pain.

Dark Dani seemed to have no argument against that.

Inhaling deeply, I told the queen everything, leaving no details out except the intimate ones. Though I was sure she could divine those all on her own. When I was done, she was quiet for a long time. I expected her to lash out, to incriminate, to blame, but when she spoke, she was sober, understanding, and empathetic to a surprising level.

"You have dealt with much, and both Kalyll and I owe you a debt. If my son had died . . ." She seemed unable to finish. "My husband is a benevolent, capable king. He has kept the peace for hundreds of years and our realm prospers. Kalyll will do the same. He has the temperament to rule, unlike his younger brother. So many lives depend on him. You can say Elf-hame's future is tied to *his* future."

I heard it clearly what she left unsaid, that this perfect

future she described did not include me. It never had, and it never would. I was one of many stones in Kalyll's road, one that could easily be removed and forgotten.

"If this dark force is increasingly gaining power over my son, it must be stopped. It's as important as his quest to Mount Ruin. Perhaps more, since *Wölfe*, as you call him, means to deceive, where the beast would have been incapable of that."

I nodded in agreement. The beast had been wild, but true to its nature. Wölfe was a snake hiding in the grass. He could attack when you least expected it. I absentmindedly rubbed my shoulder, remembering how he'd struck when I thought I was safe with Kalyll.

"So," the queen went on, "I will tell you who Kalyll's father is and put my trust in your hands. I know you want what is best for my son. I can see you care about him. I can see you understand what's at stake, and what it means to my son to fulfill his duty. I trust you will do the right thing."

I nodded, knowing full well that no other alternative existed. Stone-cold reality was the enemy of our *make-believe* affair. The rest was wishful thinking and fairytales. I was born human, after all. Happy endings, for the likes of me, didn't exist.

Slowly, without breaking eye contact, the queen set her cup down, reached under her chair, and pulled out a dagger. The silver metal glinted and gave a slight *zing*. A burst of adrenaline hit my chest, and for the first time, I considered the queen's intentions under a sinister-tainted lens.

Why would she reveal her lover's identity only to me? Why leave Jeondar out of it? She hadn't kept this secret for as long as she had by treating it lightly. She hadn't even told Kalyll until it was absolutely necessary, until the shadowdrifter symptoms manifested. And still, she hadn't revealed his father's identity.

For the first time, I wondered if Kalyll's biological father knew he had a son. Had Queen Eithne kept the truth even from him? If she had, she guarded her secret more tightly than I had previously imagined.

But now, others knew.

Jeondar, Arabis, Kryn, Cylea, Silver, Larina, and me. There was also the possibility that Silver had shared the information with Lyanner Phiran, the Unseelie Court spy he'd been working with. And if he had, how many more were now aware that the Seelie Prince was a bastard?

How angry must the queen be to see her well-guarded lie so liberally spread about?

And now, here she was, about to share yet another secret she'd faithfully guarded for over a century.

"I can see you're a smart female," the queen said. "You have reasoned things out, and your understanding goes deep. The secrets I hold can topple kingdoms, destroy worlds."

"Your mistakes as well," I said, knowing she would catch my meaning without the need for elaboration.

"Kalyll was no mistake."

What? Was she saying she'd planned to put an illegitimate heir on the throne from the beginning?

"There's one more thing I'd like you to do," she said.

Great!

"I need you to find out what Silver Salenor divulged to the Unseelie spy."

"What? But he had refused to talk and hasn't said a word since Mount Ruin."

"That is not my problem."

"It isn't fair, I—"

She smirked, then lifted the dagger. "First, we will make a blood pact to ensure you won't do anything that will risk Kalyll's position as future king, including sharing the name I'll give you with anyone outside of my son and his circle of friends. I realize you may need their help as you did before, but I trust them well enough. They've been faithful thus far. Now, give me your hand." It wasn't a request, but an order.

I tightened my fists in my lap.

"The dagger is enchanted," she explained, as if that would alleviate my concerns. "The pact will keep you faithful as well."

So she trusted the others, but not me? But of course, I was only a filthy human, after all.

"And what do I get in return?" I demanded, my anger rising. "What do you promise to do for me?"

She looked taken aback. She was used to being obeyed, never questioned.

She pressed the pad of her index finger to the tip of the dagger, pursing her lips in consideration.

"I don't suppose you desire riches since you didn't accept them from my son." She scanned my face over the dagger, reading my reaction to her comment. When she was satisfied that she guessed correctly, she said, "How about this? You properly cure my son, keep my secret, and I spare your life."

The coldness and meaning of the words hit me like a slap in the face and made me realize I was way out of my depth.

It never occurred to me that my life was of such little use that anyone would consider ending it. What had given me the idea that I could demand anything from this female? She was a master at this game while I was nothing more than a naïve child.

"What do you say, Daniella Sunder?" She brandished the dagger. "Do we have a deal?"

"No. We don't." I stood, surprising even myself. "You can figure out how to cure your own damn son."

She blew air through her nose. "I have to give it to you. You're *brave*." She said the word as if it was a novelty, something she rarely encountered. "But dear, choice, for people like you, is really an illusion. So do as I say, or you won't be the only one who suffers. My hand can reach deeply into your realm, and I'm sure you wouldn't want your loved ones to pay for your shortcomings."

"You bitch."

"No need to be crass." She ran the dagger across the palm of her hand. Blood seeped out of the shallow wound.

Feeling utterly defeated, I snatched the offered dagger and did the same. She stood, and we shook hands. I pulled away almost immediately, grabbed a cloth napkin from the tea table, and wrapped it around my palm.

"I would offer to heal that," I gestured to her hand, "but the thought of your discomfort brings me pleasure."

She rolled her eyes as if my pleasure was of no consequence to her, then she leaned forward and whispered a name in my ear, a name that turned my spine to ice and threatened to break me in two.

CHAPTER 16
DANIELLA

I couldn't erase the satisfied smile the queen gave me after she whispered her secret to me. She was deranged, sick, twisted, possibly the worst person I'd ever met.

My legs took me back to the tower of their own accord. I was lost in my thoughts, unaware of my surroundings as I tried to think of a way out of this mess. Going to Queen Eithne was supposed to help, not to make everything infinitely more complicated.

Dragging my feet, I entered my chamber and started pacing, my thoughts going around in useless circles. Looking for an escape, I walked into the library, retrieved the book I'd found earlier, and sat to read by the fire.

Soon, I was lost in shadowdrifter lore. The author explained that, due to their rareness, the creatures were deeply misunderstood and unfairly discriminated against. She said that anyone with the proper training would be able to keep the demon energy under control and enjoy the benefits it offered. She also explained that since the demon energy comes from a single source, which got passed down from the parent to the offspring, each generation became weaker.

I paused, pondering. This had to mean that Kalyll's father was a stronger shadowdrifter than his son.

As I read further, I learned that only the firstborn receives a dose of demon energy, which meant that subsequent off-spring were not gifted any powers. Interesting. That answered a few of the questions that had been swimming in my head.

I leafed further ahead, reading headers and trying to find a way to cure Kalyll, a way for the demon energy in his father to draw his out. Then I spotted it. My eyes moved down the page, then read and re-read the passage that explained just how to rid the prince of his monster.

Setting the book down, I wrung my hands.

Wölfe.

Would I really be able to—?

A knock at the door startled me to my feet. I set the book on the coffee table and walked over. Assuming it was Jeondar, I opened it straight away and was surprised to find a stout female on the other side. She was accompanied by a retinue of servants carrying boxes and wore a long purple gown, sym-bolizing her service to the queen. Her eyes were small for her round face, and her hair was a silver-gray, pulled back tightly into a bun at the nape of her neck, and judging by her self-important attitude, she was likely high in the staff totem pole.

"Lady Fenmenor, I'm Elera Venmaris, and I will be your chambermaid. Here." She extended a rolled-up letter secured with red wax.

Speechless, I stared at the royal seal while Elera ushered her people in. They immediately set about the room, cleaning, straightening, waltzing the boxes into the closet. Confused, I broke the seal and read the letter.

Your father is a Jovinian dignitary currently negotiating with the crown. The wool trade is Jovinia's main export and Elyndell has great need of it during the winter months. To show our goodwill, my husband and I are entertaining you as our special guest. I can't have you prancing around the palace for no reason. This explanation will suffice. Burn this letter after you read it.

Queen Eithne

I crumpled the letter and walked to the ever-functioning fireplace. After surreptitiously hiding the book I'd been reading behind a cushion, I threw the letter on top of the burning logs. It ignited quickly, and I watched it turn to nothing but black soot, hypnotized by the glow of the embers.

"What is all this?" Larina asked, fluttering to my left.

I snapped back to the moment and frowned at her. I hadn't seen her come in. "My chambermaid and her army of minions?"

"Chambermaid?" Larina asked defensively. "I'm your chambermaid. Unless you . . ."

I shook my head. "The queen sent her."

"Oh." She hung her head.

"This is great," I said, then cupped a hand to my mouth and whispered, "it frees you up for the important stuff."

A huge smile lit up her face.

"What are you doing here?" Elera demanded, marching in

our direction, her beady eyes homed in on the pixie. "You are not needed. *Shoo, shoo*." She made a sweeping gesture with her hand.

Larina fluttered toward the door, looking chastised.

"She stays," I declared. "I have a strong dislike for loud noises, and I find the trotting of heavy steps quite disturbing." I glanced around the room, wrinkling my nose at her battalion of helpers, who were quite efficient, but also disruptive. "I much prefer the quiet whirring of beautiful wings."

Elera looked shocked. "My lady, after this initial setup, I will be the only one to enter your room while you're here. The queen has expressly requested me to ensure you're comfortable and well cared for."

"And she shall hear no complaint from me," I said. "Not as long as my wishes are fulfilled in their entirety. You may perform your duties unobtrusively when I'm not in the chamber. The rest of the time, I will require Larina." I felt like a complete jerk and expected Elera to call me an entitled brat, but she simply curtsied and inclined her head.

"As you wish, my lady." She quickly ushered her minions out of the room, ordering them to be quiet, and closed the door behind her with barely a click.

I shook my head, bewildered. I wasn't used to acting like a jerk and getting away with it. No wonder everyone in court behaved the way they did. In their world, their whims were someone else's orders, and being an asshole seemed to have no consequences.

Suddenly exhausted, I collapsed in the armchair. Larina was quiet and when I glanced up, I found her looking at me strangely.

"What is it?" I asked. "Is something wrong?"

She shrugged. "No one has ever picked me over a *hasslyn*."

"A what?"

"A hasslyn. It's what we call *classic* Fae. They're the majority."

"Classic Fae." I'd never heard the term, but I knew she was referring to Fae that looked like the queen or Kalyll. People without hooves, horns, wings, claws, or any other similar features. "Well, guess what? I would pick you over Elera and all her minions any day. You're my friend."

Overcome by emotion, Larina fluttered in my direction, rested her head on my shoulder, and did her best to squeeze the top of my arm with her little arms. I wanted to hug her back or at least pat her head, but I was afraid to hurt her.

"I haven't had a friend in a long time," she said. "Not since I left my village and went to Imbermore."

"That's a shame. I don't have many friends back home either. I mostly hang out with my family, but you're so far away from yours. I'm honored to be your friend, Larina."

"The honor is all mine."

I shook my head. "That's not how friendship works. You have to learn to share."

We both laughed, and she fluttered away and took her spot on the other armchair.

"So what happened?" she asked. "Did you find out the identity of the prince's father?"

"I did."

Larina looked expectant.

"Before I tell anyone, I need to decide what to do. It's even more complicated than we thought."

"Oh, dear."

A knock came at the door. Larina moved to answer, but I gestured for her to stay put. Elera was back, and she had another rolled-up letter from the queen. She handed it over and scurried away as quietly as a mouse.

I opened the letter immediately and read it. "It's an invitation to lunch. She wants to officially introduce me to King Beathan and everyone else," I said, my mouth immediately going dry. "Witchlights! I don't . . . I won't . . . what do I do?"

"First things first." Larina flew into action. "We make you look as beautiful as possible."

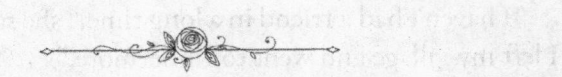

An hour later, I was walking into the most elegant dining room I'd ever seen in my life. The space was spacious and elegant, designed for hosting lavish meals. Three chandeliers infused with fairy lights hung over a massive dining table set with plates and goblets encrusted with precious gems. Large windows to the left were adorned with glittering curtains and twined with vines.

I was surprised and relieved when I found that Jeondar, Arabis, Cylea, and Kryn were there, along with a young male I'd never seen. At least they were familiar faces, even if not all of them were friendly. Kryn still seemed to hate me, judging by the way his green eyes swept over me as they would over a pile of rotting garbage. He didn't even leave room for surprise to enter his expression, not the way the others did.

Jeondar came up to me. "What are you doing here?"

"The queen invited me."

He frowned in confusion.

"I met with her."

"When? How?"

"She called me back sometime after we left her."

"Did she tell you . . .?"

I nodded. "I need to talk to you, figure out what we must do."

"That bad?" he asked, after taking in my expression.

"That bad."

"I'll get the Sub Rosa together, so we can discuss. Minus Kalyll and Silver, of course."

"Minus Kryn too."

He shook his head in disapproval. "I know you two don't get along but . . ."

"Minus Kryn too." I insisted.

"Fine. Fine. We won't be able to keep him out of it for long, though."

"I know that, but I'd like to—"

The double doors at the end of the room swung open, and King Beathan and Queen Eithne walked into the room. Close behind them were Kalyll and his brother, Cardian.

The monarchs sat at the head of the wide table, the queen taking the spot to the right of the king. The princes sat next. Kalyll took the right side of the table, to the left of the king, while Cardian sat opposite his older brother, to the right of the queen.

Once they were seated, everyone else approached the table. The young male took the seat next to Cardian, offering him a huge smile.

I followed Jeondar and felt the moment Kalyll's gaze landed on me. I also felt his shock at seeing me there, and it took all I had to sit without tripping over my nervous feet. I stared at the gold-trimmed plate in front of me, all traces of appetite petering out.

"I see you two have invited your friends *again*," the queen said, her attention going from Kalyll to her youngest son.

"Varamede and I had plans, Mother," Cardian said, sounding bored. "I was already on my way out when Elera delivered your message."

Varamede avoided the queen's gaze. He was a handsome male of about my age with smooth, light brown skin and short black hair. His dark eyes seemed to shine as if lit from behind, a very intriguing and captivating trait.

"What is *your* excuse, Kalyll?" The queen's contempt for her oldest son's friends was undeniable. I realized then that she hated that they knew her secret, that Kalyll had trusted them enough to reveal his true nature.

"Now, now," the king patted Queen Eithne's hand, "leave the boys alone. Kalyll has been hard at work this morning. He's entitled to enjoy a visit with his friends."

The queen rolled her eyes, while I took a moment to examine King Beathan. His wife was such a strong force that he seemed to blend into the background, though there was nothing ordinary about him.

He was handsome, as tall and robust as Kalyll—someone who could definitely be considered his father, even if he had blond hair and beard and a narrower face, which Cardian had definitely inherited, though the youngest prince's temperament seemed more like his mother's. It was only a first impression, but the king appeared to be a nice male, if the gentleness in his eyes and the placid smile stretching his lips were any clue.

"There is someone new at the table," the king said, turning his attention to me. "A lovely lady from Jovinia, I presume."

"Yes, Your Majesty," I managed behind my veil.

Kryn grunted and hid his disgust behind the cup of wine a servant had just poured for him.

"She is Trassin Fenmenor's daughter," the queen informed everyone. "She's visiting from Jovinia and will be staying with us for a while."

Everyone looked bored, especially Cardian and his friend, who were already busy with their wine.

"Master Fenmenor is in the wool trade," Kalyll said after a bit of thinking.

I couldn't help but be stunned by the fact that Wölfe hadn't just given me some random name as I'd suspected. He'd actually assigned me a real identity. It seemed to have worked out nicely for the queen's charade, which scared me at many levels and made me more fearful of being discovered. Somewhere in Jovinia there was a male who wouldn't look kindly at being consigned a fake daughter. Hopefully, he would never hear of me and wouldn't show up announcing that an impostor was attempting to swindle the royal family.

Because, of course, no one would suspect or blame the queen for this farce. The brunt of the responsibility would fall entirely on me.

From across the table, Kalyll watched me so intently that his gaze felt like a powerful force, determined to undress me and lay me bare for his thorough inspection. Tension hung thick in the air. Ironically, everyone was aware of the charade except for the king, Cardian, his friend, and Kalyll, though it was clear, judging by the deep frown across his forehead, that he suspected something was amiss.

Jeondar tried to make small talk with the king, asking him about his latest hunting excursion. The king spoke animatedly, making it clear that this was one of his favorite topics. The queen picked at her food, evidently not a fan of her husband's exploits with the bow and arrow, which appeared to be his favorite weapon for the sport.

He was in the middle of describing the size of the stag he last felled when Kalyll stood up abruptly, planting his hands on the table and causing the dinnerware to rattle. All conversation stopped. For a moment, I feared he would point a finger at me and call me a liar, but with some effort, he managed to get under control the emotions that prompted his outburst.

He took a deep breath and straightened. "My apologies. I have just remembered something critical that requires my attention."

"What could that possibly be?" The king asked, as if his son couldn't have any concerns outside of those he was aware of.

"Nothing for you to worry about, Father. Still, I must take my leave." He pushed his chair aside.

"I'll come with you." Jeondar moved to stand.

Kalyll waved him off. "No need, my friend. I will be back in no time at all."

I swallowed thickly, feeling for all the world as if his promise to be back quickly was some sort of threat.

CHAPTER 17
DANIELLA

"Where do you think Kalyll's gone?" Cylea asked, reclining on an ornate settee as she literally ate grapes like a goddess. She wore a blue dress, the exact shade of her hair and eyes. We were all in her room, which Jeondar had decided was the best place to meet.

Soon after lunch with the queen ended, he'd whispered in my ear for me to follow. He'd secretly communicated to Cylea and Arabis, leaving Kryn out as I'd requested.

The room was as luxurious as mine, except it was airy, with luscious flowers and vines spilling into a wide balcony. Cylea was no one's prisoner, clearly.

Jeondar waved dismissively. "It doesn't matter. It's better if he's not here right now. We need to talk." He glared at me, urging me to divulge what I'd learned. He was standing behind Cylea's settee, gripping its back.

"As much as I like the fact that Kryn isn't around," Arabis said, sitting across from the armchair I occupied, "why did we have to leave him out? He won't be happy when he finds out we're meeting and without him." Her petite frame was perched on the edge of the chair, her back ramrod-straight.

They all turned their attention to me.

I sighed. "There is no easy way to tell you all this." I pressed a hand to my forehead, too aware of how this news would throw our already chaotic situation into further disarray.

"Well, who is Kalyll's father?" Jeondar demanded.

"Earl Qierlan Goren."

The shock that ran through them electrified the room. For several moments, everyone was rendered mute. Arabis was the first one to find her voice, indignation the undeniable fuel that drove her to speak.

"You must have heard wrong," she said, more willing to believe that my hearing was faulty and not the queen's morality.

I said nothing, letting the news sink in further.

Cylea sat up, abandoning her grapes. "I knew she was ruthless, but marrying her son to his half-sister, that is absolutely . . ." She couldn't finish. Vomiting over her blue dress seemed a likelier possibility.

"We can't allow this to happen," Jeondar said emphatically. "We have to tell Kalyll."

"She said she would have me killed if I did anything to risk Kalyll's position as future king," I said. Breaking the alliance with the Fall Court probably qualified.

They all looked at me as if pondering my inevitable death.

I threw my hands up in the air. "I'm dead then. It was nice meeting you all, I guess." I stomped toward the door, wondering why I'd thought I would find any sort of support among these jerks. I knew they would never value me as much as their realm, but a little sympathy would've been nice.

"Dani, wait." Jeondar waved me back. "We're just in shock.

That's all. We need to think. Please, help us reason through this. You've had more time to think about it."

I returned, dragging my feet. Who was I kidding? I had nowhere to go.

"Now, I'm really glad Kryn isn't here," Arabis said.

For someone who claimed not to like Kryn, she surely worried enough about him. I wished they'd just get it on once and for all.

"We'll have to tell him, one way or the other." Cylea shrugged. "By Erilena!" she exclaimed suddenly. "Kalyll and Kryn are brothers."

"I think they knew that, at some level," Jeondar mused.

"Does the Earl know?" Arabis asked.

"The queen didn't say, but my guess is he doesn't." I sat down on a large footlocker at the end of Cylea's bed. "I have to assume he wouldn't let his daughter marry her brother. But you're in a better position to judge his character. You tell me if he would allow that to happen."

They all shook their heads in unison.

"Kryn's father may be an inflexible man, but he prides himself on his family name and maintaining a flawless reputation. I'm certain he wouldn't soil his legacy in such a way."

"Why would the queen do that? I don't understand." Cylea appeared truly puzzled.

Jeondar ventured a guess. "Maybe she's willing to do *anything* to prevent a war. More than her family name, she cares about what the history books will say about her in the future. You know Kalyll always jokes about her dislike for honorable historians who care not for the dignity of their betters. Losing peace during her reign would surely soil her name."

"It's all hunky-dory when she doesn't have to be the one to pay the price," I said.

Fighting the weight of it all, I stood, walked to the balcony, and looked down at the city, its placid beauty juxtaposing with the disgusting turmoil swirling inside the room. Despite our desire to despair, however, it was time to get over our shock and decide on a course of action.

"I think we need to answer a few crucial questions before we decide what to do," I started. "Anyone in favor of allowing Kalyll to marry his sister?" I expected a chorus of disagreement, but no one said anything. I turned to face them, confused. Noticing their chagrined expressions, I added, "Oh, I forgot to add . . . regardless of whether or not the queen kills me."

"In that case, I am *not* in favor of allowing Kalyll to marry his sister." Cylea raised her hand and was immediately echoed by Arabis and Jeondar.

"I think I know the answer to this," I went on, "but you three tell me . . . should we divulge the truth to Kalyll's father?"

Resonant negatives from everyone.

"That's what I thought. How about Mylendra?"

"By all the gods, no!" A more adamant chorus echoed through the room.

"Based on those answers, I believe there's only one way for Kalyll's father to help draw the darkness out."

"Shouldn't we figure out how to draw it out before we decide that?" Jeondar asked.

"I already know," I said. "I found a book that explains it."

Cylea asked, "So then what is the *only* way the Earl can help?"

They all waited for my answer, wearing similar frowns.

"He can't be aware he is helping. He has to be unconscious."

Despair replaced their curiosity.

"That means we have to abduct him," Cylea said, the realization causing her face to crumble.

I nodded.

Arabis heaved a huge sigh. "At this rate, we will promptly become professional kidnappers."

For almost an hour, we discussed ways in which we could separate Earl Qierlan from his personal guard, take him to a secluded location where no one would see us sedate him, and perform the deed that would allow the Earl's darkness to remove Kalyll's.

Easy peasy, right?

Nope.

None of the alternatives we came up with seemed good enough, but I laid it on them to figure out how to accomplish it, while my responsibility would be to create a draught to erase the Earl's memories, plus do the most important part: cure the prince.

Jeondar paced up and down, tapping his forehead. "There has to be a better way. We need to—" He stopped abruptly, his amber eyes lighting up. "I have an idea."

"Well, what is it?" Cylea demanded.

Jeondar lifted an index finger, his thoughts racing, then whirled on his heel and marched out of the room.

"Wait!" Cylea and I called at the same time.

"Typical." Arabis sat next to me. I was back on the foot-locker. Her legs dangled an inch off the floor, making her look like a child. I smiled fondly.

I played with the jewels sewn into my veil, which sat in my lap. "Damn," I cursed under my breath.

"What?" Arabis nudged me with her shoulder. "It'll be all right. We'll figure it out. We've been through worse. Even you have. Mount Ruin was no easy feat."

"It's not that. I needed to ask Jeondar for a favor."

"Maybe we can help." Cylea pushed forward and sat at the edge of the settee. "We owe you that much. We've been such jerks to you."

"You think?" I glowered at each in turn. "You treated me like dirt because . . . because Kalyll likes me, and I like him. Because you wanted him to marry his freakin' sister."

Cylea curled a lock of blue hair around her finger. "In our defense, we didn't know that."

I batted a hand at them. None of that mattered anymore. Changing directions, I said, "Apparently, you do know she can't be trusted. Why is that?"

"Well, she's a bit of a child," Cylea responded.

"A bit?" A snort from Arabis.

"Fine, a massive lot of a very spoiled child," Cylea amended.

"What do you think she would do if she found out?"

Cylea didn't hesitate in her answer. "She would throw a massive tantrum. She might even overlook the fact that Kalyll is her brother if it meant she can become queen."

"That's awful," I said.

"While the earl required Kryn to be the best at everything,

he pampered Mylendra from the day she was born. I doubt she's ever heard the word *no* from anyone but Kryn. When her whims aren't met, she makes sure someone pays."

"She sounds like a piece of work." I shook my head.

"A piece of work," Cylea repeated. "I like your expressions. I'm learning a lot. Piece of work, hunky-dory, easy peasy, hoity-toity."

Silver had also liked the expressions from my realm, which brought me back to what I'd meant to ask Jeondar. These two needed to make it up to me, anyway.

"You said you would help me."

They both nodded.

"I need to see Silver."

"Oh," Cylea breathed out, looking regretful. "Anything else but that. Silver is in confinement. Kalyll's orders."

"Are you sure they are Kalyll's orders and not Wölfe's?" I asked.

"Hmm, good question. Either way, it's not possible."

"So he's just sitting, locked up in a dungeon, and no one has seen him for days?"

Cylea nodded.

"Don't you feel bad?"

"Have you forgotten what he did?" Cylea had been indifferent so far, but now her anger mounted. "He stabbed Kalyll in the back. He was supposed to be our friend and betrayed us all."

"He must've had his reasons."

"If he did, he will take them to the grave. The traitor won't talk to anyone. He hasn't said one word. We've all questioned him, and he just sits there staring at the wall, looking like *he's* the victim."

"*I* haven't questioned him."

"If he didn't talk to us, there's no way he'll talk to you."

"Maybe he will," Arabis said thoughtfully. "Dani is the only other person who can question him, the only other person who was there and knows what happened."

Cylea waved a finger from side to side. "No. Kalyll will get mad."

"He doesn't have to know," I said.

"But don't you feel bad about him, Cylea?" Arabis asked. "I think about him all the time. I feel—"

"You're entirely too soft-hearted." Cylea sounded as if being soft-hearted was the worst possible defect anyone could possess.

"Maybe I am," Arabis responded. "But I'm taking Dani to see Silver, and you won't tell Kalyll about it."

Cylea opened her mouth, then pressed her lips together into a tight line, biting back her protest. At last, she said, "I guess it can't hurt, but just don't let him entangle you with lies," she warned me.

"I don't think I could get any more entangled than I already am."

"If I were you," Cylea narrowed her eyes, "I wouldn't tempt fate."

CHAPTER 18
DANIELLA

Arabis guided me through the bowels of the palace, moving swiftly from well-traveled corridors to areas that seemed abandoned in comparison. The decorations and vines on the wall went from abundant to nonexistent, and the lighting became sparse.

At last, we descended a set of stone steps that seemed to go down forever. I expected to find a damp, filthy space like I'd seen in too many movies, but besides inadequate lighting and a minor stale odor, the place wasn't so bad . . . for a prison.

There were two guards standing at attention just outside the entrance. They saluted Arabis with a fist to their chests, and though they looked at me curiously for a beat, they quickly regained that serious expression that suggested nothing but their job mattered at that moment.

"He's in the last cell to the right," Arabis said, pointing down a long, dark passage lined with empty cells. From the looks of it, Silver was the only prisoner.

My slippers barely made a sound as I walked across the stone floor. My heart started pounding. The last time I'd seen Silver, he'd been tied to a tree. I didn't talk to him since I was in a hurry to leave Elf-hame after finding out Kalyll was engaged to marry Kryn's sister. During our quest to Mount Ruin, I hadn't talked to him much. He'd always remained somewhat aloof, and in retrospect, I could see why. He'd been planning the unthinkable.

I stopped in front of the cell and peered into its dark interior. It took a moment for my eyes to adjust and make out Silver sitting on a narrow cot, legs drawn up as he reclined against the wall. He looked at me curiously from a distance, and after a moment, stood, walked closer, and examined my face carefully. I glanced to one side and then the other to let him examine my ears.

"Not my choice," I said. "But it is what it is." I was hoping curiosity would drive him to ask me what had happened. Anything to get him talking.

But he didn't. Instead, he gave a slight shrug and went back to the cot. I glanced around the cell, the simple wool blanket neatly folded to his side, a small table with a tray and empty dishes, a bucket in one corner, and nothing else—not even a tiny window.

I indicated the bars. "There's magic in these, I assume?"

Silver was an elemental that could control water. With a simple touch, he could freeze and shatter his prison. A powerful counterspell was the only thing that could prevent him from breaking free. It was the same in my realm. Cells had to be able to hold Skews and Stales alike. Otherwise, what would be the point?

He ignored my comment and stared at the wall.

"Why did you do it, Silver? Why did you betray your friends?"

Silence.

"Was it money? Did someone pay you?" I started pacing in front of the cell, pondering. "I don't think so. You don't seem like the kind who would do something like that for financial gain. Blackmail? Maybe someone knows some of your dirty secrets?" I shook my head. "No, I think everybody already knows your darker predilections."

Cylea had called him a whore and hadn't been the least surprised when he abandoned us in Imbermore to go to Glee Alley, a place whose name made it easy to imagine what went on there.

"Maybe it's a different type of blackmail," I whispered to myself. "Maybe the Unseelie King has threatened someone you love."

There was a slight twitch in Silver's jaw, and something told me I'd hit the nail on the head.

"Who is it? Who did he threaten?"

Nothing.

I tried to remember what the others had told me about Silver, about his family, but I couldn't recall any details.

"What did you tell Lyanner Phiran? Does the Unseelie King know Kalyll isn't a legitimate heir?"

Still nothing.

Cylea was right. He wasn't going to talk to me either. This was a waste of time.

Feeling despondent, I leaned against the bars and rested my face on their cool surface. I sighed. "I always thought that living in this realm would be like a fairytale, but it's just the opposite. I haven't been here long, barely over a month, and I've experienced more danger and deceit than in all of my years put together."

"Then it sounds to me like living in your realm is the true fairytale," Silver said, the ring of his voice surprising me.

I didn't move. I just stood there with my face against the bars, afraid to say something that would make him clam up again. I waited for more. He gave me nothing.

"Maybe you should come with me when I leave," I said. "That's if . . . I get to leave. I can't go back home looking like this." I gestured toward my pointed ears. "I need to fix this first, though, believe it or not, it's the least of my worries right now. Things aren't looking up for me. The queen hates me. I think that pretty much spells my death."

"Want to trade places?" he asked. "No one will kill you in here, no matter how much you wish for it."

Okay, definite progress. He hadn't gone back to being silent. Maybe he was tired of his solitary confinement. Whatever the case, I was grateful for it.

"I haven't given up yet." I hoped he got my meaning . . . that it sounded like he had. "I still hope to find a way out of it."

"I wish success for you, Daniella Sunder. But if you fail, may death find you swiftly." His voice was charged with a bitterness I could almost taste. He had failed in killing Kalyll, which perhaps signaled an even bigger failure. The Unseelie King couldn't be happy his mole had messed up.

Going out on a limb, I said, "I can find out if they're okay. You know, your loved one. I wouldn't tell the others. I promise."

That muscle twitched in his jaw again.

"I can't imagine how difficult it must be for you to sit here day after day without knowing." I paused. "Or maybe . . . it's easier than knowing your efforts were in vain, that betraying your friend got you nothing in return. I can understand it either way."

I waited for his answer, but he remained stubbornly quiet. It seemed he was willing to talk to me and release some of his bitterness, but that was as far as he would go. I heaved a heavy sigh, deciding to let him dwell on the idea for a few days in the hopes he'd change his mind.

"Is there anything you need?" I asked. "I can try to bring it to you." I wanted him to know I would come back, that he would have another chance to talk to me.

He asked for nothing.

I retreated a few steps, wishing there was something I could do to alleviate the anguish he was obviously in. I wondered if the others saw it. The betrayal hadn't been easy on him.

"See you later." I turned to leave.

I'd only made it a few steps when he called for me.

"Wait!"

I stopped, and doing my best not to let my relief show, I walked back. He was on his feet, standing in the middle of the cell.

"You swear not to tell the others?" he asked.

"I do." I pressed a fist to my chest because I knew that meant something to him.

He took a few steps toward the bars. I moved closer too and got a better look. He appeared weary, purple circles underlying his slate-colored gaze. His clothes were dirty and crumpled. He'd lost some weight, which made his cheekbones and jaw look even sharper. His once neatly cropped platinum hair was longer, curling around his pointed ears. Light stubble edged his face, glinting silver under the light, doing his name justice.

"You must know that none of the things I'm about to tell you are meant to elicit pity. It's simply the facts."

I put my hands up. "No pity from me."

"Good." He paused. "My mother is lady-in-waiting to the Winter Queen. After my father died in service of the Winter King, Naeduin, the queen offered my mother the post. It's not uncommon for the wife of a fallen general to be offered this kind of opportunity. The honor is meant to soothe the grieving wife, to bring her into court so she can be among other females who might keep her company and assuage loneliness. I begged her not to take the post. The Winter Queen's family has strong ties to the Unseelie Court. Of course, she knew of my friendship with Kalyll, and I suspected that might be the reason she wanted my mother close.

"My father fought for peace. Always. He was there during The Slaughter at Stone Peak. He led men to their doom for what he called a vainglorious cause. Queen Rothala, Kellam Mythorne's mother, wanted to rule Elf-hame for no other reason than to become the most renowned conqueress in the realm. She wanted for nothing. Her land and subjects were under no threat. There was no reason to go to war, but she hated that Kalyll's grandfather and grandmother were beloved by their people. She cared nothing for the suffering and destruction she wrought. She simply wanted to be revered. She didn't care if she sowed fear to accomplish her goals as long as people worshiped at her feet.

"The Winter Queen isn't much different from Queen

Rothala. On more than one occasion, I've heard her lament the outcome of that not-so-distant past. King Naeduin isn't a strong man. He is easily manipulated by his wife and has, in the past decade, formed stronger ties with the Unseelie Court. Do you see where I'm going with this?"

"I do. They threatened your mother."

"She's all the family I have. They sent me . . ." He swallowed thickly. "They sent me her hand."

I gasped.

"Her wedding band was still there on her once-delicate, lifeless finger."

"Silver, that is awful. I'm so sorry. But why not tell Kalyll? I'm sure he would understand."

"No!" he said emphatically. "You swore."

"I think he would forgive you. I think—"

"But I don't forgive myself," he growled, grabbing the bars. "My mother, she would be disappointed in me. I didn't only betray my friends, I betrayed my honor, and in turn, I betrayed her and Father. She would rather endure a thousand years of torture than see herself as the reason for my shame. She asks for nothing for herself. She only wants what's best for me."

Tears pooled in my eyes. What a horrible choice he'd had to make. Let his selfless, loving mother die or kill Kalyll to save her.

"You will keep your promise," Silver said. "If my mother is still alive, she will be safer if I remain here. If she . . . isn't, then I deserve my punishment for what I did to my friend."

I bit the inside of my cheek, doing my best to keep the tears at bay. Taking a deep breath, I gave him a curt nod. "I'll keep my promise, and I'll do my best to find out your mother's fate."

"I thank you." He met my gaze one last time, and in his clear eyes, I saw the depth of his gratitude.

He didn't deserve to be in here. His betrayal had been no trifling matter. Still, I understood his reasons, and I could see myself making a similar decision if I'd been in his shoes. Not only that, I had a feeling that, with time, the others would understand too.

After leaving Silver, it took some time to find my way back to an area I recognized. Once I did, I returned to the tower, feeling the need for solitude. I needed to think about everything that had happened today. I walked down several halls, my attention wandering toward the many adorning tapestries and portraits.

I was so distracted and lost in my own thoughts that I didn't notice someone lurking in a recessed entrance ahead of me. It wasn't until they pressed a hand over my mouth and pulled me into a dark room that I understood that nowhere in Elf-hame was safe for me—not even the Seelie palace.

CHAPTER 19
DANIELLA

A hand went over my mouth, pressing the jewels of my veil against my lips and chin. My heart knocked against my ribs as if someone were punching me from the inside. The rush of adrenaline had me kicking and shoving, trying to dislodge the hand so I could scream, but it was like fighting somebody made of granite.

"*Shh.*" My attacker pressed me against the door, closing it, and trapping me with his body. His chest pushed against mine as I waited for a dagger to twist its way into my belly. Maybe the queen had decided she didn't want to bother with me, after all.

"I'm going to let you go. Please, don't scream."

Kalyll!

I froze.

Slowly, he released me. I blinked, eyes adjusting to the dim light coming through a curtained window.

"Prince Kalyll," I said, deepening my voice, "what is the meaning of this?"

He reached out and, with one swift pull, yanked the veil off. My hands went up to cover my face, but it was a useless maneuver. If he'd gone this far, it meant he already knew who I was.

But how?

Even in the dim light, the hurt and confusion were plain on his face. "I can ask you the same question."

I shook my head at a loss for words.

"Why this charade? Why would you try to deceive me like this?"

"You're assuming too much."

"All I know is that you're trying to pass yourself off as someone else, and for whatever reason, you're lying to me. I have never lied to you, Daniella. I've always been—"

"I did try to tell you, Kalyll. You just don't remember."

He narrowed his eyes, his expression growing pinched as if a memory were trying to force itself into the foreground. He whirled, stomped to the window, and threw the curtains open, allowing the afternoon sun to spill in. Under this new light, he scrutinized my face, spending too much time on my pointed ears.

"What is happening? Why would you do this?" He gestured toward my new features, his mouth twisted to one side.

"I didn't do it. It was done to me."

"Who would dare? I'll kill them." His hand went to the dagger strapped to his side.

"You did."

"What are you . . .?" His mouth opened and closed, and at last, understanding dawned on him. "It's the darkness still left in me, isn't it?" He placed a hand over his heart.

I nodded, my heart hurting at the expression of complete defeat etched on his features.

He collapsed on a long bench situated right under the window and buried his face in his large hands. I just stood there, unsure of what to do, scared of what might be going through his head, wondering how long it would take for Wölfe to reappear and erase the knowledge Kalyll had just acquired.

After a heavy moment, Kalyll stood, took three long steps, and wrapped me in his arms, surprising me, and taking my breath away.

He inhaled my scent. "I have missed you. Every day, I longed to see you, to hold you like this." He pulled away and cupped my face with one hand while the other one remained possessively around my waist. His eyes bored into mine, then he leaned down to kiss me.

I pulled away.

He blinked, pressed his lips together, and let me go.

"I'm sorry if I assumed . . ." He lowered his head, for an instant appearing like a lost child. Though he regained his composure quickly enough to make me doubt my own eyes.

But he wasn't the only one who felt lost. I couldn't understand why I'd pulled away from him, from Kalyll. I tried to tell myself I was overwhelmed, but that dark voice inside me whispered otherwise.

"Those feelings aren't proper, Prince Kalyll," I said, my own words surprising me. Apparently, I had a bone to pick with him. He had let me go. He had chosen duty over what we shared. "Your fiancée would *not* approve."

"Daniella, you know I—"

"I don't know anything. We never talked about what happened between us. You only told me about the alliance that would save your realm from war, and I heard the rest loud and clear, even if it was left unsaid."

A war seemed to take place in his stormy dark blue eyes,

but in the end, he remained Kalyll all the way through. "Once more, I owe you an apology. You state the facts more clearly and bravely than I ever have. Despite my feelings, a greater responsibility calls on me."

His integrity was a blow that nearly knocked me to my knees. I wanted to rail at him, to beat my fist against his chest, and demand he pick *me*, but how could I do that? How could I expect him to endanger his people when I knew well that, presented with a similar choice, I would do the same?

No, you wouldn't, the darkness in me said, but I shoved it aside, silenced it. It didn't belong to me. That was not part of me. It had never been.

But it was always part of Kalyll. It belongs in there, and you had no business trying to take it out. That's why you failed. That's why you need to leave it be now.

I turned sideways and clapped my hands over my temples, forcing my true nature over that invading voice.

"Daniella . . ." Kalyll took a step closer, a hand raised as if to touch me. He stopped short, made a fist, and lowered his hand. "Are you all right?"

I composed myself and faced him again, my expression stern and distant. "We have much to talk about."

"It seems that way. Perhaps we should sit." He pointed toward the large sofa.

I ignored it and took the chair across from it instead. "How did you figure out it was me?"

Kalyll took a spot in the middle of the sofa. He sat at the edge of it, his back ramrod straight. "If I may speak honestly, even if it's improper, I could never forget the warmth in your eyes. The moment I saw you, even wearing that veil, I . . .

knew. At first, I thought I must be going crazy, and then I realized I had to make sure it wasn't you. So I went to your realm. I had to see you there with my own eyes. I had to know you were safe. I looked for you, but you were not home. You were not at work, and you were not with your family. At the risk of upsetting them, I talked to your sister, Toni. She told me she hadn't heard from you. She told me she thought you were still here with me. She nearly shifted and bit my head off."

"Toni," her name escaped my lips as my love and worry for her swelled in my chest.

"It wasn't easy to explain that I knew you were safe after I'd just been asking about your whereabouts, but I convinced her, and I promised her . . . you would be back soon."

I truly wondered if I would be back soon. Or at all. I was starting to think I would not.

"It was stupid of Wölfe to think you wouldn't figure it out," I murmured to myself more than to Kalyll.

"Wölfe?"

I glanced up from the floor, doing my best to stay anchored at this moment and not let the stress and frustration pull me under.

"You'd better make yourself comfortable," I said. "This will take some time to explain."

It wasn't easy to relate the events of the last week. I started with the night Wölfe came for me, woke me from my sleep, and locked me in a tower. I then explained how Naesala Roka had changed my appearance at his request. Lastly, I told him about Larina finding Jeondar for me, and how, together with his friends, I'd been trying to figure out what to do. But purposely, I omitted other details I wasn't proud of, details that brought a blush to my cheeks just to think about it.

I worried at a spot in my dress, a tiny embroidered rose that reminded me of the one Kalyll had given me in Imbermore.

"I don't remember any of it," he said.

"I know. Wölfe said he could control you, and he did. I saw him do it when I tried to tell you everything earlier. But it seems you're fighting back."

"When you talk, I feel like you're referring to someone else. Not me." There was a certain edge of accusation in his voice, as if he suspected the blushing facts I'd left unsaid. And maybe he did. Maybe there was a dark voice inside his head, too.

"I don't know how to explain it, but you feel like two different people."

"There's only one of me, Daniella, and it is *me*." He poked his chest with a stiff finger.

"Are you sure?"

"Certain," he said, his voice firm. "This is who I've always been. This, not a male who abducts women from their beds in the middle of the night."

My anger flared. "Of course not. You're the kind who sends others to do the kidnapping."

"That is an unfair comparison, and you know it."

I sneered. "Yeah, because you can justify anything as long as you're doing it for *your people*, but God forbid if you do it for yourself."

"I have a duty and—"

"Oh, spare me. I've heard enough about your duty. Have

you stopped to think why, if this duty is so important to you, a big part of you is willing to put it all at risk for me?"

That shut him up, and the crestfallen expression that disfigured his handsome face only made me regret my words.

"It doesn't matter anyway," I said. "Your duty . . . you'll have to find another way to save your people."

"Why?" He paused. "There is more, isn't there?"

"Yes. There's a way to draw the remaining darkness from you."

He stood to attention at this, eager to learn how he could get rid of Wölfe. A flame of animosity lit up in my chest. Wölfe wanted me. Wölfe would fight for me, while Kalyll—

Stop it, Dani. This isn't meant to be. It never was.

"Your father," I forced the word out, "your real father can help draw what's left of the demon out."

"My father?" he echoed. "I don't know who he is. My mother wouldn't tell me."

"She told me."

He raised a perfect eyebrow, looking mystified. "Who is he then?"

"Earl Qierlan Goren. Mylendra is your half-sister."

CHAPTER 20
DANIELLA

Kalyll nearly choked on the news. For a moment, he looked as if he would sprint out of the room in search of his mother to strangle the life out of her.

I tried to imagine how he must feel, but the magnitude of what this discovery must mean wasn't something I could fully comprehend. His whole life, along with the solution he'd convinced himself would save his realm, had crashed down in a matter of seconds—a sandcastle washed away by a violent storm.

Unexpectedly, he threw his head back and laughed.

I stared at him, bewildered, convinced that Wölfe had taken over again, except Kalyll's eyes remained clear and his amused laughter quickly died down to a bitter chuckle.

"Kryn is my brother," he said, a sad smile stretching his lips. "I think I knew that, somehow."

"He doesn't know yet. I talked to Jeondar, Arabis, and Cylea first. I didn't know how Kryn would react. They all agreed we should tell you. They knew you wouldn't want to marry your sister, even if your mother has no qualms about it."

At the mention of his mother, his right eye twitched. "Why would she do this? Why?"

"Was there no other alternative besides Mylendra?"

"There isn't. She is the Fall Queen's niece, whom she raised like a daughter, as she only has sons. There is no other female in that court who would foster a strong alliance. There is no one in the Winter Court either—not that that would make a difference. King Naeduin is loyal to the Unseelie King."

Despite the awful turn of events, I thought I detected a measure of relief in him. He didn't have to marry Mylendra anymore, someone he'd said he barely knew.

He went on. "But even if Mylendra was the last female in the realm, it doesn't justify what my mother is doing." He took a step toward the door. "I have to talk to her."

I blocked his path. "No. You can't."

"She has a lot of explaining to do."

"She and I made a pact."

He frowned. "What kind of pact?"

"A blood pact."

"No."

"She said if I did something to jeopardize the alliance, she would . . . kill me."

"What?!"

"It was the only way she would agree to tell me who your father is, and I needed to know in order to *cure* you." It didn't feel right to use that word anymore—not when the darkness had always been part of his shadowdrifter heritage.

"Daniella, that was so foolish." He grabbed my shoulders. "This mess . . . it's mine. My responsibility."

"I'm sorry, but this isn't the kind of problem *you* can fix, not when half of your nature is conspiring against you."

His hands fell to his sides. He hated to admit it, but I could tell he understood his dilemma all too well. "I see no easy way out. I can't go on with the engagement, and that means war. Sooner or later. How will I explain things to Father? He will think me a spoiled child, shying away from my duties, no better than Cardian."

"There has to be another way to prevent a war."

"Mylendra is determined to be queen one day. She doesn't care if that means ruling over the Seelie Court or the Unseelie Court."

"What are you saying?"

"I'm saying she will marry Mythorne, if she doesn't marry me, which will not only ensure that the now-tenuous alliance between the Fall Court and the Unseelie remains in place, but that it becomes stronger, effectively guaranteeing Mythorne has the numbers to go to war."

"What if . . ." I began, then shook my head.

"What?"

"Never mind."

"Please, Daniella."

I licked my lips. "What if you step down and let Cardian marry Mylendra?"

He looked at me strangely, making me wonder if he thought this was my selfish way of freeing him from responsibility so he could be with me. Was it? I didn't know. The more I thought about it, the more appealing the idea became.

"You have met my brother now. He enjoys causing chaos

and watching it unfurl. What kind of king do you think he would be?"

I hugged myself and shrugged.

"I must think on this." He rubbed his forehead. "I must also think on how to free you from my problems. If I had known this would happen, I would have never brought you here to begin with. You would still be happy, doing your job helping children. And I . . . I would be oblivious to the magnitude of my misery." He turned away, averting his gaze.

What was he saying, exactly? That meeting me gave him a different perspective on the path his life had been set on? That the small time we'd shared showed him there was more to life than duty? Maybe I was reading too much into his words.

"I'm glad I met you," I said, knowing I shouldn't.

He faced me, took a step forward, and seized me in his arms, pressing his forehead to mine. "Do you think me a coward?"

"What? Why would I—?"

"For not choosing you as *he* does?" He cut me off, seeming to acknowledge for the first time that Wölfe might be a separate entity from him.

I shook my head, my forehead rubbing against his. "How can selflessness not be courageous?"

He took a trembling breath, and I felt goodness swell in my heart, that generous and decent side of me growing stronger and pushing away the darkness that made it seem all right to want everything for myself.

Slowly, he lowered his mouth to kiss me.

"No." I pulled away. "I . . . I've kissed him, and I've—"

"I don't care."

His mouth crashed into mine with desperate need. He nibbled and bit and swept his tongue over my lower lip. Then, he was walking me backward and pushing me onto the sofa. His strong body settled over mine as he continued kissing me, his movements desperate, feverish. He hiked up my dress, large hands sliding from my knees to my hips. Shivers of desire raked my body, all pooling in my belly and spiraling straight to my core.

Squeezing my hip, he trailed kisses down my neck, his tongue savoring me. He pulled down my collar and bra, stretching the fabric until he freed one of my breasts. His mouth enclosed my nipple and sucked hard, making me moan.

His fingers roamed over the edge of my panties, then slid downward, downward. Pushing the fabric aside, he found my wetness and growled with satisfaction. One of his fingers caressed my folds up and down. As his thumb made circles over my most sensitive spot, he slid one finger in.

"Daniella," his voice a hot breath in my ear as he slipped in a second finger and then a third.

He pumped in and out, while his mouth seemed to be everywhere: my earlobe, mouth, collarbone, breast. Oh, and when he sucked my nipple as he pumped his fingers in and out, I felt as if I would reach heaven itself.

I found my release, waves of pleasure crashing against me. Lifting me higher and higher until I didn't care if this realm and all others crashed and burned—not as long as I could be here with Kalyll, as long as—

He buried his face in my neck and said something.

Struggling to calm down from the wave of ecstasy I was still riding, I pulled back a little for a glimpse of his handsome face.

"What did you say?" I asked, feeling drunk with lust.

"I said I love you, Daniella. I love you."

CHAPTER 21
DANIELLA

I was struck mute and lay frozen under Kalyll, unable to form a response.

Kalyll loved me.

The prince of the Seelie Court was in love with a human. My entire being quivered with emotion, my own feelings rising to meet his.

I loved him too. I—

Are you sure it isn't Wölfe you love? that dark voice asked inside my head.

But they're one and the same.

No, they're not.

I tried to hide my confusion from Kalyll, but as I'd found out, it was impossible to conceal anything from him—no matter how veiled.

"I don't expect you to feel the same way," he said. "I—"

I pressed a finger to his lips. "But I do."

His face lit up.

"Except . . ."

The light that had entered his eyes quickly sputtered out.

"Please, don't be angry. I know you think you and Wölfe are one and the same. It's hard to explain, but . . ."

He stood up abruptly, watching me closely.

Suddenly embarrassed, I rearranged my dress and sat up.

"Are you saying you love *him*?"

I shook my head. "I'm saying I don't know."

Anger flashed across his features, and I thought he would lose his temper, but after a deep breath, he got his emotions under control. He sat next to me, pried a hand from my lap, and interlaced his fingers with mine.

"I can't imagine how confused you must be. I can't say I'm not jealous, because I am. Terribly. But I can't blame you." He caressed my face so tenderly and with such love in his eyes that a knot of tangled emotions settled in my throat, making it impossible to speak.

"I would love any version of you, my Daniella, so how can I object if you love every version of me?"

I threw my arms around his neck, relief washing over me. At least I didn't have to worry about Kalyll when it came to my jumbled feelings. Though Wölfe was a completely different story.

A thought suddenly popped into my head, and I pulled away from him.

"What does melynthi mean?" I asked.

He frowned. "Where did you hear that?"

"Um, Wölfe . . . he keeps calling me that."

Kalyll nearly choked and looked worse than when I'd told him Mylendra was his half-sister. He stood and glanced around the room, bewildered. I rose too and pressed him for an answer.

"What is it? What does it mean?"

"I . . . I think that—"

Voices sounded outside the room. Kalyll's head jerked

toward the door. My heart started racing, and I cast around for my veil, which I found discarded on the floor. I picked it up and quickly secured it around my ears—not that wearing it would make this situation seem any less compromising: the prince in a semi-lit room with a female in a rumpled dress.

The door opened. Jeondar peeked his head in. He frowned, amber eyes dancing between Kalyll and me. He appeared at a complete loss for what to say. I put him out of his misery.

I removed the veil. "He knows, Jeondar."

He exhaled audibly, then glanced over his shoulder. "They're in here."

Pushing the door open, Jeondar walked in, followed by the entire Sub Rosa crew, including Kryn, who was the last one in, and stood hesitantly by the door after closing it. They had told him. It was the only reason he would act this way, since he didn't have one coy bone in his entire body.

For a long moment, everyone just stood there, then Kalyll walked to Kryn and wrapped him in his arms.

"Brother," he said, thumping his back.

Kryn thumped back.

We all exchanged idiotic smiles. If something good had come out of this mess, it was this.

"This is all too much," Kryn said. "I don't understand the half of it, especially the fact that I'm not a shadowdrifter."

I raised a hand. "I can explain that."

They all turned to look at me.

"Only the firstborn receives a dose of the parent's demon energy. I read it in a book."

"Well, now that that's clear," Cylea said, walking further into the room and casually glancing out the window, "when do we get started? I wouldn't mind a bit of action. It's been dreadfully boring."

"Get started with what?" Kalyll asked.

Cylea started to answer, but I raised a hand to halt her.

"I haven't told him *everything*," I said. "And I don't think he should know what we plan to do."

"She's right," Kalyll said.

"Wölfe could interfere," I put in.

"Who?" Arabis scratched her head.

"Kalyll's shadowdrifter persona," Jeondar explained, saving me the embarrassment, which I felt acutely every time the name came up.

"Shadowdrifter persona?" Arabis looked puzzled.

"It's like Dr. Jekyll and Mr. Hyde," I said.

"Who?" they all said in unison.

Only Kalyll got the reference and said, "It's not as bad as all that, I hope."

"So what do we do?" Cylea turned away from the window. "Your . . . um . . . Mylendra and her parents will be here tomorrow. We shouldn't delay. There's no telling what this *Dr. Wölfe* might do."

"*Mr.* Hyde," I corrected. "Wölfe would be Mr. Hyde."

"Plot twist!" Cylea exclaimed. "What if it really was the other way around?"

Kalyll grunted. "Not funny."

"Yeah, not funny," I echoed, though part of me wanted to linger on that idea.

"We should get ready for tomorrow then," Kalyll said, acquiring his princely commanding tone. "Of course, I will need to break the engagement. Though, before I do that, I need to figure out a way to mitigate the damage. Keeping things status quo, for now, will buy us some time to prepare for whatever may come once news of the break is made public. Our army is ever ready, but I need to talk to our generals to ensure our absolute preparedness."

The tension grew in the room until I felt I could scoop it out of the air in handfuls. The possibility of war never seemed so real before.

This is Kalyll's world. His decisions affect thousands of lives.

I knew well what it meant to be responsible for someone's well-being. It was my job to save lives, and every decision I made with a patient was critical, just the reason I took my job very seriously. How much harder would it be if one decision could affect not just one person but a hospital full of them? I didn't think I had big enough balls for that. Kalyll, on the other hand . . .

Arabis put a hand up as if afraid to interrupt Kalyll's intense train of thought. "What about Wölfe? The welcome reception is in the evening. He could undo your best-laid plans with one stupid action. He's reckless."

"You should move the reception to an earlier time," I said.

Kalyll shook his head. "It's not possible. The Earl arrives late in the day."

"I think there's an easy way to keep Wölfe under control," Cylea put in with a mischievous smile.

"What is that?" Kalyll asked with a frown.

Cylea snickered.

"Oh, I think I get it," Kryn said, raising an eyebrow at me. "Female guiles."

A blush heated up my cheeks.

"Don't make me regret finding out you're my brother," Kalyll grumbled, glowering at Kryn from under pinched eyebrows.

I huffed. "I'm not some pawn for you all to maneuver to your liking." I meant the comment to go to everyone, but my gaze focused on Kryn, who put both hands up in a pacifying gesture. "Besides, Wölfe isn't stupid. He would see right through any subterfuge."

"Let's put him to sleep like we did before," Arabis suggested.

"I've thought about it," Kalyll said, "but I can't get away with that here in Elyndell, not every night, anyway. There are too many things that constantly require my attention. Though, tonight I could claim a headache."

"Any reprieve we can get is a win," Jeondar said.

"Will the stillstem and marsh flower work the same as before?" Kalyll asked.

"Yes, if they could control the beast, they will control him."

"Good. I'll make sure to procure those ingredients. Meet you in my room before seven?" he asked.

I nodded.

"In the meantime, work on that plan to fix me while I ensure the kingdom doesn't implode." He gently touched my hand, and with a small bow, took his leave.

"I feel slightly better," Jeondar said once the prince had gone.

"Dani doesn't seem so sure." Cylea scrutinized my face as if by looking closely, she could decipher all my worries.

I shrugged. "We're better off than this morning, I suppose."

"This is as good a place as any to work on a plan." Jeondar pushed back the curtains of a second window, letting more light in, then reclined against the windowsill.

We all approached, too restless to sit. As Cylea and Arabis moved forward, Kryn put a hand on my elbow to stop me.

Surprised, I turned to face him.

He stared at the floor for a long moment before glancing up.

"I owe you an apology," he said.

What the . . .?! Had I somehow transferred into another dimension? This couldn't possibly be the Kryn Goren I knew.

"Are you feeling all right?" I asked. "Maybe you have a fever, and it's making you delirious."

"No fever. Just clarity. I've been an asshole to you."

"Isn't that the understatement of the year?"

"Possibly." He paused and took a deep breath, as if gathering strength. "You've done nothing but fight alongside us, working restlessly without asking for anything in return. I know you care for him, and that means a lot to me. I feared you might cost our realm its peace, and my sister her happiness. Now, I can only thank you for uncovering the queen's abhorrent plot. I don't know where any of this will lead us, but in the end, I hope you and Kalyll find a way."

"Oh, he's a romantic." Cylea clutched her chest and batted her eyelashes as if Kryn's words had swept her away.

Arabis rolled her eyes and pretended indifference, but there was a light flush around her cheeks, something that suggested she'd been swept away too.

"Enough of all of that." Jeondar clapped his hands once. "Let's get to work."

CHAPTER 22
DANIELLA

I arrived at Kalyll's room at 6:30 PM. The door was left open, and I could see him standing by a table, digging into a wooden box and retrieving small vials, cloth-wrapped bundles, glass flasks, and all the other things I would need to make the elixir.

Wringing my hands, I stood at the threshold and stared at his perfect profile. His movements were methodical, those large hands oddly delicate as he handled the fragile glass containers. He looked lost in his own mind, worried. He'd thought he was cured, rid of the darkness that stole his control. He'd thought he had a plan to keep Elf-hame's peace, but that was also gone. And though he seemed relieved he didn't have to marry someone he barely knew, the new weariness that rested on his shoulders appeared much heavier than the one he'd carried before.

As he set the wooden box aside, he noticed me.

"Daniella!" A smile illuminated his face. It was warm and genuine and made my heart thump a little faster. The unease that had weighed him down just a moment before seemed to disappear, as he focused his entire attention on me as if nothing else existed.

"Hey."

"Hey back." He took one of my hands and kissed it. As he ushered me in, he reached behind me and closed the door. His midnight gaze traveled over my face. Raising a hand, he lightly placed his thumb at the corner of my mouth and traced my bottom lip, sending a shiver skittering down my spine.

"That delicious mouth haunts my waking dreams." He kissed me gently, lingering and pulling away slowly, as if it pained him.

Reluctantly, he guided me to the table. "I got everything ready. I also sent word to Naesala Roka to talk to her. We need to get this . . . um . . ." he didn't seem able to find the right word to describe my appearance, "taken care of."

"It's the least of our concerns."

"Not to me." His mouth tightened as he threw a quick look toward my pointed ears.

He really didn't like seeing me this way, while Wölfe didn't seem to mind one way or the other. I felt oddly torn about that. I liked that Kalyll preferred me as a human, especially when I once believed he thought less of my kind. But I also liked that Wölfe didn't care about my appearance, that it was my heart he cared for. I shook the disjointed thoughts away.

"Honestly, Kalyll, looking like this will just make things easier for now. The charade is in motion, and it allows me to move freely about the palace. Let's leave it like this for now, okay?" I couldn't believe I was saying this. "Once we've done what we need to do, then we can worry about setting me back to normal."

He nodded, if a bit reluctantly. "I hate it when you're

right." He smiled crookedly, and I couldn't help but smile back.

"Let me get to work before it gets too late." I rolled up my sleeves and quickly inspected the ingredients and instruments.

For the next fifteen minutes, I worked on preparing the elixir, boiling water, grinding marsh flower, mixing everything together. I also loaded the syringe with the stillstem mix. When I was done, I handed the flask to Kalyll, whose eyes looked warily at the shimmering liquid.

"You should lay down before you drink it." I pointed toward the bed.

"I would rather you were inviting me to bed for other reasons," he said in a husky voice that had me clenching my legs together.

He sat at the edge of the bed and drank the elixir in one quick gulp. I then injected him with the stillstem. He rolled his neck, his eyelids growing heavier by the minute. As I helped him lie down, he stole a quick kiss that tasted of marsh flowers and drunkenly settled his head down on the pillow.

"It's so hot in here," he mumbled.

"I'll open a window."

The room's temperature was actually pleasant, and his discomfort was only a side effect of the elixir. I threw the window open and looked down at Elyndell. Fairy lights illuminated the idyllic streets, casting a magical glow on the massive trees, suspended bridges, and enchanting buildings.

"Is this better?" I asked, turning around to find Kalyll already asleep. He'd managed to take off his shirt, which now lay discarded on the floor.

I picked it up, folded it, and set it at the foot of the bed. I removed his boots, not without some effort, and also set them aside. My gaze traveled the length of his body and settled on his formidable chest. Golden skin stretched over perfectly honed muscles. His arms were corded, and even at rest, his veins pulsed with latent strength.

Of its own accord, my hand traced the elaborate tattoo that traveled down the right side of his body, starting at his temple. It stretched to his hip, I knew. I'd seen it in its entirety that day in the clearing before we faced Caorthannach in the depths of Mount Ruin. I never asked him what it meant or why he'd gotten it, and I could only hope there would be time for that later.

Suddenly, his hand snatched my wrist and tightened around it. I whimpered, feeling as if it would break.

Wölfe's eyes—not Kalyll's—were staring at me from that chiseled face.

"You betray me yet again," he hissed between clenched teeth.

For a moment, I feared I'd underestimated him, and that the stillstem and marsh flower wouldn't be enough to keep him under control, but in the next instant, his grip slackened, and his hand fell limply on the mattress. The feral expression on his face disappeared as Kalyll sighed and buried his head more deeply into the pillow, his features relaxing.

Strangely, my heart ached, and that voice started a recriminating rant inside my head.

I woke up to tender kisses on my neck. When I opened my eyes, I was resting on Kalyll's bed, wrapped in his arms. After watching him closely for a couple of hours, I lay down next to him and woke up at regular intervals to assess his vitals. And now, judging by the sunlight spilling through the window, it seemed I'd overslept and missed my 4 AM examination.

Damn, I was getting sloppy. This would've never happened at the hospital, even without an alarm to wake me up.

He pushed up on his elbow to look at me with hooded eyes. "I want to wake up to this every morning."

My body could have melted right then and there, but the sensible part of me wouldn't allow it. "Don't start the morning by saying things you don't truly mean."

I started to get up from the bed, but Kalyll rolled on top of me and pinned me down.

"Are you normally grumpy when you first wake up?"

I pushed against his naked chest, but it was useless. He was too heavy, and his weight on top of me was too comforting to resist.

"I have to assume that your lack of an answer means *yes*," he said when I did nothing but glower at him. "I have just the remedy for grumpiness."

He pushed my legs apart with his knees and settled between them, a full erection already in place.

"It's such a good remedy," he said. "After only a few doses, you'll start waking up with a smile on your face, anticipating it."

"Is that so?" I fought the traitorous smile attempting to stretch my lips. It was hard to resist him. He seemed so content, his disposition as bright as the sunshine spilling through the window. I couldn't help but be captured by him.

"It is so. You are an excellent healer, so I'm sure the benefits will not go unnoticed."

He lowered his mouth to mine. His kiss was a tender caress that seemed determined to taste every corner of my body. He explored me patiently.

"The first time," he said, "I was robbed of this, but nothing will rush me now."

He found a freckle over my heart and claimed it as his, kissing the spot as he fondled my breasts, his calloused hands sending shivers down to my toes.

When I tried to roll on top of him, he stopped me. "No, I also claim this time as mine, and right now you belong to me, so I may do as I please."

"Not fair," I complained.

"You can make your own claim at any other time, and I will abide, but this morning, you will let me worship you."

And he did. He worshiped every inch of my body, using his hands and lips, pushing me to the verge of madness, and when I thought I couldn't take it anymore, he settled between my legs and entered me. As he thrust in and out, moving in a tireless rhythm, Kalyll made love to me.

He stroked me deep inside, filling me to the brim.

I threw my head back as the pleasure built and built.

A hand wrapped around my throat. My eyes sprang open, and Wölfe was there, his hips thrusting harder for a moment. Panic and raw lust sent my heart thumping even harder. In an instant, he was gone, even as shame rammed against me. As if sensing my distress, Kalyll soothed me with kisses and deep thrusting motions that lingered, as he held me tight, then retreated just to touch me deep, deep, deep.

When my release came, it rocked my entire body. My nipples pebbled to aching points as he took one in his mouth and rocked with me until my body quieted. He held me in his arms as if I were a treasure he never wanted to let go of.

"I love you, Daniella. I love you like I never thought it possible to love someone."

I wrapped my arms around his neck and held him close, sweat slick between us and emotions crashing right on that freckle he'd so tenderly kissed.

I knew I loved him too, but which version of him? The one that put me first? The one selfless enough to sacrifice *this* for the well-being of others? Both?

God! Would I be able to figure it out before it was too late? Would I be selfless when the time came to choose?

I didn't know. What I knew was that, at this moment, all the realms could disappear as long as I could stay wrapped in his arms.

CHAPTER 23
DANIELLA

I didn't see Kalyll for the rest of the day. He would be busy with his father in preparation for Earl Qierlan and his wife and daughter's arrival. Jeondar told me there would be a big reception, accompanied by all the fanfare and attention befitting the future queen of the Seelie Court. I couldn't deny the idea made my insides seethe. Kalyll was going to spend all day making sure that Mylendra had an extravagant reception, while I had to hide under a veil, pretending to be Fae.

It took all I had in me not to allow dark, destructive feelings to push forward, and to remind myself that Kalyll was only trying to buy himself time to figure out how to best handle an impossible situation.

He loved *me*.

He had made love to *me* this morning, not someone else. Besides, she was his sister. I had no reason to be jealous. None at all.

So I tried to occupy myself with our own preparations. Getting Earl Qierlan alone long enough to do what we needed to do would not be easy, even with Kryn's help. He said the Earl was a restless male, given to impatience, especially with his own children.

The plan was for Kryn to ask for a private meeting, and Kryn wasn't sure the Earl would sit long enough even for that. Our hope was that the Earl would assume his son had important news to impart. Kryn had been part of Kalyll's retinue during his latest journey through the realm, after all.

"When will Cylea and Arabis be back?" I asked Jeondar as I paced in front of my bed.

They had gone to purchase a few ingredients that would allow me to create a potion that would render Wölfe and Kryn's father unconscious and erase any incriminating memories from the latter's mind. It felt dirty to think that I was pretty much about to roofie someone. A Fae prince and earl, no less.

"Um," I pulled on the sleeve of my dress, unsure of how to ask my next question.

"What is it?" Jeondar frowned, noticing my weariness.

Even Kryn, who was standing by the now open window, glanced over his shoulder. When I fidgeted a little longer, he turned to face us, eyebrows pinched.

"It's about Silver," I said.

"What about him?" Kryn asked.

"Well, he would like to . . . write to his mother."

"How do you know that?" Kryn's emerald eyes snapped to Jeondar. "You took her to see him? Why would you do that?"

Jeondar shrugged. "I didn't."

"I can figure stuff out all on my own," I lied. I didn't want to drag Arabis into this. She and Kryn were already at each other's throats enough as it was.

"You know Kalyll won't like that," Kryn said.

"And who's going to tell him?" I asked in a challenging tone.

Kryn sighed. There seemed to be more he wanted to say, but he bit his tongue. It really seemed as if he was making an effort to be nicer.

He delivered his next question with care. "So . . . Silver talked to you?"

I nodded.

"The asshole. He hasn't uttered a word to any of us."

"Perhaps it was easier talking to me. He barely knows me. It's different, less pressure, I suppose."

"Whatever the case, I don't think it's a good idea to allow a traitor to send a letter to anyone."

"Why not?" I asked. "He says his mother is all he's got. Everyone could read the letter before it's sent out to make sure nothing sensitive was revealed. What harm could it do?"

"Have you so easily forgotten what he did to Kalyll?" Kryn watched me through narrow eyes.

"Of course not, but maybe . . . he had his reasons."

"A good enough reason for what he did does not exist."

"Why are you always so harsh, Kryn? Don't you feel the slightest bit of sympathy for him? He's locked up in a dungeon all by himself." I asked, truly puzzled. It seemed his father had been hard and inflexible with Kryn. Was that the reason he was also so obstinate?

He turned away, facing the window once more.

I exchanged a glance with Jeondar. He raised an eyebrow and shook his head as if to say I'd lost Kryn in this conversation. It seemed topics that involved discussing emotions weren't Kryn's cup of tea.

"Kalyll would have to agree," Kryn said. "And I doubt he will."

"Okay, I'll ask him."

After lunch, which I shared with the Sub Rosa in Cylea's room, I went back to my chamber to continue my research on shadowdrifters and make sure the method I'd found to cure Kalyll was sound. My pile of books had grown, though not by much. Either Kalyll's library was short on the topic, or there wasn't much recorded on the subject. My bet was on the latter since the Seeley Prince's library seemed very thorough on every other subject.

I reached for another book and laid it open on the table. Though we had a sound plan to take the darkness from Kalyll, I needed to ensure the same method would fix me, and any little bit I could learn about how shadowdrifter energy worked, the better my chances.

My research, however, wasn't the only thing that led me to separate from the others. I wanted to visit Silver again, to take pen and paper to him before the day was over. I figured it might be easier to convince Kalyll to send the letter if he read it and saw it was harmless. I knew I risked angering him, but despite everything, I felt for Silver. I begged to never be in a situation like his. I never wanted to find out what I would be capable of to protect my mother, my siblings, Kalyll.

So, after spending a few hours lost in the pages of several thick tomes, I made my way down to the dungeon. I feared the guards might give me grief since I was on my own, but they let me pass with no problem. It seemed Arabis hadn't given any instructions to block me from visiting further.

Silver was pretty much in the same position as the last time

I'd visited: sitting on the far corner of his cot, knees bent. This time, however, his clear gaze rose to meet mine immediately. For a moment, I detected eagerness in his expression, but he quickly schooled his features into blandness. It seemed he had been expecting me, or more accurately expecting news of his mother. Either way, he didn't want me to see his eagerness.

"Hello, Silver," I greeted him.

He rose slowly and met me at the bars.

"No news yet," I said. "I'm sorry, but I came up with an idea." I offered him the paper and fountain pen I'd found in the library. He frowned at the implements. "It's the only thing that occurred to me in order to keep things secret, like you asked. My plan is to have you write a letter to your mother. I'll make sure it gets delivered, and if she answers, then you'll know she's fine."

A shadow crossed over his features, something like anger, but it was also gone in a flash and pity replaced it.

"Oh, Dani, how little you know of this realm. How naïve. A letter can be coerced, faked."

I felt stupid and started to pull the paper and pen away, but he reached for them through the bars and took them. I stared back, confused.

"There might be a way. Though it won't be as simple as you might have imagined. It will require additional effort on your part?" He said the last bit as a question, as if he wasn't sure I would be willing to go the extra mile.

"Whatever it is, I'll do it."

He nodded, though his expression was skeptical, which made me wonder exactly what I would need to do to get this letter delivered.

Without another word, he sat on the cot and began writing. When he was done, he folded the paper and handed it back, along with the pen. I hid the letter under my dress, close to my heart.

He nodded. "Read it. Later."

"Is there anything else I can do?"

"Don't get yourself killed."

I grimaced.

"I like you, human." He smiled crookedly, which surprised me.

All I had seen from him since that day at the cave was sullenness. It was strange to catch a glimpse of his old self. I felt as if I should say I liked him back, but he *had* almost killed Kalyll, despite his defensible reasons.

"Even if you hate my guts," he added as an afterthought when he noticed my discomfort.

I turned to leave, and after a couple of steps, I glanced over my shoulder. "I hope I can help you get the news you want."

Back in my chamber, I sat by the fire and carefully unfolded the letter. I read what Silver had written, and my heart sank.

Thank you for trying, Dani. Forget about me. I deserve my fate.

I crumpled the paper, threw it in the fire, and watched it turn to nothing. Silver's fate didn't seem fair despite what he'd done. I felt as if there should be something I could do to help him and his mother, but I was deceiving myself. I had no power here, or anywhere else, for that matter. All I had were my healing skills, and they were useless in this situation.

My ribs ached, and I hugged myself against the now-familiar pressure. Feeling restless, I walked into the closet, hoping to distract myself by selecting a dress for the evening ahead. But even as I ran my fingers through the rich silks and taffetas, my mind kept swirling around the topic of Silver.

I had to try harder.

CHAPTER 24
DANIELLA

When Cylea appeared before 5 PM, and I still hadn't decided what to wear to the reception, I realized I'd been obsessing over Silver's situation in order to avoid thinking about my own.

"I've got what you asked for." She set a bag on the coffee table by the fire, then quickly left, saying she needed a long hot bath before the event.

I grabbed the bag and set to work on two potions, one for a prince and one for an earl. It was fast, as no cooking was necessary, and when I was done, I placed the potions in two small vials, then slid them into a pouch.

A few moments later, Larina showed up to help me get ready.

"Those are all very pretty," the pixie said, hovering over my shoulder as I contemplated three dresses, which I'd laid on top of the bed.

I tilted my head to one side. "You pick. I can't make up my mind. To be honest, I don't want to attend this *thing*."

"I don't blame you." Larina pointed toward a vanity she'd conjured, where she'd laid out makeup and all the implements to do my hair. There was a silver comb and brush, along with jeweled hair pins, inside a small wooden box.

"Where did you get all of this?" I asked, a hint of suspicion coloring my tone. I hated the way the question came out, but there was that necklace she'd given me in the Summer Court.

"Prince Kalyll provided it. You may ask him," she responded, her head lowered.

"I'm sorry, Larina. I didn't mean it to come out that way."

"Oh, it's no problem. I don't blame you. I did lie to you. I didn't really have much of a choice, but I guess that's a weak defense."

I shook my head. "I know it isn't weak. I'm beginning to understand how difficult life can be for the likes of us here, among these court people. I don't even want to think about how it must be in the Unseelie Court."

Larina shivered. "Me neither."

"Let's get started then." I sat in front of the mirror, and the pixie got to work weaving her magic into my hair and makeup. When she was done applying pixie dust to my carefully arranged hair—a treatment that worked much better than hairspray to keep things in place and give them a little lift—she fluttered to the bed and pointed to the turquoise dress.

"This one."

I didn't think much of her choice until I was standing in front of the large mirror in the closet and saw how well the makeup and hair complemented its style.

"You look stunning, Dani," she said. "It's a shame you have to cover your face."

She helped me put the veil in place. This time, it didn't hook around my ears. Instead, it hung from a couple of specially designed, rose-shaped hair pins she'd secured to my hair. The eye makeup she'd applied was dramatic and enhanced my eyes, making them look larger and full of life.

"You outdid yourself," I said.

A knock at the door surprised me. We walked out of the closet, and I quickly hid the potion pouch in my dress. Larina opened the door using her magic. To my surprise, Kalyll stood on the other side dressed in a white, gold-trimmed coat, black trousers, and high, polished boots. He looked arresting, his presence immediately filling the room, a tangible energy that made my heart beat faster.

"May I come in?" he asked.

All I could do was nod. Larina fluttered out of the room with barely a sound and closed the door behind her. The Seelie Prince stalked in my direction and stood a pace away from me, his cobalt gaze admiring the pixie's work.

"Those beautiful brown eyes," he said. "They speak a thousand words all on their own."

I smiled under the veil, gratified by the compliment. "Were you able to get everything ready?"

He nodded and reached down to take one of my hands. He lifted it to his mouth and planted a soft kiss on my knuckles. A shiver skittered up my arm as his eyes remained set on mine. They also spoke a thousand words, and they were telling me very clearly what he wanted to do to me right that second.

I pulled my hand away and smiled mischievously. "You will ruin Larina's hard work."

"It would be worth it."

I walked away toward the fireplace, worried he would make good on his promise. It would be easy for him to get himself presentable again if we ended up tangled in the bed-sheets. Me? Not so much.

"Um, I've been wondering," I started, hoping that Jeondar and Kryn hadn't spilled the beans about my visit to the dungeon, "where is Silver?"

I placed my hands on the back of the armchair and peered sideways at him, trying to judge his reaction. There was none, which made it impossible to guess how he felt about his friend and what he'd done. It seemed his tutors had helped him master the art of neutrality all too well.

"He is imprisoned," he answered simply.

"Has he told you why he did what he did?"

"He has not. In fact, he hasn't spoken a single word since Mount Ruin."

"Will there be a trial?"

"A trial isn't possible under the circumstances. We cannot talk about what happened in Mount Ruin without discussing why we were there."

"So . . . what? He will remain in prison indefinitely?"

"Why your sudden interest?" Kalyll asked, frowning.

"I don't know. The Sub Rosa just isn't the same without him, so I feel his absence, I guess."

"I must agree with that." He smiled.

I opened my mouth to say more, but he artfully disengaged himself by looking at the clock on the mantle and saying, "*He* will be here soon, and I'm worried he'll do something reckless and ruin everything tonight." He wrung his hands in front of him, looking concerned.

Suddenly, I felt guilty for talking about Silver and not

what was to come. I approached him and placed my hands over his. "I'll do all I can to prevent that."

"How?"

I shrugged one shoulder. "His mind seems to work on one track only."

Kalyll's face darkened. "You mean that he thinks only of you?"

I hated to admit it, but it was true.

A grunt of disapproval sounded in the back of his throat, and a muscle trembled in his jaw. He broke contact and walked away from me, looking frustrated.

"It's the most ridiculous thing to be jealous of myself." He walked to the window.

I wanted to tell him it wasn't at all ridiculous. Kalyll felt as different from *him* as a lion felt from a wolf, but I doubted admitting such a thing would offer any help.

Suddenly, his hands gripped the windowsill. He leaned forward, bearing his weight on them, his entire body trembling. I stepped closer, unsure of what was happening only for an instant, until I realized Kalyll was fighting against that encroaching being who had taken residence inside his body. Claws appeared at his fingertips and dug into the wood. A growl rumbled in his chest.

Just as abruptly as it started, the fight ended, and in a flash, Wölfe was on me, his hands wrapped around my shoulders, fingers digging into my skin as he bore down on me, sharp fangs bared.

"Why?" he demanded with a hiss. "Why do you keep betraying me like this?"

"Let me go."

"Not until you give me an answer."

"You're hurting me. Isn't that reason enough?"

He let me go, taking a step back and looking horrified, though still mad. I feared he really wanted to throttle me, but I didn't let it show on my face. Instead, I raised my chin, trying to appear righteous instead of scared shitless.

"Don't you ever lay a finger on me again," I spat.

"I promise you that I *will*." His tone was charged with double meaning. "Just like I did this morning."

So he had been there. I hadn't imagined it. I wanted to rail at him, but it wouldn't help the situation—not when I needed him to be on his best behavior tonight.

"I don't want to fight, Wölfe."

"Easy for you to say when you drugged me and then—"

"Please. Do you know what's happening tonight? Your betrothed is coming."

I was afraid he would tell me he didn't care about his betrothed. He wanted to rule with me, after all.

Instead, he chuckled. "It seems I didn't inherit all the darkness from my father, did I? My mother would have me marry my own sister. I should perhaps *talk* to her about it." His fists tightened, and it was clear that talking was the last thing on his mind.

Would he dare hurt his mother? Not that she didn't deserve it, but still. Kalyll had been extremely mad at her too, and I'd had to stop him from seeking a confrontation.

"That's not important right now," I said. Even though I didn't want to get closer, I took a step forward and got right into his field of vision. "You have to focus. You don't want to inherit a kingdom fractured by war, do you? Keeping the pretense will buy you time to decide what to do."

"You only say that because it's what Kalyll wants," he responded between clenched teeth.

"That doesn't make it any less true. Your goals remain the same."

He narrowed his eyes. "You're too clever for your own good. At least it means that, in this, you're on my side."

Wölfe ran the back of his fingers down my bare arm, his touch igniting me despite my best efforts. What was wrong with me?

"A warning," he added, "when you help me get what I want, don't hold it against me."

He grinned with satisfaction, his self-assured attitude planting a foreboding seed in my chest. What if we were falling right into his trap? He always seemed to be a step ahead of us.

Smirking, he added, "I know you're planning something to get rid of me. I'm not stupid. But it won't work, princess. You might as well give up all hope on that account." He started toward the door. "Oh, and by the way, I'm going to let Kalyll remember everything I do from now on. He will particularly enjoy it when you give yourself to me *again*." He crooked his elbow, inviting me to loop my arm with his. "Shall we?"

I ignored it and marched out of the room, a wild mixture of emotions crushing inside my chest. The fate of thousands of people could take a turn for the worse tonight—not the least of them my own.

CHAPTER 25
DANIELLA

W e didn't enter the ample ballroom together, the same one where Cardian's birthday party had been celebrated. I went in first through a side door, while Wölfe joined his parents and entered later through the back of a raised dais flanked by golden curtains. A large shield carved with an eagle at its center hung above two thrones, one for King Beathan and one for Queen Eithne. The Fae monarchs sat down, the queen to the right of her husband. Wölfe stood next to his father, while Cardian took a spot by his mother.

Wölfe's piercing eyes zeroed in on me immediately, even though I was standing by myself in the back of the room, away from the other members of the Sub Rosa. After the spectacle we'd caused during Cardian's party, I was hoping to go unnoticed. Not that I'd succeeded, despite my best efforts. Many people had noted my presence already. They pointed, whispering in each other's ears. The fact that the Seelie Prince was now looking straight at me didn't help matters. I spotted Naesala among them. She waved at me with two fingers, appearing strangely satisfied. *The bitch!* I had the urge to pluck her pale eyes out.

I shook my head slightly. Wölfe seemed to give a sigh, but at least he turned his gaze away.

Within minutes of the Seelie royals' arrival, trumpets sounded beyond the main doors. They were thrown open and the earl and his wife walked in. Earl Qierlan regally held a hand up, his wife's resting on top of it. He wore a brown jacket with leaf-shaped buttons and a cape with an ample fur collar that immediately made me think of a gray wolf's pelt. His wife wore a beautiful off-white gown that flared out like a bell.

Behind them, the loveliest female I'd ever seen walked with her chin held high. She had flowing red hair that fell to her waist in luscious, silken waves. She was tall and voluptuous, her creamy breasts straining against a tight bodice that also helped accentuate a small waist. She walked confidently, hips swaying from side to side. Her resplendent emerald gown seemed to billow around her as if stirred by a magical breeze. She waved with grace as she walked down an aisle formed by Fae bodies, nobility eager to see their supposed future queen.

As I watched her closely, I had to remind myself she was Kalyll's sister, and I had no reason to be jealous. Never mind the fact that he was meant to marry someone that looked just like her—not like me—someone who was also a Fae royal, raised in the lap of luxury, and blessed with godlike features.

I watched Queen Eithne and Wölfe closely. The former gave nothing away, not a hint of the shame she should be feeling. The prince was nearly as stern, except a twist of his mouth revealed a hint of disgust.

Kryn followed behind his parents and sister, wearing a shiny suit of armor, carved so finely it made me think of filigree. He also wore a slightly disgusted expression, which was more obvious than Wölfe's. Of course, Kryn seemed to have a sour disposition anyway, so I doubted anyone who knew him thought anything of it.

The earl bowed to the king and queen while his wife curtsied. The royals on the dais inclined their heads. They all seemed to be following some sort of choreographed dance, one that had been imprinted in their DNA since conception—while plebeians like me were born with blueprints to the dollar store instead.

The earl stepped aside to allow his daughter to go forth and take center stage. Her mother remained by her side, however, and it was she who took the young female's hand, held it gently, and offered it to the Seelie Prince. It was the queen's turn to do the same. She stood, took her son's hand, led him down the steps, and deposited him in front of his betrothed. Both mothers helped the couple interlace fingers and patted their joined hands with a smile.

Bile rose in my throat, and from the acerbic expression on Wölfe's face, it seemed he was on the verge of vomiting. Kryn was no different. Only his sister appeared delighted by the situation—her emerald eyes, so much like Kryn's—sparkling with smugness, as if she'd scored the prize only she deserved.

Witchlights! What would she do when all of this came crashing down? Her heart would be broken for sure, though not necessarily for the normal reasons a female would suffer at the loss of her betrothed. Her pain would be felt more acutely when she realized her butt would never sit on Queen Eithne's throne. *Boohoo.*

The crowd, which up to this point had observed in silence, erupted in cheers and claps.

"She's stunning," a lilac-haired female standing in front of me said.

Her friend stuck a pointy nose up in the air and huffed. "Prince Kalyll should marry someone from the Seelie Court. This engagement is a betrayal to our city. The Fall Court can't be trusted. They've always been loyal to the Northerners."

I listened with interest, surprised by the comment. I'd figured everyone would welcome an alliance that would spare Elf-hame from war, but it seemed that wasn't necessarily the case. My eyes swept the ample ballroom, wondering how many shared the same sentiment, how many would be glad to see the alliance broken.

Light music began to play, floating from one of the second-floor balconies that surrounded the ballroom. The crowd mingled, moving like social butterflies, touching here and there, sharing gossip, and a myriad glances that went from hateful to lustful.

I squirmed, feeling out of place, my *otherness* stabbing my chest more acutely than ever. I didn't belong here and never would. No matter who took Mylendra's place, they would hate her, and it wasn't hard to imagine how much greater that hatred would be for an outsider. It wasn't that I wanted everyone to like me. I knew that was impossible, but unrequited hatred? Anonymity was more my style. No one wished you any harm if they didn't know who you were.

I considered the scene, weighing the need for my presence here. I had shown my face and was inclined to think that was enough. Couldn't I just stand outside the room and wait for the Sub Rosa's signal that it was time to act?

Slowly, I meandered toward the side door I'd used to enter, crinkling my eyes to fake a smile to all of those who took note of me and searching for Cylea. She'd been standing somewhere around here. When I spotted her, standing by a wide column, wineglass in hand, I made a beeline in her direction.

She wore a white gown that left her back bare and barely covered her breasts. A large sapphire necklace hung at her neck and rested on her breastbone, a nice compliment to her blue hair and eyes.

"Where is Kryn?" I asked.

He was supposed to get his father out of the ballroom and into one of the many waiting rooms that surrounded it.

"Over there." She pointed a blue-tipped finger in his direction. His red hair stood in stark contrast to his shiny armor. He was hovering close to his father, who was talking to King Beathan. Kryn's impatience was clear, reflected in restless fingers tapping the hilt of his sword.

"Does he ever relax?" I asked. Not that this was a *relaxing kind of situation*, but still.

"He's forgotten how, I think. It's Arabis's fault, really."

"How so?"

"He's desperately in love with her, as I'm sure you've noticed, but he messed up. Big. He's never been the same since she left him."

"How long ago was that?"

Cylea bobbed her head from side to side. "Umm, about ninety years. Give or take."

"Ninety years?! Are you serious?"

She looked at me as if I was a peculiar, clueless thing.

"Sorry." I waved a hand in the air. "It's just—"

"I know. I know. I always forget a human's lifespan is . . . brief."

Brief.

Witchlights. She made me feel like a mayfly. Yet another reason why I didn't belong here. I tried not to think about how futile a relationship between Kalyll and me would be. Our time together would certainly be brief, my entire existence nothing but the blink of an eye to him. And once I was a middle-aged woman, and he still looked the way he did now, my love would turn to shame as my body barreled into its sunset, no longer vibrant, utterly incapable of being the match he needed.

I shook myself, doing my best to hide my distress. Instead, I asked, "So Kryn and Arabis used to be together, huh?"

"Inseparable," Cylea said. "They were sickening, to be honest. Always holding hands, kissing, and giggling like children. The first time they met, they were nothing but children. It was during The Starlight Festival. The second time was many years later, and the chemistry was immediate."

Arabis had told me about the first time they'd met, how at seven years old Kryn schooled her on swordplay for daring to scrape him with her wooden sword as they played. But when we'd talked, Arabis had also hinted at more, and it seemed Cylea was about to tell me the sordid bits. At least, I hoped so. I couldn't help but be curious.

Cylea went on, "When Kryn next returned to Elyndell, he was a cocky male of twenty-one years. He fell in love with Arabis on sight. But even though he'd forgotten what he'd done during the festival, she hadn't. She can surely hold a grudge." Cylea rolled her eyes. "Kryn was just a kid then, so she had no reason to be so hostile still. I mean, Kryn can be a real jerk, and he wasn't different at twenty-one. If anything, he was worse. He acted as if Arabis should fall at his feet, if he but flicked his red mane in front of her. That made his pursuit of her much harder than it should've been because she also liked him. She tried to hide it, but we all could see it. We knew it was just a matter of time. For all his faults, Kryn loves her. She made him chase after her for nearly two years."

"Oh, wow."

"Right? But when she finally gave in, she fell hard. They were together for nearly ten years. Not even the distance between them—which was a common occurrence with him needing to spend time in Thellanora—could get in the way. They were apart for months at a time, and it only seemed to strengthen their bond. I thought for sure they would marry."

"Couldn't they use a token to travel and see each other more often?" Their separation seemed unnecessary when tokens could use veil magic to allow quick travel.

Cylea shook her head. "Not something the earl would allow. He didn't approve of the relationship. He wants his son to . . . improve the lineage. Marry a duke or a princess. He kept a tight leash on Kryn."

"The earl sounds lovely." I was about to ask if Kryn and Arabis's breakup was the earl's fault when Cylea lifted a finger, directing my attention toward the male.

"Lovely, indeed," she said, voice dripping with sarcasm.

I glanced over to find Kryn talking to his disgruntled-looking father. Kryn was gesturing toward a side door, clearly trying to pull the earl away from the reception. I lay my hand on the small pouch hiding between the folds of my dress. My heart started hammering at the thought of what we were about to do. If someone caught us . . .

Taking a deep breath, I dismissed the thought and didn't let the pressure in my chest build with nerves. I'd been through worse. This was nothing.

We will get this done, and no one will be the wiser.

Traitor. You're worse than Silver, Dark Dani said, but I pushed her down in her proper corner.

My gaze drifted from Kryn toward where Wölfe stood with Mylendra. She was batting her eyelashes and casually touching his hand as she talked animatedly. Many of the male guests had their sights set on her, practically drooling as they admired her from head to toe. Their looks were no different than those from the majority of the females. They also seemed unable to take their eyes off their presumed future queen, though in their cases, lust was replaced by jealousy. Did they crave the power that being queen would afford them? Or did they crave the commanding male that would bed them and give them heirs? I didn't care about the former, but the latter made my blood boil.

"Dammit!" Cylea cursed, pulling my attention back to Kryn, who now seemed to be in an argument with his father, judging by the way the older male was gesticulating and glowering at his son. After an intense exchange, the earl walked away, leaving Kryn behind.

Kryn cursed under his breath, fists tight at his sides. After a moment, he marched in our direction.

"Sometimes I want to strangle him," he hissed between clenched teeth as he reached us.

"No luck?" Cylea asked.

Kryn shook his head. "He says he has no time for me right now, that he has matters to discuss with King Beathan. But the king is done with him."

Which was true. The king had moved on to talk to a group of important-looking people—members of his council, Cylea pointed out—and he didn't seem the least bit concerned about Earl Qierlan.

"So what now?" I asked, feeling at a loss.

"We hope that *Wölfe* doesn't ruin everything somehow?" Kryn sounded as if he didn't think that was possible in the slightest.

We all turned our attention toward the male in question. From the looks of it, he was doing a halfway decent job entertaining Mylendra. His mouth formed a downward curve, and he appeared as if he found whatever she was saying as boring as watching paint dry, but he bore it with dignity.

"At least he isn't trying to dance with you," Cylea said, throwing a sidelong glance my way.

"Don't even mention it." I shivered.

"Where is Jeondar?" Kryn asked. "Maybe he can tell my father that King Elladan has a message for him."

"Elladan hates your father," Cylea said. "It would raise suspicions."

"Why does he have to be such a dick?" Kryn murmured.

I wrung my hands. "Maybe it will all be all right, and we'll—"

But when one of the stained-glass windows that adorned the balcony directly above us shattered into a million pieces, any hope of salvaging the situation went up in smoke.

CHAPTER 26
DANIELLA

A masked figure dressed all in black sailed above us and landed in the middle of the ballroom, sending people scattering in all directions. Many screamed in panic, but others quickly acquired defensive stands and drew their weapons, which, as it turned out, were not only for show.

Shards of glass rained down, a few biting into my skin and causing me to hunker down with my hands over my head. When the onslaught stopped, I stared wide-eyed at the lone, dark figure, unable to comprehend what was going on.

Was this some sort of . . . *show*? Maybe it was part of the night's entertainment because if this was meant to be a hostile attack, this person, a male, must be completely out of his mind. There was no way he could accomplish anything other than getting himself killed.

My mind raced, offering possibilities. Maybe he wasn't alone and others were just about to storm into the room. I glanced all around just as Kryn and Cylea did the same, but no one else came in. Okay, maybe this was some sort of suicidal mission. Maybe he had a bomb, a magical one. Or one from my realm. Or—

Wölfe stepped forward, pushing Mylendra away without ceremony and unsheathing his sword.

"What is the meaning of this?" he demanded.

The king joined his son, also pulling out his sword.

"Show your face, coward." Wölfe twirled his sword over his head, making it zing.

A flash of Kalyll fighting the decayana in the Zundrokh Barrens swept across my mind. His ferocity and virility seemed the same as they had on that day, except he appeared to be holding back, very unlike Wölfe. Was Kalyll able to exert some control? If he was, he'd picked the wrong day.

It was a stand-off.

No one moved, not the intruder, not Wölfe, not the armed guests. Time seemed to stop. I held my breath. A long moment passed, then the dark figure's hands twitched and flames erupted at his fingertips. A collective gasp went over the crowd.

"A flamewielder," Kryn hissed, exchanging a glance with Cylea, then moving forward in unison to stand behind Wölfe. Jeondar, Arabis, and others—guards mostly—also pressed forward, creating a circle around the male, who seemed as relaxed as if a litter of puppies were surrounding him. I almost called Cylea's name to tell her to get back—she had no weapon to fight with, her crossbow not a friendly accessory to her beautiful dress—when she pulled the belt that circled her waist and came up with a long whip. It uncurled and undulated like a snake, then she cracked it menacingly against the floor.

As others ran past me, fleeing through the side doors, I felt useless. There was nothing I could do. I was so . . .

Not true, the dark voice inside me said.

Shakily, I lifted my hands and stared at them. I wasn't helpless anymore. These hands, these bare hands, could kill. I had pushed the thought aside, denying what I had done to that poor male. The pressure in my chest grew tighter. *Witchlights!* Was this tight feeling against my ribs my unprocessed guilt?

It wasn't my path to take life, but to give it. I curled my fingers, made my hands into fists, and let them fall to my sides. I was no fighter, no warrior.

I glanced up. The face-off continued. Something told me the intruder was enjoying this. I couldn't see his face, not even his eyes—the mask, gloves, and clothes covered every inch of skin—but something about his stance, which appeared casual despite the threat around him, made him appear thoroughly unconcerned.

Suddenly, the male's hand moved. It went up so fast that a semicircle of fire formed in the air, then a large orange ball shot forward, going straight for Wölfe. My heart jumped into my throat, and I nearly cried out, but he moved as fast as his attacker, blocking the searing projectile with his sword. He split it in two, sending sparks flying in every direction. For the first time, I wondered if his sword was imbued with magic, metal reinforced with spells to counteract this sort of attack. It only made sense the Seelie Prince would possess the best weapons.

Several guards lunged forward to protect their prince.

"Stand back," Wölfe shouted, but it was too late.

The intruder's hands moved at a staggering speed, doling out fire projectiles to all of those who dared attack. They didn't possess the speed and agility of the Seelie Prince, and in the expanse of a second, they were all struck squarely in the chest.

As the fire hit, it morphed into something like lava. It seared and ate away at their armor, clothes, skin. The guards screamed, but their agony lasted but an instant as the substance quickly dissolved their very bones, leaving only a gaping hole in the ribcages as they collapsed.

My knees wobbled at the horror of it all. No wonder the male hadn't been afraid to conduct such a blatant attack. But it couldn't be that easy. There had to be someone here besides Wölfe who could neutralize his power. The prince couldn't face this alone. He needed help.

Just as the thought materialized, King Beathan, Kryn, Cylea, Jeondar, and Arabis took defensive positions to the left and right of the Seelie Prince.

Wielding his own fire magic, Jeondar released an attack, a scorching orange ball not unlike the intruder's. I almost whooped in victory when the fire hit the male, but to my utter astonishment, nothing happened. He simply seemed to absorb Jeondar's energy.

"Surrender now!" Arabis's Susurro command boomed through the room, the sound waves rippling in the air and hitting the intruder head-on.

Even though the command wasn't directed to me, I felt it in my bones and knew few would be able to disobey. But the male did, which meant he was strong, at least as strong as Kalyll had been in his beast form. Not good.

A deep chuckle came from the dark figure, an utterance meant to belittle Arabis's power, but she wasn't that easily cowed. Baring her teeth, she removed what looked like a baton from a cleverly concealed holder at her back. She twirled it above her head and the weapon extended from both ends, turning into a long staff that ended in two very pointy, very sharp daggers.

In the next instant, this standstill became a melee.

Wölfe charged forward, at the same time that he shielded the king and pushed him back. The prince attacked recklessly with no concern for himself, and yet he had the presence of mind to protect his father. But the king would not be dissuaded, and he shoved forward, sword in hand, throwing an annoyed glance at his son.

I had a moment of clarity in which I spared a thought for the queen, Kryn's mother, and sister, but as I glanced around I saw no sight of them anywhere. In fact, very few people remained in the ballroom, and all of them were surrounding the intruder. It begged the question of whether or not I should leave, too, but who was I kidding? I couldn't abandon my friends to this—not when one of them might get injured, and my healing skills could save their lives.

As Wölfe reached his opponent, he sliced his sword downward, ready to cut him in half. The weapon met with a column of fire that quickly solidified, forming what looked like an igneous rock. The sword hit the surprisingly strong material and sparked as it glanced off of it.

The intruder prepared another attack and released it before Wölfe could recover.

"No!" I cried out.

Just as the fire was about to hit Wölfe's middle, a blue-white sphere of the same size flew through a gap between Kryn and Jeondar and engulfed the fiery projectile. The sphere hovered in midair, trembling for an instant, then it shattered into a million pieces that scattered to the floor like sleet.

Every member of the Sub Rosa—except Wölfe—seemed to freeze in shock, as if there was something about the intervening assault that they recognized. I glanced toward the source of the counterattack. My jaw dropped.

Silver strode into the room, a sheen of ice outlining his imposing figure like a force field.

CHAPTER 27
DANIELLA

Silver! He was here and not in the dungeon where I'd left him earlier today. Not only that, he'd just saved the very male he'd tried to kill only a week ago. He was also joining the melee, which had started in full force, with the intruder lobbying fireballs right and left, and the others blocking them with magical swords, staffs, and more ice attacks from Silver.

Despite the commotion, I could feel the ripples of confusion coming from the other Sub Rosa members. They had no idea what Silver was doing here. Despite everything that had happened, however, they seemed content with letting him help, at least for now.

The intruder held his own.

There were over twenty Seelie Court members and guards fighting against one male, and yet, he was giving them a run for their money, fighting like a small army all unto himself.

As I watched, holding my breath, it became apparent what the intruder was trying to do. When someone attacked him, he spared defensive attacks to save his hide, but the bulk of his energy and concentration was directed at the king and his son.

He wanted to kill *them*.

The realization must have hit Wölfe at the same time it hit me, because he turned to Jeondar and issued a command.

"Take the king out of here."

Jeondar didn't hesitate. He rushed toward King Beathan and attempted to grab him, but the king scurried to one side, bent on staying and fighting.

"I'm not a child to be ushered out. I will defend my home," he bellowed, pressing forward heedlessly, sword raised above his head.

It was all the intruder, the assassin, needed. He saw an opening and didn't waste it. Jerking a hand forward, he shot the fireball he already held in his hand.

"No!" Wölfe jumped forward, his sword reaching out to block the attack, but he wasn't close enough and missed it by mere inches.

The searing sphere hit King Beathan in the neck. I cried out as the infernal heat worked as effectively as a guillotine and severed his head. It thudded to the floor, rolled a few times, then stopped. His blank, blue eyes stared fixedly into mine. Horror washed over me, and I squeezed my eyes shut, shaking my head in denial. Still, that vacant stare remained imprinted in my mind.

A roar of fury echoed through the hall. My skin rippled with a shiver at the unadulterated quality: rage in its purest form.

When I opened my eyes again, making a point not to look toward the severed head, Wölfe was marching toward the assassin, just as heedlessly as his father had. Except he was faster than the king, and he whirled his sword like a windmill in a storm. It moved so fast it looked as if he were holding a large shield in front of him. Fiery attacks hit the twirling sword and dissolved into thousands of sparks that floated harmlessly to the floor.

Wölfe advanced on his enemy, and for the first time, the attacker's movements seemed uncertain. The figure took a step back as Wölfe barreled forward, his sword creating its own wind, making his midnight blue hair fly in every direction.

From where I stood, I spied Cardian hiding behind one of the thick curtains that adorned the dais. He was staring at his father's severed head with a strange look in his eyes. Maybe I was imagining things, but I thought I saw a slight smile stretching his thin lips.

I diverted my attention back to Wölfe. The fight had been reduced to the two of them, everyone else unable to do anything without potentially hurting their prince.

The attacker quickly formed two more fireballs in his hands. One was larger than the other, and they appeared weaker—not as dense or bright. He took two steps back and threw his hands out, one high and the other low. The first one hit Wölfe's twirling sword and disintegrated into nothing. The second one grazed the side of his calf.

Wölfe fell to one knee, teeth bared as he growled. His sword hit the marble floor, releasing sparks, then came to an abrupt stop.

"Wölfe!" I screamed as his opponent quickly formed another fiery sphere and directed it at him.

I rushed forward as if I could do anything to stop what was coming.

One moment, Wölfe was in the path of a magical attack

that would surely end his life, and the next, he was gone, nothing but a gliding shadow on the marble floor.

In the next instant, he reappeared right in front of his enemy and drove his sword straight through his heart. It happened so fast that if I'd blinked, I would've missed it. I froze on the spot, taking in the crowd that surrounded Wölfe as he slammed his dead opponent against the ground.

I perceived movement out of the corner of my eye, and when I glanced back, I saw that Cardian had come out of his hiding place. He was descending the dais steps, an astonished expression shaping his features.

Like me, it seemed he hadn't blinked and had seen Wölfe dissolve into a dark puddle of shadows. I could practically hear gears turning inside his head as he stared unblinking at his brother, the male who would be king of the Seelie Court, now that their father was dead.

When Cardian caught me watching, he retreated a few steps, then fled the ballroom. I pressed a hand to my mouth and walked closer to the circle that had tightened around Wölfe. You could have heard a pin drop inside the massive hall as Wölfe removed the assassin's mask and threw it to one side.

There was a general murmur of curses. Wölfe pulled back, favoring his right leg, sword still in hand.

The male that lay in the middle of the circle, resting in a widening puddle of his own blood, had fine features under a mop of white hair. His skin was the color of obsidian and his blank-staring eyes, which matched King Beathan's to perfection, were as pale as a snowflake.

"Is that Garrik Mythorne?" Cylea asked, her face as pale as I'd ever seen it.

Mythorne? That was the Unseelie King's last name. Was this a relative of his?

"How, by all the gods, did he get in?" a female guard with green hair asked in disbelief.

"He sent his son?" said another.

"This means war!" a male bellowed, beating his chest.

Wölfe pulled away from the crowd, sheathing his sword. He walked in his father's direction. He passed by me, his gaze lost in grief and anger. Dark veins formed patterns around his eyes. He paused and looked from the decapitated body to the severed head, which lay several feet away.

Limping, he moved to pick up the head. My heart shrank to almost nothing as he placed it in the puddle of blood by the cleaved neck. Then he kneeled next to the king and took his hand.

He was facing away from everyone, but the emotions that must be raging inside of him were clear to see by the way his shoulders rose and fell. After a long moment during which no one dared move a muscle, Wölfe rose, walked to the dais, yanked one of the curtains down, and covered his father's body.

Barely placing any weight on his right leg, he turned to face everyone.

"The king is dead," an imposing male with long brown hair pulled into a ponytail said. He wore a uniform similar to that of the guards, but judging by the emblem embroidered in his tunic, he held a higher rank.

"Long live the king," someone else called behind him.

Wölfe shook his head, almost imperceptibly. He didn't want this. He wanted his father back.

"Captain Loraerris," he said in a broken voice that betrayed his pain.

The brown-haired male stepped forward. "Your Majesty."

"Take care of my father. Make sure all arrangements are made with the utmost respect. I'll come find you in an hour, so we can discuss the next steps."

Next steps? What did he mean, exactly?

The captain pressed a fist to his chest. "Yes, my king."

Wölfe's pained gaze met mine. Like a light bulb going out, I saw all vulnerable feelings vanish from his face to be replaced by a stern, determined mask. He inclined his head toward the Sub Rosa members and, with a jerk of his head, gestured for them to follow.

I sensed a level of resistance from them. This wasn't Kalyll, but Wölfe. Silver was the first one to step up. Kryn blocked his path, looking defiant. The last thing we needed was a fight in front of everyone. Thankfully, a pointed glare from Wölfe diffused the situation, and everyone followed, giving Silver a wide berth.

I waited a couple of minutes, and when no one was looking, I scurried out of the ballroom. I didn't want anyone to think I was part of the prince's—the king's, I corrected myself—retinue. Out in the hall, I glanced left and right, but saw no one. Raised voices and a trickle of blood led me to a set of closed double doors.

"What the hell is he doing here?" Kryn was saying.

"That's the least of our problems," Arabis intervened.

I tentatively knocked on the door. Jeondar opened it a crack.

He seemed relieved when he realized it was me, then let me in. Silver was standing off to the side. I noted he'd shaved and wore clean clothes. His fists were opening and closing as he kept his eyes on the floor, appearing both angry and embarrassed.

Jeondar flicked his amber gaze in Wölfe's direction, who was standing in front of a fireplace, staring into the burning logs. I approached him with hesitant steps and stopped by his side. I raised a hand to touch him, then put it down again. I wanted to tell him how sorry I was he'd lost his father, but none of the words that came to mind felt adequate. Instead, I turned to what I knew best.

"Let me heal your leg." I pointed toward an armchair. "Please, sit."

I thought he would refuse, but like a robot, he took a few steps back and sat. I kneeled on the side of the chair to examine his leg. Bile filled my throat at the sight of the wound. I was used to much worse, but seeing him injured was nearly all I could handle. As I'd been taught, I tried my best to detach myself from my emotions and focus on the healing. I had enough practice, and it should have helped, but it didn't.

My hands trembled as I aimed them at his calf. Most of the muscle was missing and cauterized by the heat, though there was some blood sliding down what was left of his boot. A section of bone was visible in the middle. His Fae healing powers were hard at work, trying to repair the damage, but it was too extensive and, left unattended, the wound would take days to heal and might not even do so properly. I had no idea how he was still upright, and not passed out from shock.

The glow of my hands illuminated the ghastly wound. I

focused on easing his pain first. A few seconds in, he gave an audible exhale that let me know I'd provided some welcome relief.

As I worked, he glanced up, his gaze meeting Kryn's, who seemed at a total loss for words, same as me. It was Jeondar—the most sensible of us—who said what we were all thinking.

"There are no words to express how deeply I feel for your loss, my king." He inclined his head with respect, which surprised me.

It was Kalyll who had been their prince, and now was their king. Not Wölfe.

Oh, God! What would happen now? The prince couldn't become king, not with Wölfe partly at the helm.

CHAPTER 28
DANIELLA

The other Sub Rosa members offered their condolences, placing a fist on their chests and lowering their heads. They remained silent for a long moment, holding that pose, honoring their dead king solemnly.

I worked fast, pouring all my power into Wölfe's wound. Tissue knitted itself until there was nothing but smooth, golden skin covering the muscular calf. I rose, sending my head spinning. Wölfe stood fluidly and wrapped an arm around my waist to steady me.

"Are you all right, melynthi?" he asked in his rumbling voice. "Did you exhaust yourself? You shouldn't have. Not for me."

"I'm fine." I pushed away from him, feeling self-conscious of his hands on me while the other ones were present. His calm surprised me, made me wonder how much of Kalyll was pushing through.

"Wait!" Kryn exclaimed. "She's his mate?"

Jeondar shook his head. "Not the time."

"Mate?" I asked. "Is that what melynthi means?" I looked at everyone in turn, but no one said anything.

Silver, Cylea, and Arabis just looked shocked, and as

unwilling as Jeondar to go there. Kryn was the only one who seemed willing to let me have it, so I focused on him.

"That can't be right," I told Kryn.

He just shook his head, appearing completely at a loss. The Kryn I knew should've been ranting and raving, saying that a lowly human couldn't be the Seelie Prince's—Seelie King's— mate, that someone, namely Wölfe, had completely lost their mind. Except he only managed to look as shocked as the others.

Jeondar was the only one who didn't appear flabbergasted. Instead, he seemed resigned. I had already asked him what melynthi meant, after all.

Regardless, Wölfe had to be wrong. I couldn't be his mate. I was very familiar with what that meant. In my realm, some types of Skews had the possibility of encountering mates. Mainly, it was a thing for shifters, merpeople, and, of course, for Fae. But not for Skews like me. I was only a human healer. Mates didn't exist for my kind, much less mates of a different species. It was unheard of.

My sister, Toni, who owned a mate tracking agency, would be able to find what she called a *soulmate* for me, but all that meant was that she'd track someone who was compatible with me, someone I could easily and willingly fall in love with. It didn't mean she would find me a true mate, a person that destiny had designed specifically for me. The *only one* you could fall in love with. The *only one* who would give you offspring. The person who would love you no matter what, who would let the entire world burn if it came to it.

I pressed a hand to my mouth to repress a sob.

"I guess that explains everything," Kryn said.

Why wasn't he raging? I wanted him to rage the way he had when he discovered Kalyll and me kissing in that cave. I wanted him to say that Wölfe was wrong, that the king's mate couldn't be a human who everyone in Elf-hame would hate, that I wasn't doomed to love someone I could never be with.

I would be able to have a family with someone else. I would, even if I didn't love him the way I loved this male.

I looked up at Wölfe pleadingly. He ran the back of his fingers down my cheek.

"Don't fret," he said. "You're mine, and I'm yours, and no one and nothing will keep us apart."

"This is fucked up and shocking," Cylea spluttered. "But, I'm sorry to say, we have a very delicate situation on our hands. That was Garrik Mythorne out there." She pointed a finger in the general direction of the ballroom.

"Are you sure that was him?" Silver asked.

Kryn whirled on him. "That's not the only delicate situation we're dealing with. What is this asshole doing here?"

"This asshole," Silver said, "saved your asses out there."

"You did no such thing. We had it under control."

Jeondar intervened. "There's a lot going on in this room right now, each thing as delicate as the next, but I'm sure Kalyll can quickly clear the air and explain Silver's presence here, so we can move on to the most pressing subject of the attack."

"I'm not Kalyll. My name is Wölfe, as you well know." The prince—the king, I had to get used to this—squared his shoulders.

"With all due respect, we can't call you that. If someone overhears—"

"There's no one around to overhear anything but *my* Sub Rosa."

The emphasis on *my* seemed to rub them the wrong way. To my surprise, they didn't protest, which was wise. Wölfe's darkness was ill-contained. It was swirling around him in smoky tendrils. He raised an eyebrow at Jeondar in challenge.

The Prince of the Summer Court cleared his throat. "I'm sure *Wölfe* can explain why Silver is here."

"That is easy," Wölfe said. "Dani wanted him free."

"Come again," Kryn said.

"You heard me."

They all turned to look at me with a mixture of anger and incredulity. Only Silver appeared grateful.

"Not true," I said. "I didn't ask you. I asked Kalyll." If he was going to make such a distinction between Kalyll and himself, then I was going to do the same. He couldn't have it both ways.

Wölfe narrowed his eyes at my challenge. I thought he might scoff at me, but in the end, he gave me a crooked smile. "My feisty, clever Dani. That's why I like you." He paused. "But don't worry. Kalyll is also in agreement."

"Is he?" I asked doubtfully.

"He freed my mother," Silver said, emotion thick in his voice. "Kalyll sent Kaya Olocarym to retrieve her. They're now on their way back."

"Wait," Cylea held one finger up, "you sent The Whisper to free Silver's mother from . . ."

"The Winter Queen was using her as leverage to blackmail me," Silver said. "I know that's no excuse for what I did, but she's all I've got. I couldn't let her endure the horrors they were putting her through. She's innocent in all of this."

"I don't hold it against you, Silver Salenor," Wölfe said. "I wouldn't be here if not for you. *Kalyll* doesn't hold it against you either. He would have done the same in your place. And all of you, too."

Kryn shifted from foot to foot as if he wanted to contradict Wölfe's statement. In the end, he said nothing, making it clear he'd truly weighed his options.

"So, if I don't hold any grudge against him," Wölfe said. "None of you have the right to do so."

Despite Wölfe's words, the air in the room still smelled of rancor. It was Jeondar who stepped forward, extended a hand in Silver's direction, shook his hand, then pulled him close and thumped him twice in the back.

"I'm glad to have you back, brother. The Sub Rosa wasn't the same without you."

Cylea and Arabis followed, embracing him and kissing him on the cheek. Silver's pale skin turned red, and I could've sworn I saw moisture sparkle in his eye. Kryn was last, if a bit reluctant, but he still shook his hand and by the time he stepped back, the future earl seemed to have made his peace with Silver.

"So back to Garrik Mythorne," Cylea said.

Silver repeated his question from earlier. "Are you sure that was him?"

"Yes, I met him once. He was *oh-so* charming. I can't understand how he got in."

Wölfe sat back down, running stiff fingers through his long hair. He looked overwhelmed, and I wanted to wrap him in my arms and let him grieve for his father. Instead, he had become king in the blink of an eye, and now he had to deal with the fallout.

He glanced up, meeting my gaze. I sensed his desire to throw it all away, to give up the throne and the responsibilities that came with it so that he and I could simply . . . go away. But there seemed to be enough of Kalyll present in him because when he spoke, he left no doubt in our minds about what would come next.

"Kellam Mythorne will pay for what he did," he rumbled.

"Wölfe," Jeondar sat on the chair across from his king, leaned forward, and spoke in a conciliatory tone, "it's possible Garrik acted on his own. He's said to have a rash nature."

"That is true," Cylea corroborated. "I've heard he thinks the Unseelie King weak for not taking action."

"I've heard the same thing," Arabis said.

Wölfe shook his head. "Either way, it doesn't matter. My father will be avenged."

"If Garrik acted alone," Jeondar said, "you have already avenged King Beathan."

"That's a big *if*. An *if* I don't give a fuck about. Mythorne spawned that bastard, and he raised him to hate us, to wish our doom. Besides, what do you think the Unseelie King will do when he finds out I killed his precious son?"

"He's right," Kryn agreed. "Mythorne has been waiting for an excuse to go to war. Now, he has the perfect one."

No one disagreed with that, which meant the peace Kalyll had been working so hard to maintain would soon evaporate. I carefully scanned Wölfe's face, as if I could ferret out Kalyll's view on the matter, but all I saw was hatred and resolve. I looked to the others. Surely they were keeping Kalyll's interests at heart. What I found in their expressions chilled me to the bone. They all seemed to be in agreement with Wölfe, and it seemed that, for the first time, Kalyll and his darker side were also on the same page.

Wölfe rose, stretching to his full height. He turned to me. "You should rest, melynthi. I need to talk to my uncle."

I frowned. Uncle?

"Captain Loraerris," he elaborated when he noticed my confusion. "He commands the King's Guard."

"I don't need to rest. I'm fine."

I wanted to stay with him. Grief was a brutal thing. It could hit you when you least expected it. I knew from experience. I'd lost my father too.

Cylea stepped closer. "It won't seem appropriate if you're there. It's best if you do as he suggests. I'll go with you." She exchanged a curious glance with Jeondar.

"Fine." I wasn't happy about it, but I wouldn't add to Wölfe's worries.

I started to leave, but Wölfe trapped me in his arms and buried his face in my neck. "I'll come before the night is over."

The words rumbled in his chest, and I felt them to the tips of my toes.

Kalyll. Wölfe.

Wölfe. Kalyll.

My emotions flared for both of them. How could I feel this way about two completely different males?

It felt wrong. Oh, so wrong.

Back in my chamber, I threw my veil to the floor and paced around, my nerves frayed, my mind whirling with endless questions. Fear sank its claws into my heart. War. Freaking war was coming, and I was smack in the middle of all of it.

Cylea closed the door, rushed toward me, and got right in my face. "We have to get Kalyll back. We need him more than ever."

Taking a couple of steps back, I freed myself from her hold. "How?"

"You still have everything, right?"

My hand involuntarily rose to the pouch hidden in my dress.

"But the others," I said. "They went with Wölfe."

"They'll be here soon."

"How do you know?"

"Trust me. None of us want anyone but Kalyll dealing with this situation."

I faced away from her, my heart beating out of control. If I did what we'd planned to do, Wölfe would be gone forever. Was that what I really wanted? Before, when Kalyll's presence had been so fresh in my mind, it had seemed right, but now . . . I wasn't sure.

You can't. It would be murder, that dark voice said inside my head.

My hands flew to my head. My breathing grew agitated.

"Is everything all right?" Cylea asked. When I didn't answer, she came around and grabbed my arm. "Dani, you're not having second thoughts, are you?" She examined my face carefully. "Please." Her voice was full of reproach. "You've only known Kalyll for a short time. I can assure you, he's a better choice than Wölfe."

"None of you seem to mind Wölfe's decision to go to war. So he must not be that different."

"More and more, war seems inevitable, Wölfe or no Wölfe. That's not the issue. The issue is that we need level-headed Kalyll to be in charge, especially at a moment like this. You have to see that."

"Are you sure about that? Wölfe killed Garrik. I don't think Kalyll could have done that. Did you see exactly what happened?"

She whipped her head, her long blue hair sweeping to one side. "Yes, I saw. That's another thing we should've discussed, but there is so much going on it feels like the sky is coming down on us. We can only hope no one else noticed or will think to question it."

"The shadowdrifter power saved him," I said. "If there's to be war, those abilities may be crucial to keeping him alive."

Her mouth opened and closed. She couldn't deny the truth of my words.

A knock came at the door that made us both jump. Cylea opened it, and Jeondar came in.

She gave him no chance to say anything. "She's having second thoughts. She thinks the shadowdrifter powers will give Kalyll an edge in the war to come. I hate to admit she's not wrong."

"You can't be serious." His amber eyes flicked from Cylea

to me. "Wölfe is a liability even in the best-case scenario, and I hate to say that, by far, this is the worst-case scenario."

"Things can always get worse," I said under my breath.

"I don't see how." He shook his head. "Kryn will go to his father when we're ready. After what happened, I'm sure the earl will agree to meet him in private."

No! Dark Dani shouted inside my head.

"Kalyll would be dead *right now* if not for those shadow-drifter powers, Jeondar," I said.

"What are you talking about?" he demanded.

So he hadn't seen how Wölfe had evaded Garrik's attack. Cylea quickly explained.

Jeondar rubbed his forehead. After a few moments of deep thought, he said, "It's not up to us to decide. It's what Kalyll wants."

"He may not want the same thing after what happened tonight," I offered.

He took a moment to examine my face as if he could read my mind. "And will you do what he asks when the time comes?"

I opened my mouth to answer, but nothing came out.

"I have been reasonable." He took a step closer. "I have defended you when others would condemn you. I consider you my friend, but if you betray Kalyll, I will personally make sure that you pay for it. We'll wait until tomorrow, and then he will decide."

A knot formed in my throat. Jeondar delivered his verdict with calm resolve, his gaze never leaving mine, and at that moment, he was scarier than Kryn and Wölfe put together. I didn't doubt for one second he would undo me if I did anything other than what Kalyll asked of me. He turned on his heel and walked out of the chamber. Cylea hesitated for a moment, then left too.

I collapsed on the bed and buried my face in the pillow, emotions crushing inside me, forming a powerful whirlwind that threatened to tear me to pieces.

What you want doesn't matter, Dani.

This realm, these people, even Kalyll himself, existed before I was even a thought in my parents' minds. What right did I have to decide their fate?

You have every *right. Your happiness comes first,* that voice said, the same selfish voice that likely took residence in Wölfe's head. Was it so wrong to listen to it? Wars could be waged with or without me. With or without the Seelie King.

When he comes, if you ask him, he will leave with you.

Did I dare? Could I, for once, put myself and my happiness first?

CHAPTER 29
DANIELLA

I waited for Wölfe, going over the words I would use to convince him to leave all of this behind.

We can be happy elsewhere, just you and me.

Come away. We can go wherever we want.

I sat in bed, twisting the sheets between my hands. The hours wasted away, and he did not come. I stared at the light through the window, watching as dawn approached, fighting the urge to go search for him. I knew once the sun peeked through the horizon, it would be too late. Kalyll would never agree to abandon his people. And he would be disappointed in me if I asked, maybe even enough to lose his fondness for me.

He was loyalty, honor, and duty personified. He would not abide by someone who put her selfish needs first.

My dark side fought to drive me out of bed, to run out the door and search every room until I found him. But the true Dani prevailed, stifling her sobs and wondering if the pressure under her ribs would undo her.

In the end, Wölfe never came.

I wasn't really surprised, not after the events that had

surely upended the entire palace and that must make his presence as king indispensable.

Rubbing my eyes, I got out of bed and went into the washroom. After a quick bath, I got dressed in another Jovinian-style dress. As usual, it had its own matching veil, which I eyed resentfully and reluctantly placed over my face. Even more reluctantly, I hid the pouch with the sleeping potions under my dress.

I was too impatient to wait for Larina, and instead, I headed for Cylea's chamber, the only one whose location I knew. When I got there, I knocked on the door, but received no answer. I stood there for a long moment, my head pounding from the lack of sleep. I didn't know where else to look. I had no idea where kings and generals met to discuss war.

"There you are!" Larina's wings whirred as she flew toward me.

The urgency in her expression sent my heart into overdrive. "Everything all right?"

She nodded uncertainly. "The king and the Sub Rosa need you. They sent me to fetch you. I worried when I didn't find you in your room."

"Lead the way."

"They said to make sure you had the soporific potions with you," she said as she started flying back the way she'd come.

I patted the pouch. "I have them."

She looked relieved at that, as if enough time had been wasted in search of me already. The need for the potions told me everything I needed to know. Suddenly, the desire to run away and never be found assaulted me, but I knew there was nowhere to go, nowhere to hide.

Larina led me to a room off the beaten path. Every member of the Sub Rosa was there, standing around a massive table with a map of Elf-hame painted on its surface. Figurines that represented soldiers were set at even intervals around the "X" that marked Elyndell. I thought such things were restricted to war movies, but it seemed they were truly used to concoct plots of doom and destruction.

Kalyll was leaning into the table, hands pressed to the edge and a deep frown parting his forehead. Everyone appeared as exhausted as I felt. It was clear they hadn't caught a wink of sleep either. Surprisingly, no one had a black eye or split lip. They had all survived Wölfe unscathed. A miracle? Or Kalyll's influence over Wölfe?

Pushing away from the table, Kalyll looked up as I approached. The others did the same. Their weariness seemed to hang in the air like toxic fumes, which I couldn't help but inhale.

"Leave us," Kalyll said, the order unequivocal.

Jeondar filed out first, his expression stern, as if to remind me of his threat. I had no doubt he'd told Kalyll I was having second thoughts. Great!

I wrung my hands together, unsure of what to expect.

In two long strides, he was in front of me. Sighing, he gathered me in his arms and pressed me to him, burying his face in my neck. His strong body trembled with emotion, and his large chest expanded and contracted as he breathed raggedly.

I hugged him back, overwhelmed by this unexpected show

of vulnerability. Leaning my cheek against his, I spoke soothingly.

"We'll get through this," I said. "I lost my father too. I know how hard it is."

He cleared his throat. "I know it's selfish, but I'm glad you're here."

Slowly, he pulled away. He didn't look me in the eye as if he were embarrassed for allowing himself this moment with me. He took a seat on an ornate sofa and stared straight ahead. I joined him, gnawing on my lower lip.

"This morning," he started, his words halting, "a slew of new memories assaulted me."

I swallowed thickly. Wölfe had resolved to let Kalyll remember everything that had happened between us. It seemed he'd stuck to his promise.

Kalyll stood abruptly and walked to the bookshelf on the opposite wall. He placed a hand on one of the shelves, his gaze set on the gilded tomes that rested there.

"You prefer him." The wood groaned as he tightened his grip on the shelf.

I rose to my feet. "That's not true."

He whirled on me. "Then you choose me?"

"I . . ."

His behavior had me baffled. He was acting more like Wölfe than himself, letting anger and frustration control him.

"You what?" The shelf cracked with a splintering sound. Kalyll stared at what he'd done, completely startled. I expected the plank to break completely and collapse under the weight of the books, but surprisingly, it held.

For a moment, I thought I saw a glimpse of sharp claws

instead of nails, but it was too fast to be sure. I searched for a glimpse of Wölfe in his face, but I found none. This was Kalyll, if somehow tainted by the darkness.

His hand flexed as he lowered it to his side.

I took a deep breath and gave him the honest truth. "I don't know who I would choose."

His azure eyes narrowed, revealing how much my words injured him.

"Jeondar told me I don't know you," I said, "and maybe that's true. Maybe, to them, Wölfe is entirely unrecognizable, but not to me. Don't forget who you were when I first met you. I . . ." I hesitated, unsure about admitting the depth of my feelings, even if *he* had. But what point was there in trying to hide what must be painfully obvious? "I fell in love with the prince and the beast. With you."

He stood perfectly still for a long time. When he finally spoke, his words took me aback.

"You like it rough then." He reached for me and pulled me forcefully. My chest collided with his. He pulled my hair back, causing my head to tilt. His full lips hovered over mine.

A jolt of heat ran to my core, and my heart pounded out of control. I felt certain this must be an action incited by Wölfe, but I only detected Kalyll in those lustful features.

He smiled wickedly, then lowered his lips to mine. His kiss was tender, not at all what I was expecting.

When he pulled away, he said, "And I fell in love with you." His expression sobered, and he slowly let me go. "The issue remains . . . Wölfe wants war, and I don't."

"What?" I glanced over the table with its carefully arranged tiny troops. "I thought . . ."

"*He* did that, and I understand why he feels the way he does. He would act this instant, whether or not Mythorne decides to use his son's death as an excuse to declare war. However, I would not act so rashly. There are thousands of lives at stake."

The Sub Rosa seemed to have agreed with Wölfe last night. Had they simply been humoring him? Or had the grim talk of war sobered them?

Kalyll paced. "Now, more than ever, the fate of the realm lies in my hands. I am the king, and the decision falls solely on me. I will not condemn my people to death, nor those who manage to survive the atrocities and destruction of war. I simply can't."

I heard what he left unsaid *and you can't ask me to*.

And he was right. I couldn't. Despite that dark voice in my head. I wasn't a selfish person. I wouldn't have dedicated my life to healing children if I were. As if he'd heard my thoughts, he appealed to my compassionate side.

"War affects everyone. Children lose their parents, are injured, *die*," he said, placing special emphasis on the last word. "I know that if we don't do everything we can to prevent a conflict, we would both regret it. We would not be able to live with ourselves. Time would cause our guilt to fester, to morph into self-hatred. It might even drive us to despise each other. We can't do that to others, to ourselves."

A knot lodged in my throat. He was right, so right. There was nothing decent I could say to argue with him, even if the thought of losing even the smallest part of the male I loved was tearing me apart.

Unable to utter a word, I reached for the pouch under my dress and deposited it on the table next to the tiny armies.

When I lifted my hand, I knocked the figurines down, letting the virtue of my actions fill me with resolve.

Kalyll stood behind me and placed a hand on my shoulder. "It's the right thing to do, Daniella. I love you more for it, and in time, it may do the same for you."

CHAPTER 30
DANIELLA

There was a tiny knock at the door. Kalyll stepped away from me, taking the warmth of his hand with him.

"Come in," he said.

The door opened on its own, and Larina fluttered in. "They are ready for you, my king."

"Thank you, Larina."

Kalyll picked up the pouch from the table. The pixie moved out of the way as he guided me out the door. She followed us as we made our way down the hall. We didn't walk for long. In fact, we went back to the waiting room where we'd been last night.

Kryn was standing by the door, and he urged us forward. "He's waiting," he whispered.

Handing back the pouch, Kalyll asked, "Which vial is for the earl?"

I picked the largest one and handed it to Kryn. The smaller one wouldn't be needed, since Kalyll was doing this willingly.

Lowering my head, I realized that Kalyll had known I would agree with him. He hadn't expected me to deny him or put myself and my interests first. It meant he knew me well, and yet, I couldn't help but resent him for it.

"My father . . . he'll be all right?" Kryn asked. The earl may not have been the most tender father, but Kryn cared about him still.

I smiled gently. "Yes, he will."

Kryn hurried into the room where, presumably, his father was waiting. A moment later, the murmur of conversation seeped through the closed doors.

Larina landed on my shoulder, and her whirring wings quieted. I glanced at her sideways. She made a sheepish face. I nodded to let her know it was all right to perch on me. She weighed nothing at all.

Several minutes passed, and Kalyll started to look impatient. He seemed on the verge of charging into the room when Kryn came out, nodded, and gestured with his hand for us to hurry inside.

"Larina, tell the others," Kryn said.

The pixie bowed her head and flew off my shoulder, making her way down the long corridor.

We followed Kryn and found the earl slumped in an armchair, eyes and mouth half open.

"What now?" Kryn asked.

Kalyll looked at me.

"Remove his jacket," I instructed Kryn, pointing at his father. "You too."

Kalyll blinked away from the slumped figure. That was his biological father sitting there, and I figured this was the closest he'd been to the man since he learned the truth. In a way, he'd lost one father and gained another one. Though I doubted—based on what I knew about this male—that he could fill any type of void.

Quickly, Kalyll removed his jacket, then went to help Kryn as he struggled to maneuver the earl's dead weight. Once they managed to get rid of his jacket, they turned to me.

Wasting no time—the potion would only last for so long—I rolled up the flowing sleeve of the earl's shirt to reveal a pale forearm. With a bob of my head, I instructed Kalyll to do the same. He quickly complied.

"Pull that chair closer," I asked Kryn, pointing to a spot next to his father. "Now, sit," I told Kalyll.

The two now sat side by side, their forearms exposed.

I extended a hand toward Kryn. "Your dagger."

He pulled a beautiful piece from under his long coat and handed it over. It was perfectly balanced, with a ruby set in its hilt.

Without a preamble, I set to work. Magic poured from my left hand to Kalyll's arm. I instructed my power to minimize the pain and bleeding, then applied the same treatment to the earl. With that done, I proceeded to make matching deep incisions on both forearms.

The wounds gaped open, small amounts of blood coming to the surface. Attuning myself to the dark energy I'd experienced in Mount Ruin, I returned the dagger to Kryn and extended my left hand to the earl's wound and my right to Kalyll's.

I felt the shadowdrifter energy in both males. It was strong in the earl and weaker in his son. And, as the book had said, they called to each other.

Immediately, I recognized Wölfe's jagged edges and bravado, his rashness and wild abandon—a darkness that called to my own. My right hand trembled. Biting my lower lip, I hesitated. Kalyll shifted in his seat as if to recall my attention to what I was supposed to be doing.

Don't do it, that voice whispered inside my head. *You'll lose him forever.*

"Daniella," Kalyll said in a pleading voice.

There was no reproach in his dark blue eyes. He knew why I hesitated, knew this wasn't easy for me. In the end, it was this understanding that made it impossible to deny him. His reasons were noble, selfless, and if I went against his wishes, I feared that the side of him who was Kalyll would, one day, stop loving me. The thought was unbearable, even more than knowing I'd never see Wölfe again.

Kalyll searched my face. "Daniella, you have to do this."

"What's the matter?" Kryn asked, glancing nervously toward the door. "You need to hurry."

Pushing all thoughts aside, I concentrated on drawing the dark energy out of Kalyll. He grunted as I got hold of it and coaxed it toward the surface. Wincing, he watched as his veins grew dark and began pulsing.

The energy inside the earl came forward, also disfiguring his arm. I gasped as a plume of shadows lifted from his wound, reaching for Kalyll's. My left hand trembled as I allowed more healing energy to push out with its purifying light. The earl's darkness shriveled back where it belonged. With that under control, I focused on steering the darkness out of Kalyll and into the earl.

My eyes flicked to the king in front of whom I kneeled.

Through gritted teeth, he nodded in approval. The shadow-drifter force that had saved his life last night snaked out of the wound, a searching tendril resembling dark smoke. It didn't take much to guide it toward the earl. It went willingly, like calling to like.

A bit of the earl's own darkness came out to meet it. As the two tendrils connected, Kalyll threw his head back and hissed in pain. Dark veins broke around his eyes, and when they next met mine, I saw Wölfe and felt the sharp hurt my betrayal caused him.

I hesitated for only an instant. Then it was too easy to allow the earl's greater darkness to take Kalyll's weaker one away.

Shouts sounded outside of the room. My head jerked in that direction. A loud bang followed, and the door was thrown open.

A line of guards fronted by Prince Cardian stepped inside.

"Arrest the usurper!" the young prince commanded, pointing at his brother.

The guards rushed in our direction. My focus broke and so did my control over the shadowdrifter energy I was so carefully manipulating. The earl's eyes sprang open. Teeth bared, he jerked to his feet, the darkness within him exploding like a bomb.

The impact hit me square in the chest, and I went flying across the room, a failed and hollow marionette.

CHAPTER 31
DANIELLA

I shook my head. I was on the floor, lying on my back, bits of shadow falling around me like snow. Blinking, I pushed up to my elbows to find both Earl Qierlan and Kalyll on their feet, staring at each other in some sort of battle of wills while shadows throbbed in the middle like a giant heart.

The guards, Kryn, Prince Cardian . . . They stood frozen, gaping in disbelief.

I scrambled to my feet.

Kryn rushed to my side. "What's happening?"

I shook my head.

"Do something!" he urged, but I had no idea what.

Chest pounding, I took a step forward and raised my hands, unsure of whether my healing magic could do anything against the demon energy that pulsed between the two snarling males.

Doing the only thing I could think of, I pushed my hands forward and blasted all of my healing energy at the darkness. As it hit, there was a loud bang, and tatters of light and shadows scattered through the room. I threw my arm up and covered my face.

As the fallout dissipated, I stared at Kalyll. He was hunched over, breathing heavily, dark veins writhing under every visible bit of skin. Dark claws tipped his fingers, and writhing shadows pulled under his feet.

"Bear witness," Cardian shouted over the din. "This is *not* my brother. This is an impostor who has taken his place. Arrest him. Now!"

The guards hesitated. Captain Loraerris—Kalyll's uncle—stood at the head of the group, his expression riddled with confusion.

"Do you need any more proof?" Cardian shouted.

Still looking conflicted, the captain waved his guard to follow through. Kryn took a step forward and blocked their path.

"How dare you take such action against your king? Stand down."

"You have no authority here," Cardian spat.

Kryn ignored him and turned to Captain Loraerris. "This is ridiculous."

The captain spoke firmly, even if his expression betrayed doubt. "This, combined with what happened last night . . ." He shook his head. "My nephew has never possessed such powers." He pushed Kryn out of the way and stepped toward Kalyll.

When Kryn pulled on his shoulder, the captain turned to his guards.

"Arrest him, too," he ordered.

I gasped.

My weak exclamation seemed to remind everyone that I was there.

"Arrest this female, as well. They have many questions to answer."

Two guards came to grab me by the arms. Near the door, Cardian stood, smirking, a satisfied glint in his eyes.

When the guards grabbed Kalyll, I thought he would fight. Instead, his legs shook and he nearly fell. His uncle offered a hand and steadied him. Kalyll blinked. Slowly, his wild features cleared. He glanced around as if waking up from a nightmare.

"What is happening?" he asked, glowering at the guards as they flanked him and took hold of his arms. "What are you doing?"

"Take them to the dungeons," Captain Loraerris ordered.

"Uncle? What is the meaning of this?"

The captain was at a loss for words and glanced at Cardian. The young prince, unlike his uncle, was more than pleased to enlighten Kalyll.

"Stop pretending, impostor, and tell us where my brother is."

"Have you lost your mind? *I am* your brother."

"My brother is not a *shadowdrifter*," Cardian pronounced the word as if he were saying a *piece of trash* instead.

At this mention, the earl shook himself and glanced around, looking like a caged animal. He took in the cut on his arm, his discarded jacket. His green eyes searched Kryn.

"What did you do?" he demanded. "What happened here?"

Cardian narrowed his eyes. "You don't know?"

"I . . . I came to talk to my son. Last I remember, it was only us in this room, and now . . ."

Cardian's eyes moved from side to side as his mind raced

for an explanation. I could well imagine him searching for a way to use the earl to his advantage.

"Please, sit. You seem unwell." Cardian walked further into the room and practically pushed Earl Qierlan into an armchair. He lifted a hand, and without looking up, said, "put them all away."

The earl's attention went to his son as the guards pushed him toward the door.

"Now, Earl Qierlan, please tell me what happened," Cardian raised his voice, distracting the addled male.

The guards pushed us outside the room.

Kalyll roared in anger. "Unhand her!"

He lurched in my direction, murder in his eyes. He was so strong, the guards couldn't hold him. I braced myself for a fight, but Captain Loraerris stepped behind Kalyll and struck a mighty blow against the back of his head. Kalyll's eyes rolled into the back of his head, and his extremities unhinged. Unconscious, he thudded to the floor.

The captain's face twisted in a combination of regret and wariness. It was clear he didn't want to do this, but he saw no other alternative.

"We'll get to the bottom of this," he murmured in a barely audible whisper, and his tone indicated he'd be hunting for arguments to help Kalyll, not hinder him.

As he gestured for the guards to pick Kalyll up, he threw a sidelong glance at Cardian, that told me exactly what I thought of the young prince. He didn't like him. Not one bit.

They threw me inside a cell without ceremony. I heard the thump of Kalyll's body as they flung him inside a separate stall, an indication that some of these guards' sympathies lay with Prince Cardian.

"That's your king," Kryn growled. "Don't think I will forget your faces. You'll pay for this."

When they were done locking my cell, I rushed to the bars, straining to look down the aisle. It seemed they'd put Kalyll in the next cell, and Kryn in the next one over. Kryn had no magic to attempt to break us out, but when Kalyll woke up . . .

I didn't know what would happen. Would he be able to use his shadowdrifter strength to break out? Did he still have it? I had to assume he did, considering the way he'd looked after I blasted the shadows with my healing magic.

And if he did, would the cell be able to hold him? Or would it also be able to suppress his physical power, since it was rooted in magic?

"Godsdamn asshole," Kryn roared, his voice echoing in the cavernous space.

I assumed he was referring to Cardian. Or maybe his father? It was a toss.

Holding my head in my hands, I collapsed on the cot. It seemed I had traded places with Silver. I could only hope he would endeavor to free me the way I had endeavored to free him. Also Jeondar, Cylea, and Arabis . . . They wouldn't let Cardian get away with this. Right?

I wanted to yell across the way and ask Kryn, but there were guards stationed outside. Best if I didn't call any attention to our allies. Though it was ludicrous to hope Cardian wouldn't try to arrest them, too. He knew how loyal they were to Kalyll, and I suspected they might soon be joining our ranks.

Kryn's ranting and cursing didn't stop for the better part of an hour. He only quieted when we heard a rustling from Kalyll's cell.

"*King* Kalyll," he called, placing emphasis on the title. "Order these bastards to let you out."

There was no answer.

"I will personally hang you by the balls," Kryn threatened the guards, "and won't take you down until they shrivel away."

"Kryn," Kalyll said, "that's enough. It's not their fault."

Surprise seemed to silence Kryn, though not for long.

I held my breath, trying to imagine how Kalyll must feel.

"It *is* their fault," he barked. "Bunch of traitors." He grumbled for a few minutes and finally quieted.

We sat in silence for a long while. I pulled at my hair, following the train of events that had brought me here. Only five weeks ago, I was a healer in my realm. My only worries were the welfare of my patients and my simple life. Now, I couldn't even recognize the person I'd become.

God! If I hadn't hesitated, if I had swiftly drawn out Kalyll's darkness, maybe things would have turned out differently. Maybe it—

"Daniella," Kalyll called from the other side of the wall.

Legs wobbling, I stood from the cot and walked closer. Kalyll's large hand was reaching for me. I stuck my hand through the bars. He seized it and interlaced his fingers with mine, exhaling with relief at the touch.

"Did they hurt you?" he asked.

"No."

"And your strength? Did the transfer take too much out of you?" At the last question, he lowered his voice to a tiny whisper that I barely heard.

"I feel better already, but I . . . don't think it worked?" I whispered back in the form of a question.

Through our interlaced hands, I felt him pause.

"Did it? Do you remember what happened?" I asked.

He released my hand and pulled away.

I hugged myself, feeling unanchored.

"I . . . I don't know," he said.

I explained, speaking so quietly that I wondered if he could hear me.

When I was done, he said, "But . . . I don't feel him inside of me anymore."

Apprehension flooded me. I seized a handful of my dress. Maybe it *had* worked. Maybe Wölfe was gone, and it was only my wishful thinking that wanted him to still be there. Of their own accord, tears filled my eyes. I swatted them away, angry at myself. We had bigger problems than my selfish desire for a male that wasn't supposed to exist.

Once more, we grew quiet. I sat back down. Nothing seemed to stir in the dungeon until quiet steps approached. Curiosity drove me to my feet once more. I pressed my face between the bars to find Queen Eithne approaching her son's cell. She spared a withering glance in my direction that seemed to spell the death she'd promised me.

I retreated, my ear straining to hear the whispered conversation that took place between Kalyll and his mother.

My foolish hope that she would free him vanished when

she retreated as quietly as she'd arrived, only the whisper of her steps echoing against the walls.

"What did she say?" Kryn asked. "Is she going to get us out of here?"

Kalyll said nothing, which I figured was answer enough. It seemed not even the queen could help us.

Hours passed until I felt sundown approaching. I gnawed on my thumbnail, feeling both fearful and hopeful. Would Wölfe come back? Would I never see him again? And if I did, would he forgive me for trying to vanish him forever?

My stomach growled in complete contrast with my mood. I couldn't stand the thought of food, but my body seemed to disagree. I had spent a lot of energy today—evidenced by the way my arms shook when I moved them. I needed to replenish my stores. Except there were no signs that anyone intended to feed us.

A strange guttural sound came from Kalyll's cell. I stood, fearfully approached the wall, and listened. Something ripped. Fabric.

My heart thundered.

"Kalyll," Kryn called.

Nothing.

"Kalyll, answer me!"

The answer that came was not from a person. It was a low rumble that sent goosebumps rippling through my body. I'd heard that sound before.

It was the beast.

CHAPTER 32
DANIELLA

The throaty rumble turned into a full roar that rattled my bones.

Trembling, I leaned toward the bars for a better view, staying close to the far wall. The guards abandoned their posts and came running. They stared into Kalyll's cell, their jaws hanging open. The screeching whine of twisting metal filled the space. The guards drew their swords and pointed them forward, looking uncertain and scared.

"Stab him," one of the guards told the other.

"You stab him," the other one said.

"Good idea! Stab your king, why don't you?" Kryn spat.

There was another loud screech from the metal bars.

One of the guards feigned with his sword. "Get back."

A clawed hand swatted at the weapon, and it clattered to the stone floor. The guard quickly picked it up and took several steps back.

"We need reinforcements," he announced, then ran out, raising the alarm.

The second guard hesitated a second too long. The beast stepped out of his cell and roared skyward. I stared, dumbfounded. This wasn't the creature that had chased me into the Zundrokh Barrens. This was a blend between Fae and wolf, a hybrid that walked upright on weirdly jointed legs. The tatters of a shirt hung from his back. He swatted it away. Only the torn pants remained, stretching precariously over bulging muscles.

His body was nearly eight feet tall and covered entirely in fur. A mane of dark blue hair went down the back of his neck and wrapped around the front. He had a long snout full of large, sharp teeth, and two-inch long claws. His eyes glimmered blue as the remaining guard came at him, sword raised. Almost carelessly, the beast swept a massive muscular arm and knocked the guard off his feet. The poor male went flying and hit the far wall with bone-crushing force. He slid to the floor in a limp heap.

The beast turned and looked at me. I took two steps back and swallowed thickly. He took hold of the bars and, as if they were made of putty, bent them out of the way, creating a space big enough for me to walk through.

I didn't dare move. With a shake of his mane, he stepped away and left. I came out of my cell and watched as he freed Kryn, who also hesitated to come out until the beast gave him space.

Kryn hurried to my side, and we warily watched the enormous creature.

"I guess the transfer didn't work," Kryn said.

I opened my mouth to say something sarcastic, but closed it again as the beast slowly morphed back into Kalyll.

What the hell?!

"We don't have time for you two to stand there gaping like idiots. Let's move," he spat in a tone I knew all too well. This wasn't Kalyll. It was Wölfe.

My heart leaped.

Wölfe was still here.

He ignored us and rushed out of the dungeon. Kryn and I exchanged bewildered glances, then snapped out of it and ran after him.

When we made it up the many stone stairs, we stopped and glanced right and left, searching for Wölfe. We caught a glimpse of him as he turned the corner.

"Where is he going?" Kryn asked.

"Probably to tear Cardian to pieces, if I had to guess."

"Shit. Let's go." Kryn took off.

Ahead of us, at a fork with several corridors, Wölfe scented the air, then sharply took a right. His back was rippling as if he were on the verge of shifting, but he was managing to stay in his Fae shape somehow.

"Stop!" Kryn called. "You shouldn't let anyone see you like this. You'll fall right into Cardian's trap."

Kryn was right, but Wölfe wasn't listening to reason.

"You tell him." Kryn pushed me forward. "He'll listen to you. We have to regroup, get out of here, or they'll arrest him again."

I rushed forward, running as fast as I could to catch up with Wölfe.

"You have to listen," I practically yelled. "You want Cardian to win?"

Wölfe's steps seemed to hesitate.

I pressed on. "He will dishonor your father."

He let out a growl and pressed forward.

Shit! Wrong thing to say.

"Cardian will just throw you back in a cell." I tried the Cardian angle again.

"So I'll break out again," he bellowed just as he threw open a set of gold-painted double doors and burst into a room full of people.

A host of what looked like Fae dignitaries sat around a long rectangular table presided over by Cardian. I caught sight of Jeondar sitting among them. Cardian jumped to his feet, causing his chair to tip over. His eyes were wide and scared, but as a few guards peeled away from the walls and surrounded him, he composed his expression into a cocky mask. He looked Wölfe up and down, a satisfied smile slowly stretching his thin mouth.

I shrank inwardly. Wölfe was doing Cardian a favor by appearing here like this. It was clear to see by the appalled expressions of those present.

"You cowardly weasel," Wölfe said in a rumbling voice. "I'm going to kill you." He charged forward, and there was no doubt in my mind that he was about to tear his brother to pieces.

"No," I cried out.

More guards poured into the room from different side doors. Some carried swords, but most of them had magical attacks at the ready. It seemed Cardian had realized that simple weapons weren't going to cut it when dealing with a shadowdrifter.

"Stop him," Cardian cried out, gesturing to a familiar-looking male, the same one I'd met the day we had breakfast with the king and queen. Varamede was his name.

At Cardian's command, Varamede released a jolt of electricity from his fingertips. It crackled white-blue, but before it hit Wölfe, Jeondar released a stream of fiery energy that crashed against the lightning. The collision caused an explosion of energy that scattered wild streams of fire and electricity. People screamed, many ducking under the table for protection. The adjacent wall caught on fire, and a bolt of lightning made a crack in the ceiling.

Varamede flew back, and he fell at Cardian's feet, who barely had time to blink before Wölfe was on him, sharp claws at his neck. He squeezed, drawing blood. Cardian made a strangled sound as his eyes rolled back.

I knew he would be dead in the next instant. Wölfe couldn't be stopped. He was tearing down everything Kalyll had fought for. In a flash, I saw everything destroyed: his reputation, the hope for peace, the glimpse of the future that might have been between us.

With an angry cry, Varamede reared up, reached for Wölfe's leg, and released a blast of electricity. Wölfe's back arched. He convulsed and released his brother, falling to the floor and twitching violently. Varamede held on to Wölfe's ankle, even as his energy sputtered to nothing, and Wölfe went still.

Kryn and I rushed toward him as Varamede scrambled away. Kryn had gotten a guard's sword somewhere, and he used it to fend off more incoming guards as I fell to my knees next to Wölfe. I took his face in my hands and shook him. He opened his eyes, looking bewildered.

"What . . . what . . ." He seemed unable to form a question, and there was something in the depths of his eyes that . . .

"Kalyll?"

He nodded.

What in the world? It seemed the jolt of electricity had sent Wölfe into hiding.

I helped him sit up. He looked around at the chaos that surrounded us. Cardian was retreating through a side door, followed by Varamede and a group of guards that seemed loyal to him, judging by the way they shielded him and urged him forward.

But even as he escaped, more guards poured in.

Jeondar hopped over the table, slid across it, and landed in front of me. "We have to get out of here. Now!"

He helped Kalyll to his feet and ushered him toward the gold-painted door. Pushing forward, Kryn brandished his sword, trying to open a path for us to escape, but there were too many guards. There was no way we could get past all of them.

Someone grabbed me from behind. I screamed. Kalyll went for them, but before he could do anything, I whirled and pressed a hand to the guard's neck. Without thinking, I reached for his life force and drew it into me. He gasped, his face going pale, his lips blue. In horror, I let him go. He collapsed in a heap. Was he dead?

My chest grew tighter, that awful guilt inside me building and building.

Kalyll and Jeondar blinked, confused. But there was no time to explain what I'd done. Especially when a current of energy rippled over the crowd accompanied by a command.

"No one move."

I froze in place, unable to even blink. A petite shape

squeezed through the guards, jumped on top of the table, and walked toward us. Arabis hopped off and landed with grace. She whispered in Kalyll's ear, then Jeondar's, then mine.

"Move."

My entire body seemed to go limp for an instant, then I caught myself.

She hopped back onto the table. "Follow me before they wake up. It won't last long."

We ran over the long table, our shoes scratching its polished surface. Jeondar jumped off first. Once down, he pushed guards out of the way, knocking them down like bowling pins. We navigated over their fallen bodies and got out into the hall, where still more guards crowded. At last, we came out at the other end of the throng and broke into a run.

Behind us, the guards started waking up, if their mumbled curses were any indication. Soon, pursuing steps and shouts chased us. Ahead of us, Silver and Cylea waited. They urged us into a waiting room. Silver shut the door behind us, then used his elemental magic to barricade it with a wall of ice.

"It'll buy you some time," he said.

Cylea was on the other side of the room. "This way." She twisted a sconce on the wall and a panel slid out of the way. We rushed into the secret passage, and I dared think we were safe. Darkness enveloped us as the panel slid back into place.

Jeondar lit the way with a small flame in his hand. We rushed forward, our steps echoing in the cramped space. We came out in an unfamiliar room, a place that looked like some sort of greenhouse, full of plants and with a glass ceiling.

The sweet scent of blooming roses filled the air as we rushed past several bushes and exited through a narrow door that spilled into a garden.

Shouts echoed through the night. Already guards searched for us out here.

Cylea and Silver led the way down a grassy slope. They headed for the tall wall that surrounded the palace. There seemed to be no exit in that direction, but I knew enough not to worry. In minutes, we would be on the other side of that wall, and maybe, just maybe, completely out of Cardian's reach.

At the wall, we slipped behind a line of trees. Kalyll pressed a hand to an indentation in the wall. The stone yielded, the blocks sliding in and out until a narrow gap wide enough for one person opened up.

We had to turn sideways and push ourselves through the six-foot-deep fortification. When we were all out, Kalyll touched the wall again, and the gap closed.

"This way," someone shouted over the battlement.

An arrow whistled past and embedded itself at Arabis's feet. They had spotted us and were shooting to kill.

"Run!" Silver headed toward the city.

More arrows whizzed by. I dared a glance over my shoulder and spotted a host of guards hot on our heels. We might have left a full battalion inside the castle, but they seemed to be all over.

There was no escape.

As we went around the bend, Silver came to an abrupt

stop in front of a busy street. Carriages pulled by majestic horses made their way up and down the passageway. He looked right and left, appearing unsure of where to go. He started to move right when the door to the carriage sitting right in front of him opened, and Naesala Roka stuck her head out.

She gave us her cold, cutting smile and said, "Get in."

CHAPTER 33
DANIELLA

W e all blinked up at her, our expressions no different than if the devil himself had invited us to tea.

"You won't be able to escape," she said in a buttery voice. "They'll have you surrounded in minutes."

"We'll take our chances," Kryn said and started down the road.

"Wait." This from Kalyll. He was looking at the sorceress wearing a deep frown. "I think we can trust her."

"Are you insane?" Kryn demanded. "She's one of Cardian's sycophants."

She blew air through her nose. "Hardly."

Before anyone could argue anymore, Kalyll climbed in, leaving us no choice but to follow. The carriage was large, but not large enough for eight people. We crammed inside, and I ended up next to Naesala. I gave her a withering glare, my hand itching to draw out her energy and turn her into a dry husk.

The carriage moved forward, the ride bumpy over the cobblestone street.

She smiled haughtily, her chin held high, sheets of silken jet-black hair framing her face.

"I left the palace as soon as the commotion started," she said. "Lucky for you."

Kalyll glowered from across the way. If he thought we could trust her, why did he look so tense? My heart thundered as shouts sounded outside.

"Stop!" someone ordered.

A pounding came at the door. We all exchanged panicked glances as the carriage came to a halt.

"No one move or say anything," Naesala whispered as she threw open the door.

I bit my lower lip, cursing Wölfe, who was responsible for making Kalyll think he could trust this horrid female.

"Is there a problem?" Naesala asked as a guard peered in.

His sharp, narrow eyes scanned the compartment, his gaze sliding across us as if we weren't there.

"No problem, Lady Roka." The guard bowed and closed the door. "Search every single one of them," he shouted as we started moving once more.

I exhaled in relief, throwing a reassessing glance at the sorceress. She had used her magic to conceal our presence. Could we really trust her?

We rode in silence for over fifteen minutes. When the carriage came to a stop and we got out, we were inside a large courtyard. A massive wooden door was closing behind us, apparently of its own accord. As I glanced around, I noticed, for the first time, that the carriage had no driver.

Naesala headed toward an arched door, and I stared in astonishment as the harnesses around the horses began to undo themselves. The door to the stables opened and brooms, brushes, and buckets hopped out in a single file. They quickly set to work on cleaning the animals and making them comfortable.

"What the hell?" I scratched my head.

"What the hell, indeed?" Silver stood next to me, looking as weirded out as I felt.

We snapped out of it and followed the others into the gloomy-looking, ominous house. *Witchlights*, the female didn't only look like Morticia Addams, her house did too.

Inside, however, it was a different story. The place was warm and inviting. Fresh flowers in large vases sat at regular intervals, filling the space with a pleasant aroma. Sconces shone with fairy lights, illuminating walls covered in patterned wallpaper and matching furniture. I searched for portraits and found none. Instead, oil paintings of idyllic landscapes hung in gilded frames. I swear only doilies were missing from the surfaces of the wooden furniture.

"Have we crossed into an alternate realm?" Kryn asked under his breath as he eyed the place.

"You must be exhausted." Naesala pointed toward a large wooden staircase that led upstairs. "Make yourselves comfortable. You will find warm baths and clean clothes in your rooms. Come back down for dinner in two hours."

"Our rooms?" Cylea pursed her lips, looking doubtful. Hands on hips, she examined every inch with a frown. "How will we know . . .?" She trailed off when she realized that Naesala had disappeared.

"Where did she go?" Kryn turned a full circle, looking ready to draw his sword.

"Calm down," Kalyll said. "She means us no harm."

"How do you know? What in Erilena's name is going on here?"

Kalyll rubbed his forehead, his bare chest flexing. "She befriended Wölfe. Helped him do this." He pointed at me, at my ears. "He knows she has ulterior motives, but he didn't care."

"What motives?" Jeondar asked.

"I don't know." Kalyll continued rubbing his forehead. A muscle jumped in his jaw.

"Are you all right?" I asked.

He shook his head. "He's trying to push to the forefront."

Kalyll was holding Wölfe back? That had never happened before.

He whirled and turned his back on us. His entire body seemed to quake with effort.

"He's going to blow," Silver warned.

"What do we do?" Arabis made as if to reach for Kalyll, but stopped, a hand frozen in midair.

Kalyll collapsed to one knee. Arabis hurried forward and touched his shoulder. He reared back, teeth bared as he growled. She flinched back. Kalyll curled over his knee, arching his back. He stayed like that for several long moments, then slowly stood, taking several deep breaths. When he faced us, I couldn't tell whether we were looking at Kalyll or Wölfe.

"We should do as Naesala said." He headed for the stairs.

No one moved.

Jeondar sidled toward me and whispered, "Is there still any hope of making him right?"

"How the hell should I know?" The outburst surprised even me. "Look, I'm sorry. I'm no expert in any of this. It all went wrong, and it's not my fault."

Kryn took my hand. My head snapped in his direction as surprise washed over me.

"You did everything you could, Dani," he said. "It *wasn't* your fault. My father, Queen Eithne, Cardian. We can blame all of them, but never you." He let go of my hand and addressed the others. "We could all use some rest and clean clothes. That dungeon smelled like piss."

"But how will we know our rooms?" Cylea asked. "I would love to get out of these uncomfortable clothes." She wore a tight leather outfit with a million straps and daggers.

Silver sauntered up the steps. "Let's find out."

When we made it upstairs to a long hall with many doors, there was no sign of Kalyll. Presumably, he had found his room.

Cylea walked down the carpeted corridor, surveying each door. A sconce a few doors down shone in blue, like her hair.

"Will you look at that? My favorite color." Without pre-amble, she sashayed through the door and disappeared behind it.

A sconce flashed red next.

"I guess that's you," Arabis said, gesturing toward Kryn.

"And that must be Silver," I added when another sconce flashed white. "And we must be screwed, since we all have brown hair."

Jeondar tilted his head to one side and took several steps forward. A door at the end of the hall flung itself open. He glanced over his shoulder and shrugged. Arabis followed and quickly found her own room. When I was the only one left, the door behind me opened slowly, whining a little.

I sighed. No matter the strangeness and chaos of this whole situation, a bath sounded divine. Padding softly, I entered the room and immediately froze.

Kalyll stood naked by the bed. The door slammed shut.

CHAPTER 34
DANIELLA

He glanced up in surprise. My eyes raked the length of his strong body. My knees wobbled.

"I'm . . . I'm sorry. The door just opened and I . . ."

In four long strides, he reached me and wrapped me in his arms, crushing me against his bare skin. He held me for a long moment before his lips started moving ravenously against my neck. His kisses reached my mouth, and he tugged on my lip desperately, his teeth biting down enough to hurt.

I pushed him back, panting. His eyes were dark and full of lust. I shook my head, unsure of what name to use on him.

"Please, slow down, I . . ."

But he didn't listen. Instead, he wrapped an arm around my waist and whirled me towards the bed, his erection tight against my belly, sending a jolt straight to my core. I wanted him. Badly. I wanted to feel him inside me, but it didn't seem right at this moment.

I slipped from his grip and did my best to look him in the eye.

"What is it? You don't want me?" he demanded.

"Oh, I want you." I dared to look down and nearly jumped his bones. "What is there not to want?" I chuckled, nerves twisting tightly inside my stomach.

"Then what's the problem?"

"That I don't know who you are."

"Kalyll. Wölfe. What does it matter? That didn't stop you before." He wrapped a hand around his shaft and held it, taunting me. "Besides, this is the same."

"Wölfe, then," I said as his words cut me deep.

He smiled crookedly, giving nothing away.

"Only Wölfe would say such a thing."

"Are you sure?"

"Of course, I'm sure."

"Then I have you fooled."

Witchlights, I was so confused.

I headed for the door. "I can't stay in the same room with you."

He got there at the same time, and before I could grab the knob, he pressed the length of his body along mine, pushing my front flush to the door.

"Will you make me beg, my queen?" he asked, hands sliding along my sides.

Queen?

It wasn't easy to do, and I felt more of his body than I wanted, but I turned around and faced him.

"In case you haven't noticed," I said, "you're not the king anymore, and well . . . I'm far from being anything that resembles any sort of monarch."

"You're wrong on both accounts."

I gaped at him. "Everyone saw you. They *know*."

"Shh," he pressed a finger to my lips and dragged it down.

He lowered his mouth to mine and kissed me. The kiss started tender enough, but by degrees, it turned more insistent, demanding. Something rose in me to meet his roughness, and I dug my fingernails into his strong pecs, causing him to growl deep in his throat, a delicious sound that let me know he liked it.

Panting, he pulled away. He lifted a hand and wiggled his fingers in front of my face. His claws unsheathed. My eyes widened. Before, they'd seemed to have a mind of their own, but now it appeared as if he'd made them appear on command.

With his other hand, he pulled my dress away from my body and poked a claw into the delicate fabric. With a small tear in place, he easily tore the dress off in one swift motion and flung it to the floor.

His darkened eyes drank me in. Desperately, he tore my bra and panties next, using the same method.

"Now we're even," he said.

Pushing to my tiptoes, I tried to kiss him, but he bypassed my lips, lowered his head, and sucked one of my nipples into his mouth, while his thumb and forefinger squeezed the other one. Both nipples tightened into buds as I threw my head back.

He spent some time savoring my breasts. My arousal and heat gathered between my legs as I squirmed. One of his hands slid downward and cupped me.

"I've been craving your taste," he said, abruptly dropping to his knees.

Draping my legs over his shoulders, he parted my sex open. His tongue lapped up as he made a sound of pleasure.

"Umm, delicious," he said as I sat on his shoulders, my back leaning against the door.

One of his hands held me open for his teasing tongue, while the other one cupped my ass, holding me at just the right height and angle. He was so strong, no effort was required from me to remain propped up as I was.

His tongue explored my folds, following their contour. Each lapping movement ended at the apex, where he paused to suck and flick and drive me crazy when he moved away to keep exploring. My breaths were frantic, punctuated by little moans of protest.

I almost went mad when his tongue entered me and moved inside me. It was no substitute for what I craved most, but it was a feeling like no other and it sent me squirming as I pressed myself against his face.

His chest rumbled with pleasure as he sensed my climax approaching. As I neared the edge, he focused his entire attention on that aching knob, sucking it into his mouth and caressing it with his tongue at the same time.

Waves of ecstasy rolled over me, my skin tightening with shivers of pleasure. I cried out with my head thrown back while my entire body quaked. As the last ripple ravaged me, he rose to his feet and carried me to the bed. He sat me at the edge, then flipped me over. My feet were on the floor as my bent torso draped along the bed.

I barely had time to know what was happening when he thrust his length inside me, causing me to cry out. His fingers dug into my hips as he held me in place and moved in and out, driving himself deep and touching unexplored depths that brought tears of delight to my eyes.

He fucked me hard, as I pushed on my tiptoes to ensure he had full access. I would've never thought it would be possible for me to climax like this, but he soon brought me to the edge once more, his massive girth thrusting against all the right places and then some.

As my second climax arrived, I moaned with abandon, not caring who heard me. He fell forward, his front pressing against my back as his own climax rocked his body like an eruption. He sank sharp fangs into the back of my neck, like an animal taking possession of his female. To my surprise, my orgasm was intensified and prolonged, breaking some sort of record.

When he was done, he lifted my limp, exhausted body and placed it in the middle of the bed. He lay next to me, resting his head on my chest. I sank my fingers into his silky hair and marveled at the amazing chemistry between us.

After a long moment of quiet, I couldn't help but ask, "What are we going to do now?"

"Shh, worry not." He tenderly kissed my eyelids. "Sleep. Just for a bit."

I didn't want to sleep, but it had been a long day and my lids were so heavy I couldn't keep them open.

When I woke up some time later, I heard water running.

A shower?

I followed the sound, padding naked to the door in the back of the room. I pushed it open and steam snaked out. Through the haze, I saw him standing behind a glass door. Indeed, he was taking a shower.

I approached and tentatively opened the door. He had a bar of soap in his hand, which he was rubbing against his chest.

He seemed startled by my presence.

"You need a loofah for that," I said.

"A what?"

I stepped inside, grabbed the bar of soap, and took over for him, sliding it in circles over his strong chest and abs.

Smiling, he planted a quick kiss on my lips.

"Who are you?" I asked.

"Kalyll."

"And earlier?"

"Kalyll."

I shook my head. "I don't—"

He placed a finger across my lips. "I don't want you to worry about it anymore. It's me. It's all me. You don't have to feel bad for loving every aspect of who I am."

"But you don't want to be like this. You want to—"

"I didn't understand," he interrupted. "Now, I do."

"What made you change your mind?"

"Something happened when you tried to draw the darkness out of me. Suddenly, I didn't want it to leave, and I started fighting it. I think that's why Earl Qierlan woke up. He felt me drawing from him, so he fought it. Even if that part of me was dormant for so long, it was always there." He lay his hand over mine and smiled tenderly. "Will you ever forgive me for what I put you through?"

"Well," I pretended to think about it, "I may need payback."

"Payback?" He frowned. "What do you mean?"

"I dunno. Perhaps I'll come up with a plan to make you suffer."

He narrowed his eyes, his expression playful for a moment before it turned serious. "Earlier tonight when you . . ." he started.

I turned away from him and got straight under the spray of the shower. I knew what he was about to say, and I didn't want to talk about it. "You need one of these in the palace. I love showers."

His hand squeezed my shoulder. "When I saw what happened, another memory returned to me. Some of my darkness got inside of you. You discovered it that night . . . with the guard that came to your door."

My heart squeezed as I remembered the guard's withered face. Had I also killed that other male tonight?

"I know it troubles you, Daniella, but the first time was an accident and today . . . you were defending yourself."

"I'm not supposed to take lives. I took an oath."

Like any professional healer in my realm, before I could get my diploma from college, I had to take the Hippocratic Oath.

He turned me around to face him. "You can blame it all on me."

"That's not how it works. We're all responsible for our own actions. Those two guards were only doing their job."

"You have a big heart, melynthi. But sometimes, in our lives, there are situations that are out of our control, and how can you be responsible for that which is not within your influence?"

"But it was. I did it with these hands." I held them up.

"Can you honestly tell me the darkness wasn't in charge?"

"Maybe, but there's something within me that rose to meet it."

"I suppose that means you're not perfect then." He frowned, pretending to look disappointed. "I guess you had me fooled."

I shoved him, poking his hard pec with my fingers.

He let out a hearty laugh, but quickly sobered. "Maybe, like me, you need to learn to embrace *everything* that you are. Time doesn't pass in vain. Life changes us, and you can't remain the same. We grow."

"Shouldn't growth be for the better?"

"Who says it isn't?"

I wanted to contradict him, but he quieted me with a kiss, his mood changing on a dime. In an instant, he was hard, that same savage look in his eyes. I didn't know I wanted more until he lifted me, and my hips wiggled in search of his hardness until I felt it in my center.

We made love, and at least for a moment, I managed to shut out the rest of the world.

CHAPTER 35
DANIELLA

Sometime later, we found ourselves sitting at an ornate table, a sumptuous dinner laid in front of us. The sound of a tiny bell outside our bedrooms had served as an announcement, and we made our way there, following the flickering sconces.

Naesala presided over the table with Kalyll to her right and Jeondar to her left. I sat next to Kalyll followed by Silver and Arabis, while Cylea occupied the space next to Jeondar and Kryn sat straight across from Arabis, those emerald eyes watching her closely. Everyone looked freshly showered and wore comfortable leggings and tunics. Except for Kryn, they all kept peeking in Kalyll's direction, probably wondering which flavor of him had shown up for dinner.

The sorceress waited contently as the dishes floated around, serving slices of roasted meat, vegetables, gravy, dinner rolls, and something that looked suspiciously like a casserole. Leaning forward, I squinted at it, trying to figure out exactly what it was. I'd never seen anything like it in Elf-hame.

"Do you have something against green bean casserole?" Naesala asked.

I straightened, looking apologetic, though I couldn't help my surprise. "Green bean casserole?"

"Yes, did you never have it for Christmas?"

"Christmas?"

I wouldn't have taken Naesala Roka for a Fae with a penchant for human customs, and judging by everyone else's expressions, neither did they.

"I will tell you something that very few people know," she said, spearing a piece of roasted beef. "I think I can trust you."

"And what is that?" Kryn asked, spreading the green bean casserole apart with his fork, as if he expected to find razor blades hidden in it.

"I am human."

Jeondar's fork clattered. He quickly picked it up, looking chagrined. He exchanged a glance with me, acting like I was the authority in everything human and I should balk at the ridiculous claim. But what did I know? She had made me look Fae. She could've done the same to herself.

It was Kalyll who spoke, echoing my thoughts. "Why would you make such a ridiculous claim?"

Naesala looked offended.

"Everyone knows you have lived in Elyndell for nearly two centuries."

Human witches and mages could definitely extend their lives and remain youthful, but they rarely lived past a hundred and fifty years, and they definitely didn't go on looking like thirtysomethings.

"One hundred and eighty-nine years, to be precise," she said. "You weren't even born. I doubt any of you were." She glanced around the table. "But it is rude to point out a lady's age."

"Humans can't live that long," I said. "Even powerful witches."

She wagged her fork. "No one has ever called me that in a long time. Here, they prefer the term sorceress."

"You should get your facts straight before lying," Silver suggested, taking a bite of the casserole and working it around in his mouth. "Um, not too bad."

"It's disgusting," Cylea put in.

"Show some respect," the sorceress snapped. "That is my granddaughter's recipe."

Witchlights! Did she still have a granddaughter who lived in my realm and made green bean casserole for Christmas? That would certainly explain why such a "delicacy" was being served in Elyndell. It might also explain the shower in the bedroom. This was all kinds of messed up.

Arabis had pushed her casserole to the edge of her plate, not daring to touch it. "One way or the other, what difference does it make if you're human or not?"

"A huge difference," Naesala said, steepling her fingers. "When I first came to Elyndell, my biggest priority was to infiltrate the Seelie Court."

Kalyll and the others bristled.

"Wait!" I said. "*Infiltrate?* What are you? Some sort of spy?"

"Precisely."

My jaw dropped, and I blinked several times, hoping to clear the jumble of questions that sprang to life inside my head.

"Humans have spies in Elf-hame, the same way that Fae

have spies in our realm, Dani," she said. "Despite all the treaties, there is fear that one day some despot will get it in their head to take the other realm over. So everyone takes precautions. Ask *him* if you think I'm lying?" She dipped a hand toward Kalyll.

Six pairs of eyes flicked in his direction, including mine. I gave him a *what the hell?* expression.

He ran an index finger down one eyebrow. "It's true."

"Are you sure that's what all those spies are doing?" I asked.

"Of course."

Naesala sighed. "Maybe your people, but the Seelie Court isn't the only one that has spies there, darling. Surely you aren't that ill-informed or naïve."

Kalyll's jaw tightened.

"Mythorne," Arabis said.

The sorceress nodded. "As well as Cardian."

"Cardian?" Kalyll looked completely thrown off his game.

"Yes. Your little brother fancies himself one of those despots we all fear. I'm sure you will have no trouble picturing him as such. It's the reason I got close to him. I needed to keep a close eye on him. But he doesn't trust easily. He would backstab his entire family, so it isn't hard to imagine why he keeps his cards close to his breast. But lately, I've been able to glean enough to be very concerned."

"And why is that?" Kalyll asked.

"He is working with Mythorne."

"What?!" everyone asked in unison.

Kalyll shook his head. "That's impossible. Our moles would've noticed something."

"Cardian is smarter than you give him credit for," she said.

He still looked skeptical.

"He was the one who let Garrik in."

"No. No. No." Kalyll gripped the edge of the table, unable to believe that his own brother had caused the king's death.

"Garrik's objective was to kill you and your father."

Kalyll shook, and we all watched with concern, wondering if Wölfe would make an appearance and knock all the pretty dishes off the table in a fit of rage. But somehow, he controlled himself, though not without a visible effort.

"You see," Naesala continued, "he knew about you. He knew you weren't Beathan's son. He learned the truth while you were gone on a quest to Mount Ruin."

Silver's already pale skin went the color of paper. "That means that I . . . I helped Cardian." His breathing grew ragged as anger assaulted him. He was furious with himself for the role he'd played and for the dire consequences his seemingly unrelated actions had wrought.

Naesala seemed surprised at this. Apparently, her spying endeavors hadn't gone as far as to figure out where the damning information had come from.

"At any rate," the sorceress continued, "Cardian saw his opportunity. He knew that with your father out of the way, he could become king if he was able to prove you weren't Beathan's son."

"He will *not* be king," Kalyll pronounced with unmovable surety.

Like me, everyone else threw questioning glances in his direction. He had sounded certain before, but why? What did he know that we didn't?

"They saw you, Kalyll," Kryn said.

"It doesn't matter."

"It does matter." Jeondar opened his mouth to argue further, but Kalyll cut him off with a raised hand.

"It *doesn't* matter."

For a long moment during which no one dared disturb him, Kalyll's azure gaze rested on a fixed spot on the far wall. A million thoughts seemed to race through his mind before he finally spoke.

"If Mythorne has an alliance with my brother and expects Cardian to become king, where does that leave the war the Unseelie King has been threatening against the southern lands?"

"I knew you were smart," Naesala said. "Now, you're getting to the heart of the matter."

"There is no war. At least not the one we've been expecting," Arabis said, the realization barely an audible whisper.

Silver frowned. "So then, what exactly are they planning?"

Panic filled my chest. Did they want to attack my realm? Was that the reason Naesala was involved?

No.

That would be the worst decision in the history of bad decisions. No matter how greedy or stupid Cardian and Mythorne were, they couldn't risk nuclear weapons. They knew about nuclear weapons, right? I was about to ask when Kalyll spoke.

"The courts. They want to take over the courts."

The sorceress raised a perfectly manicured eyebrow. "I'd hoped the rumors of your shrewd mind were true. You don't know how glad I am to find that they are. I may be human at heart, but I've lived in Elf-hame for a very long time, and I would hate for two idiots to destroy its beauty and peace. Neither Mythorne nor Cardian are content with the minor courts' alliances. They want to control them, want access to their resources so they can become richer and more powerful."

Jeondar squeezed his fork, knuckles turning white. He set it down carefully. "My father and I won't take any such threat lightly. Let it be known that the Summer Court would fight to defend our land and our people."

"The Fall King would fight too," Kryn assured us.

"And the Spring King," Cylea put in.

"And let's not forget the Winter King," Silver added.

Jeondar shook his head. "Which means an all-out war if Cardian gets away with this."

"Cardian will be in a dungeon soon," Kalyll said. "And he will spend the rest of his long, miserable life in one."

"How are you so sure?" Kryn asked.

I turned my shoulders to face Kalyll squarely. "That's what *I* want to know. What aren't you telling us?"

"I will explain." Kalyll picked up his fork and started eating, explaining nothing. "Everyone should eat and rest. We will need to lie low for a few days."

Kryn tightened a fist on the table. "How is doing nothing going to help?"

"We need to wait until my father's send off to The Blessed Fields."

"Not wise." Naesala shook her head. "I can assure you Cardian will not follow any sort of protocol or wait the appropriate amount of mourning time before he proclaims himself king."

Kalyll speared a green bean, lifted the fork up, and twirled it around, examining the mushy vegetable. In the end, he set it down, clearly unconvinced by its edible nature.

"You do not cook this . . . casserole?" he asked, looking at me with a disappointed frown.

"No," I said, "but I cook kickass potions that can render you useless, as we all know."

Naesala pursed her lips. "Oh, a fierce woman after my own heart."

Silver hid a cough behind his napkin.

"You've got a mouth on you, *woman*," Kalyll said, a glint in his eyes.

"I also got a boot that can go up your ass."

Kalyll or Wölfe—I wasn't sure—let out a rumbling growl.

"Is this some sort of foreplay or something?" Kryn asked. "Because if it is, I've lost my appetite." He threw a sidelong glance at Arabis, who was caught stealing a glance at him. Cheeks lighting up, she snapped her attention back to her plate.

Kryn cleared his throat and shifted in his seat. "Um," he seemed to search for a different topic and found it. He turned to the sorceress. "There's still one thing that doesn't make sense. How can we believe anything you've said when you've based it all on a lie? You can't be human. Humans don't live as long as you have. How do you explain that?"

Naesala tapped the side of her nose. "That's for me to know, and for you to find out."

Her gaze cut in my direction as she gave me a tiny, almost imperceptible smile.

CHAPTER 36
DANIELLA

After dinner, Naesala ushered us into a study with décor that made me think of some old-fashioned library in my realm. There were supple leather sofas, Persian rugs, paintings depicting landscapes that seemed to connect with me and gave me a sense of belonging. It was an interesting feeling, the sensation of being drawn to my own land.

Whiskey tumblers magically filled themselves and made their way into our hands. After a couple of rounds, the sorceress disappeared.

Sipping my drink, I glanced around the room, feeling at odds with the situation. Everyone seemed relaxed, drowsily enjoying their drinks, and kicked back comfortably in their chairs, while I sat at the edge of a large sofa, ready to bolt.

I felt sure a host of guards would burst in and seize us all at any moment. But this bunch didn't seem to break a sweat unless demons were at their heels. One benefit of being well-seasoned warriors, I supposed.

"Relax, Dani." Cylea sipped her whiskey and lifted the tumbler in my direction.

"That obvious, huh?" I shrugged.

Kalyll was standing by the fireplace, a hand resting on the

mantel, while he stared at the fire, the flames dancing in the depths of his midnight eyes. He'd been standing there for several minutes and hadn't moved a muscle. Not one. It was unsettling. No one dared intrude into his silence. I couldn't help but detect a pattern.

"Ease your mind, Dani," Arabis put it. "No one will find us here. They would never think to look in Naesala's house."

"How are you so sure?"

"Cardian believes she's one of his loyal fanatics. He thinks himself too clever, but he has no clue the sorceress has been playing this game for much longer than he has."

"I agree with Arabis," Kryn said. "He's an arrogant fuck."

"I do wonder what's happening at the palace." Cylea's clear blue eyes lifted to look at Kalyll as she tapped a fingernail against her tumbler. She was reclined on a wingback chair, feet up on an ottoman. "I imagine Cardian in front of a mirror, trying on the king's crown for size."

Everyone waited to see if Kalyll would react to the comment, but he went on staring at the fire, sharing nothing about what he'd said earlier.

Sitting tight didn't at all seem to fit his friends' style, but he didn't appear concerned about them. There were other things on his mind, for sure.

Kryn downed his whiskey in one go and slammed the tumbler on a side table. He pushed to the edge of his chair, looking as if instead of whiskey, he'd drunk a shot of courage.

"Arabis," his emerald eyes met her blue ones, "can I talk to you?"

She crossed her legs, making herself comfortable around a set of cushions. "Sure. Speak."

"In private."

"You and I have nothing to talk about in private. Whatever you need to say to me, you can say it here."

Silver stretched his arms over his head. "I haven't slept in a nice bed for too long. I think I'll retire."

Cylea jumped to her feet. "Me, too."

Jeondar followed, and I wasn't about to be the only one left here with Kryn, Arabis, and the statue named Kalyll, so I did the same.

Arabis suddenly didn't look so comfortable at the thought of staying alone with Kryn. She rose to her feet. "Bed sounds like a great idea."

"When are you going to stop avoiding me?" Kryn demanded.

"When are you going to stop hounding me?"

"Hounding you?"

As the others filed out the door, Kalyll seemed to wake. He blinked several times, then looked chagrined as what was happening in the room sank in. He sidled toward the door without saying a word, grabbed my hand, and pulled me along.

"No, you're not leaving this room until we talk." Behind us, Kryn shut the door to make sure Arabis couldn't escape.

"We've talked enough. When will this harassment stop?" Arabis shot back.

"This never ends well." Kalyll led me down the hall, shaking his head as he glanced over his shoulder.

"Why is Arabis so angry at Kryn?"

"You don't know?"

I shook my head.

"I thought she might've told you."

"She hasn't."

"I guess it's still painful for her."

I waited for an explanation. Kalyll was quiet for a moment, and I thought he might leave my curiosity hanging, but at last, he spoke.

"You may know enough about Kryn's father—my father," he gave a derisive laugh, "to understand that he's a very proud, very elitist snob."

"Yes, I think I do."

"When he found out that Kryn was in love with someone without a title, he adamantly opposed the relationship. Kryn was ready to propose."

"He was?"

Kalyll nodded. "Unfortunately, he decided to wait. He hoped to change his father's mind. Instead, Earl Qierlan publicly announced Kryn's engagement to a duchess."

"Oh, no."

"Kryn couldn't reach Arabis before she heard the news. She suffered terrible mockery at the hands of shallow court mischief-makers, friends of the duchess, you see. She told them they were wrong, that Kryn loved her, but then the duchess herself confirmed the engagement. She had the earl's word, after all. Arabis still stood by Kryn and told the cruel female she had her facts wrong. Arabis asked me for a travel token to go to the Fall Court. I tried to convince her to wait, but she wouldn't have it, so I gave it to her, which I still regret. When she got there, Kryn wasn't there. He was on his way here. On horseback. He had no access to a token. The earl made sure of that. When Earl Qierlan learned that Arabis was there looking for his son, he took it upon himself to destroy whatever he could. She never shared with anyone exactly what he told her, but it was enough to drive her away."

"What a bastard!"

"Indeed." He paused. "After that, Arabis didn't return to Elyndell. In fact, she remained absent for over two years."

"Are you serious?"

"I believe it took her that long to harden her heart to him. As soon as she returned, Kryn found her, talked to her, but nothing sufficed. No explanation, no matter how heartfelt, has changed her stance."

"It's awful," I said.

"That it is."

We walked the rest of the way in silence, as I wondered if, today, Kryn would be able to find the right words to say to win Arabis back.

Back in our assigned bedroom, I went into the closet and came out with a set of flannel pajamas with unicorns imprinted on them.

"This reminds me of my scrubs," I said, nervous hands undoing the buttons of the soft top. I still didn't feel comfortable around Kalyll. He barely seemed to be in control of his dark power, which made him volatile and apparently extremely aroused. Not that I could complain in that department.

Except, he still seemed distracted, and only removed his boots and lay on the bed, crossing one foot over the other and interlacing his fingers on top of his stomach. I padded back to the closet and changed. When I went back, his eyes were closed and his breathing steady.

He looked terribly peaceful and handsome in his sleep. I

crawled into bed quietly, relishing the cozy feel of the pajamas and marveling at the unexpected peacefulness. Just hours ago, I was sure we would end up slaughtered by Cardian's soldiers, and now . . .

I allowed myself to relax. My mind whirled with questions. I slowly sifted through them, putting away those I knew I couldn't answer. There was no point in having a sleepless night over things outside of my control. Eventually, I started to drift off into sleep.

A light tap had my eyes springing open.

Kalyll stood by the door, boots *and* a cloak in hand, his back to me.

I sat up. "Where are you going?"

He cursed under his breath and looked over his shoulder. "Go to sleep."

"The hell with that." I threw the covers aside and got out of bed. "Wherever you're going, I'm going with you. You're not leaving me here."

He put the boots and cloak on a chair and approached me. "You need not worry about me. I will be back shortly." The words were polite, but not his tone.

"Forgive me if I don't trust you," I said, "but you're acting fishy, so, like I said, I'm going with you."

"You obstinate creature."

I jutted out a hip and put a hand on it.

He appraised me up and down. "Do you mean to protect me with your . . . colorful unicorns?"

"Don't be an ass. You aren't aware of the joys of flannel. Besides, have you forgotten," I flexed my fingers in front of him, "that I now have a power no one should sneer at?" I had no idea where my bravado was coming from, but I was glad for it. No way was he leaving without me.

"Does that mean you're ready to embrace what you've become?"

I hesitated.

"I didn't think so." He turned to leave.

"Dammit! You will not treat me like some weak female," I said, my anger rising.

"But you *are* weak." He whirled and grabbed my wrist, squeezing it tightly.

I bit my tongue to stop a cry that would prove his point. The pressure around my wrist increased until I felt sure my bones would snap.

"Let me go, you bastard."

He only squeezed harder. "What are you going to do about it?"

Anger and darkness surged inside of me. I slapped my free hand on his neck and dug my nails in, pulling his energy toward me. Kalyll's face paled in seconds. At first, his expression was satisfied, but it quickly turned to panic. He let go of my wrist and made a croaking sound in the back of his throat. It was that tiny noise that snapped me back to my senses.

Hissing in a breath, I took a step back and pulled both hands to my chest, feeling terrified of myself.

"I'm sorry. I'm sorry."

Kalyll wobbled on his feet. I wrapped my arms around him, held him in place, and gave back the energy I'd taken.

"I didn't mean to do that," I said. "I'm sorry."

It took him a moment to recover himself, but when he did, he cleared his throat and spoke.

"I'm glad you did."

I pulled away to better look at him. "Are you crazy? I could've killed you."

"And I would have deserved it. I was being a bastard, as you well pointed out."

A realization hit me. "You were taunting me. You wanted me to do that."

He managed a crooked smile. "If you promise to do that to anyone who gets in our path, you can come with me."

CHAPTER 37
DANIELLA

We both wore heavy cloaks with hoods that obscured our faces. My heart was hammering out of control as we wended down a dark alley, its wet cobblestones shining with moonlight. It seemed there had been a light shower moments before. The smell of wet earth that saturated the air also attested to it.

Kalyll hadn't told me where we were going, and even if he had, the sword strapped to his back—one that he'd taken down from a wall display in Naesala's house—didn't make me feel reassured about our destination. It was a terrible idea to be stalking around a city where his head would fetch a pretty price if he was spotted.

He put a hand up, gesturing for me to stop. I stood behind him as he peered around the mouth of the alley. Abruptly, he pulled back in, driving me deeper into the shadows. A group of palace soldiers appeared, weapons at the ready, eyes searching every corner. One of them peered into the alley. My hands itched with my dark power and the desire to clap them over the male's mouth, so he couldn't utter a sound. Kalyll's arm held me steady.

I was sure the guard would see us, but his gaze traveled right over us, and he moved on. We stayed there for a few long minutes until we couldn't hear their steps anymore. It wasn't until we pulled away from the wall that I realized Kalyll had swathed us in thick shadows. As moonlight illuminated his face, I saw those dark veins around his eyes.

He guided me from alley to alley, avoiding the main roads. I thought of them as alleys in the least strict sense of the word—only because they were narrow. In truth, they didn't resemble any alleys I knew. They were narrow passages heavily draped with vines, some with cobblestone paths, but most carpeted by thick moss. Here and there, roots stuck out from adjacent dwellings, those magical structures that seemed to have grown from the ground rather than have been built by any living person.

In one particularly narrow corridor, Kalyll stopped and stood very still. He took my hand in his. "Don't move."

What looked like a rough wall, but was actually a thick tree trunk, stood in front of us. He whispered something under his breath, some sort of conjuration if I'd ever heard one.

The texture of the tree changed, growing blurry or transparent. I peered closer, squinting. Before I could decide what it was, Kalyll pulled me through. I felt a phantom touch all over my body as we crossed into . . . into what?

A dark place with circular walls took form around us. Oil lamps resting inside small crevices cast a dim illumination.

I glanced around, hands tingling, ready to grab and drain anyone or anything that might come at us. My eyes adjusted slowly while my heart kept its crazy rhythm. Despite the million nervous questions inside me, I didn't dare utter a single sound.

By degrees, a dark pool materialized on the floor. It shone like a puddle of oil, pulling in what little light came from the lamps. Circles rippled from the center, growing outward. I interlaced my fingers with Kalyll's. He wouldn't take us to the pit of hell, would he? Because that was what this place made me think of. For some reason, it felt worse than that cave in Mount Ruin. The hairs on my arms and neck stood on end.

The ripples continued, then something appeared right in the middle. It rose slowly, impossibly white and suspiciously shaped like a head. I swallowed.

Oh yeah, it was a head, all right, then a neck, and then the rest of the body.

The female—because the figure was female, if the shape of its breasts was any indication—was fully wrapped in pristine white gossamer from head to toe and floated lightly above the rippling puddle.

Kalyll bowed his head. I'd never seen him defer this way to anyone—not even his father. It made me shiver.

"Envoy," he said reverently.

Envoy?!

This was the person . . . creature . . . being . . . who had told Kalyll I was the only one who would be able to take the shadowdrifter darkness out of him, the reason I'd been kidnapped and dragged to Mount Ruin.

Some freaking Envoy! She'd been absolutely wrong. Why had Kalyll come to see her again? Hopefully to chop her head off for lying.

"Vague as always," Kalyll said, as if picking up on an old conversation. His deep voice seemed to take a turn around the chamber, then come back with renewed force.

Vague as always. Vague as always. Vague as always.

Yet, you are back, a voice neither male nor female responded.

As the words were spoken, the Envoy's mouth opened, revealing a full set of sharp teeth, blood and rot coating each of them. A set of all-black eyes not much different from the pool of oil at her feet looked on. They seemed to take in everything in the cavernous space.

I blinked, and again, the Envoy's face was nothing but a conglomeration of encircling rags—no mouth or eyes in sight. My insides trembled, along with my knees.

"My brother . . . will I prevail over him?" Kalyll asked.

He should die, but he won't.

Again, that horrible mouth and eyes flashed, then were gone. Was she inside my head making me see things? And what the hell did that mean? *He should die, but he won't?* I had a feeling the Envoy was a demon. Some of them were huge tricksters.

"Will the one I love be my queen?" he asked next.

I sucked in a breath. I wasn't prepared to hear the answer to that question or think about the implications of a positive response. If I became queen, my life in my realm would be forfeited. Was I ready for that? And why ask this of all things?

You will mourn her. Deeply.

Kalyll took a step forward, going pale. "What?!"

The words hit me like a blow to the chest.

Mourn?

I was going to die? This had to be some kind of joke, and the Envoy was nothing more than a charlatan adept at parlor tricks.

"You lie!" Kalyll bellowed.

The Envoy said nothing, just floated over the dark pool, her gossamer rags swaying slightly as if in a gentle breeze, though the air was as still as death.

"I don't want to be king if she's not by my side." His voice boomed, bouncing against the walls and echoing throughout.

The pool rippled again as the Envoy began descending into it. Those hideous features flashed in my mind once more as she disappeared, though this time her mouth was twisted in a grotesque smile that seemed to promise the fate she'd proclaimed for me.

"You will tell me how to save her!" Kalyll made as if to walk into the pool and seize the ghostly creature.

My heart leaped, and I leaped with it, grabbing his arm. I knew that if he went into the pool, he would never get out again. But he was too strong for me, and I saw only one way to stop him. I let my power out and dug my fingers into his bicep, drawing his life energy into me and immediately stopping when he went limp. I tried to ease his fall as best as I could, but he was heavy and thudded to the stone floor. My ribs ached with that strange pressure I was slowly starting to understand.

Like earlier tonight, he went deathly pale. I willed the pool to disappear quickly, and when it finally did, I gave him back his energy, the pressure under my ribs easing slightly.

He lifted his head. Coughing, he thumped his chest.

"I had to stop you," I said. "I don't think it would have been wise to go in there with her."

He sat up and hung his head.

"I'll be all right," I said. "Nothing will happen to me."

His eyes lifted and met mine. "She wasn't wrong before."

"What did she say to you?"

"She guided me to you."

"How?"

"When I asked her if the shadowdrifter curse could be cured, she said only the sister of the only human I considered my friend could help me."

Kalyll had met my sister, Toni, before he met me. That was how he'd known who the Envoy meant.

"But I didn't cure you," I said. "Not completely."

"She never used the word *cure*. Anyway, you did more than that. You saved my life."

I pushed away from him and rose to my feet. "So you're saying you believe her? You think I'm going to die?"

Slowly, he stood and stared at the place where the pool had been, anger flashing in his eyes. "I refuse to believe that."

"Okay, so then what?"

"Death is not the only reason that would cause me to mourn you."

I opened my mouth but didn't know what to say.

"You don't belong in Elf-hame, and I've thought long and hard . . . I have no right to ask you to stay here. You should go back to your realm, to your family, to your life."

My heart seemed to shrink. "Are you asking me to leave?"

He let out a sharp exhale and turned toward the wall where the entrance had been. "We should go. It isn't wise to linger here."

I didn't argue. I simply followed him on shaky legs. I knew the time to choose had come, and I wasn't ready for it.

CHAPTER 38
DANIELLA

I slept on the large bed alone. After we got back, Kalyll didn't come into the room with me. Instead, he stayed downstairs, saying he needed time to think. I didn't argue with him. There were many questions circling inside my own head that I needed to contemplate.

For four hours I lay on my back, staring at the ceiling, weighing everything up. I was in love with Kalyll, with Wölfe, with every bit of who the male was, and there was no doubt in my mind that, if I left him, I would never feel the same way again for anyone. The mere thought of having a different male as a partner made me nauseated. Literally.

I'd never had such intense feelings for anyone, and it made me realize that Kalyll was right. I was truly his mate, which meant that if I left him and went back home, I would condemn myself to never having a family of my own, even if I married.

Yes, I would have my mom, my siblings, and my career, but deep in my heart, I knew it wouldn't be enough.

And yet, how could I stay with him when my life would be nothing but a single page in the book of Kalyll's life? Only twenty years from now, I would start looking old while he remained unchanged. Then soon after that, I would be dead, and what would he have but pain and the mourning the Envoy had promised him?

And maybe that was exactly what she'd been talking about. Warning him against a too-short life with me, one that would be followed by loss and grief.

The thought of putting him through that was nothing but selfish, and much worse than giving him a chance to find someone else, a female of his kind who could offer him companionship for as long as he needed it.

At some point during the night—all of these thoughts hammering inside my head—I fell asleep. No more than an hour had passed, and I was once more awake, aware that the sun had come out, even if its light didn't pierce the thick curtains.

Begrudgingly, I got out of bed, a decision set in my heart.

I took a quick shower and got dressed. I descended the stairs and made my way toward the dining room, where I found everyone sitting around a luscious breakfast, a feast of Fae and human proportions. There were eggs, bacon, pastries, fruit, bagels, waffles, pancakes, buttermilk biscuits, and more.

"What are these things called?" Silver speared a waffle and held it up in the air. "They have become my favorite." There was a thick layer of syrup already on his plate, which served as a bed for what I assumed must be his second waffle.

"I have no idea," Cylea said. "But I like these ones more." She pointed toward a stack of biscuits. "They are flaky and buttery, and I'm sure they have them in The Blessed Fields. What's your favorite, Jeondar?"

"I like it all," the Summer Court prince said.

Everyone seemed cheery and at ease as they tasted the

different foods, as if they were true delicacies. Only Kryn and Arabis seemed on edge, which made me think their argument from last night hadn't ended well.

Only Kalyll was missing, and for a moment, I panicked, wondering if he'd left the house again.

"Where's Kalyll?" I asked without preamble. "I need to talk to him."

They all turned to look at me, realizing for the first time that I was there.

"Good morning to you, too," Kryn said, putting on a smile that seemed forced.

I stared him down, and he rolled his eyes.

"He's in the study," Cylea provided. "He said he'd join us soon. Come, let's get you something to eat."

But I didn't want to delay matters any longer, so I turned to exit the dining room, just as Kalyll walked in.

He looked exhausted, with huge circles under his eyes, and deeper hollows under his strong cheekbones. His appearance was worse than the day he battled Caorthannach and nearly died.

The chatter around the table and the clatter of silverware stopped as everyone noticed his appearance.

"Is everything all right?" Jeondar asked, pushing to his feet.

"We went to see the Envoy last night," he said.

"What? Without us?" Kryn demanded. "You could have been captured."

"We were not."

Kryn's face grew red. It was clear he wanted to keep arguing, but what was the point?

Arabis pushed her plate away. "Curious, I'm not hungry anymore. What did that bitch say this time?"

"Don't tell me." Cylea put a hand up in the air. "We have to dive into the depths of Rotwyn Lake, lop Huskul's head off, and bathe in its blood to ensure that you remain king."

I had no idea what she was talking about, but it sounded about as fun as another trip to Mount Ruin.

"Nothing as entertaining as that," Kalyll said. "She said I will be king, as I already knew, but she also said something else."

I shook my head. "Wait? She never said you would be king. What are you talking about?"

He turned to me. "I'm sorry, Daniella. I should have explained. When you ask the Envoy a question, she will reply with a *no* if that is the answer. However, if the answer is *yes*, her reply will be something else, something that relates to your question somehow. So when I asked her if I would prevail over my brother and she responded that *he should die, but he won't*, that means her answer was *yes*."

"So when you asked her if the one you love would become your queen, and she said that you would mourn her, that means that . . ." I couldn't finish.

That couldn't be. I had decided not to stay, and now more than ever, after understanding exactly what the Envoy had meant, I needed to leave. I couldn't become his queen so that he would end up alone when my inevitably short life expired.

Everyone around the table looked at me as if I'd already died and become a ghost.

"Stop looking at me like that," I snapped. "I'm not becoming queen, and Kalyll will mourn me for other reasons. I'm leaving. I'm going back to my realm. You don't need me anymore. Kalyll can control his shadowdrifter powers now." At least, it seemed that way.

Kalyll grabbed my elbow and made me face him. "I'm barely in control, and all it would take for me to lose my precarious hold would be to lose you. Have you forgotten I couldn't spend even one night away from you? If you leave, you'll find yourself back at square one."

"You can't." I shook my head. "You have to let me go. I have nothing to offer you. I will be dead before you even have time to blink. You will not mourn a dead queen."

"You're not going to die. I won't let that happen."

I let out a bitter laugh. "And how are you going to manage that?"

As if on cue, Naesala walked in. "I will let you in on my little longevity secret, dear, and he will owe me another big favor."

CHAPTER 39
DANIELLA

"**F**ucking Erilena!" Silver said, kicking back in his chair. "This is getting interesting." All he needed was a bucket of popcorn to complete his *edge-of-his-seat* fascination.

Kalyll threw a cold glower in his direction, but Silver didn't seem in the least bit affected by it.

Suddenly, I lost it. I whirled on Kalyll, anger boiling in my chest. "So I have no choice? Is that it? You tell me that if I go back to my realm, you'll bring me right back and that you've decided I'll live forever and become your queen. You haven't even asked me to marry you?"

"Yeah," Cylea put in. "The girl needs some *bling-bling*, like they say in her realm."

Kalyll looked flustered. "I'll get you a ring. The biggest one you can imagine."

"Are you all crazy?" I shouted. "I don't care about a fucking ring. I care about not becoming your little marionette. I have a right to decide what I want to do with my life, but your entitled princely ass," I poked a finger into his chest, "thinks you can just snap your fingers, and I'll dance to the tune. You're seriously wrong, mister." I poked him again.

"I told you. You should've asked." Naesala meandered

around the table, picking up a crispy piece of bacon and crunching on it.

"Then stick this in my heart." Kalyll pulled a dagger from his belt and extended it in my direction, hilt-first.

"I have been there, and done that," Silver said. "Did I get that expression right?"

Cylea put a hand up and made a so-so gesture. "Been there, done that. Snappier, you know?"

I threw my hands up in the air. "Infuriating brats!" I knocked Kalyll's hand out of the way. "And overly dramatic. I'm not stabbing you in the heart." I stomped out of the room.

Kalyll followed. "I'm not being dramatic, dammit. It's the only way to stop me from coming after you if you go back to your realm."

"Then grow a pair and exert better control over your instincts."

"Ouch," I heard Silver say behind me. I was starting to wish I'd left him in that cell. He was quickly getting comfortable and back to his old self.

I reached the stairs and started climbing.

"So that's it? You're leaving me?"

Emotions ricocheting inside my chest, I froze mid-step. My chest pumped up and down, and that pressure in my chest seemed to push out. My ribs ached. My fucking heart felt about to explode. The floor below me trembled. I threw my arms out and held on to the handrail. Head swimming, I imagined there must be an earthquake, but it was only my emotions. The earth wasn't shaking.

"Yes, I am," I answered, climbed the rest of the stairs, and locked myself in my room.

I paced in front of the bed until I lost track of time. When a knock came at the door, I spun, ready for another fight. The knob turned, and the door cracked open.

What the hell? I had locked it.

Naesala waltzed in. Of course, this enchanted house wouldn't stop its mistress from going where she pleased. She made her way to the bed, sat at the edge, and patted the spot next to her.

I gave her a dirty look. "I still haven't forgotten what you put me through."

"Did your mama never tell you that holding a grudge would sour your soul?"

"No. My mom is Italian. Grudge is her middle name."

She laughed. "Hopefully, it isn't yours." After a pause, she said, "You realize you're not going anywhere, right?"

"And who's going to stop me?" I really was losing it. I was helpless against Kalyll's or any of his friends' strength. They could stop me if they wanted.

"No one needs to stop you. You know that because you *will* stay."

"You're bat-shit crazy." I crossed my arms.

"Am I?"

"Yes."

"The Envoy is never wrong. Never. You will be queen."

"No," I said between clenched teeth, anger and impotence building and building.

"Don't fight it. Accept your destiny."

"But she said he would . . . mourn me."

"All that may mean is that you'll die before he does, which could be many years from now after I teach you what you must do to extend your life. Or it could mean a host of other things. The Envoy is at once exact and vague."

Exact and vague. How quaint!

If Naesala could help me prolong my life, the mourning bit could, indeed, mean something else than what I'd first imagined, which . . . changed everything. Well, sort of. The idea of becoming queen wasn't something that sat well with me.

The sorceress smiled knowingly. "Now, will you take that male out of his misery? I don't need him moping around the house. Besides, there are other matters that need his attention."

I nodded.

"And about your face . . . I can change that when you're ready. Though I have a feeling you aren't there yet."

I nodded again.

She stood and padded out of the room, leaving me feeling like a total idiot.

It seemed the woman could read me like an open book and seemed to know what I wanted before I did.

I'd been so sure I would go back home and pick up the pieces of my past life. But who was I kidding? I couldn't stay away from Kalyll any more than he could stay away from me. Ever since Jeondar, Kryn, and Silver took me from Pharowyn, I'd been by his side, falling deeper and deeper in love with him. And after Mount Ruin, when I thought I'd lost him, I'd been devastated. I cried myself to sleep, fearing I would never see him again, knowing that my life without him would be an endless string of meaningless days—one after the other, pining for the love I'd lost.

On the brink of tears, I rushed to the door and pulled it open. I nearly ran into Kalyll, who was standing in the hall looking as if he'd been trying to decide whether to knock or hold back. His eyes were red, and his fists held tightly at his sides.

Without a word, I threw myself at him and wrapped my arms around his neck. He was frozen for an instant, then seemed to deflate a little as he let out a long exhale. His arms came around me, then crushed me into his chest. He nuzzled the side of his head against my neck, and we held each other for a long time.

Then he lifted me off the floor, took a twirl that landed us inside the room, slammed the door with his foot, and started kissing me. He devoured me in bursts of tenderness and passion. We stripped each other naked with desperate hands, tugging at cords and buttons and belts.

He made love to me and fucked me thoroughly all at the same time. He was rough when he needed to be, when I wanted him to be, and gentle when I felt vulnerable. He was Kalyll and Wölfe all at once and then separately. The perfect combination of everything I loved about him.

We came together for the first time, and our shared ecstasy was like a salve to our strained tempers. I didn't know what the future would hold, but any second I was allowed to spend by his side was worth whatever anyone could throw at us.

CHAPTER 40
DANIELLA

On the fourth day of hiding in Naesala's house, the sorceress came into the study, wearing a tight expression.

Kalyll and I sat on the leather sofa, leaning on each other as we read and sipped tea. The last few days had been bliss, but from the looks of it, they had come to an end. We had been waiting for a bit of news, and it seemed it had arrived. Kalyll had finally explained his plan, but no one felt as confident as he did about it.

"Gray smoke billows in the blue sky," Naesala announced.

Kalyll sat up and put his book away. His teeth tightened, a muscle ticking in his jaw. I placed a hand on his back, my heart squeezing as I saw his pain.

The smoke in the sky meant his father's body had been burned over the pyre, releasing his soul to The Blessed Fields.

And Kalyll hadn't been there.

"It's time to go then." He rose and offered me his hand. He helped me to my feet, offering me a gentle smile. "Ready, my queen?"

I frowned. It would take a long time for me to get used to that title, even coming from him.

We told the others, then went to our room to get ready.

Kalyll dressed in a stately long coat in royal blue and gold, and I wore a gown more in keeping with Elyndell's style, not the Jovinian one, which meant I wore no veil. As for the others . . . they wore the uniform of the king's personal guard.

Naesala had no trouble providing the clothes, even on short notice. There seemed to be no limit to what the sorceress could accomplish. She also provided a carriage, one that was definitely fit for a Fae king. It was pulled by six white horses, gilded in gold, and large enough to fit everyone. Though Kryn and Silver had insisted on driving.

"Thank you for everything." Kalyll inclined his head toward the sorceress. "I owe you more than one debt."

He glanced at me sideways. The promise to teach me how to extend my life was the second debt, which Kalyll seemed to value the most. Though I appreciated the first one more. She'd helped us when Cardian's guards were hot on our heels and had possibly saved the entire kingdom from a ruthless leader—not a trivial thing to repay.

"I hope it all goes well up there." Naesala's eyes flicked in what I assumed was the direction of the palace. "I will call upon you when the time is right, King Kalyll." She made a slight bow, and there was nothing but deep respect in her gesture. She turned her pale eyes on me. "I'll be seeing you for our lessons."

All I could do was nod. I couldn't lie. The thought of prolonging my life scared me. I'd always thought of my time as brief, finite. My entire mindset had to change, and it would take some getting used to . . . not to think of things like rushed bucket lists and retirement savings—not that money would ever be an issue for a queen.

We climbed into the carriage. Arabis, Cylea, and Jeondar were already there, looking sharp in their uniforms. We started moving. The large gate opened and we rolled out of the sorceress's house and onto the street.

We cut across the city undisturbed, though our ostentatious ride garnered the interest of many people. When we arrived at the palace's open gates, Kalyll got out and walked straight to the guards. Kryn jumped off the driver's seat and joined him.

I watched through the open door, heart in my throat.

At the sight of Kalyll, the two guards stared in near horror. I almost felt sorry for them. They had no idea what to do. Their orders were probably to kill Kalyll if he showed his face, but that was easier said than done. They'd known him as their future king for who knew how long.

When five other guards joined in, however, I started to question Kalyll's decision to show up so openly.

"Arrest him," a guard I'd seen with Cardian called out.

No one moved.

Kalyll stood passively, looking back with Wölfe's predatory eyes. "Lieutenant Preleth, why don't *you* arrest me yourself?"

The lieutenant didn't move a muscle.

"I assure you, anyone who stands in my way will find themselves tried and judged for obstructing your king."

The guards all exchanged panicked looks. The lieutenant glanced back and frantically started waving more guards over.

Kalyll stepped forward and grabbed the male by the neck. He squeezed and lifted him off the ground, letting his pointed canines flash. He wasn't hiding who he was anymore. It was all part of the crazy plan.

"He's a shadowdrifter," the lieutenant croaked, fighting uselessly against Kalyll's hold. "He's not our king. Arrest him, you idiots."

Still, no one interfered.

With a jerk of his arm, Kalyll cast the lieutenant aside. The male crashed in a heap against the gate, coughing and sputtering.

"Take me to *Prince* Cardian," Kalyll ordered.

A female guard stepped forward and inclined her head. "I will escort you. Move out of the way," she called over her shoulder at the line of guards who blocked the entrance. When no one obeyed, she pointed at two guards. "You and you, make them move."

They hesitated for only an instant, but then ran back and started urging the other guards to break formation. No one put up a real fight. In truth, they had no reason to. Kalyll wanted to enter the palace. Once inside, it would be easier to arrest him when Cardian inevitably gave the order.

Jeondar, Cylea, Silver, and Arabis jumped off the carriage.

Kalyll came to the door, offered me a hand, and said, "We shall walk. The front gardens are beautiful."

I returned his smile, took his hand, and maneuvered the narrow step, trying not to get tangled in my dress. He folded my hand into the crook of his arm and started forward.

"Perhaps your personal guard should stay behind," the female said nervously.

"They're coming with me." He left no room for argument.

She nodded. Then the palace guards surrounded us, and I couldn't help but wonder how Kalyll could remain so calm and look so in control in the face of so many weapons and hostile glares.

As we walked toward the main door, the guards stared at us sideways, some appearing intimidated rather than unfriendly. No doubt, they knew what Kalyll and his retinue were capable of. More than just their number would be needed to stop them. They had fought a legion of demons in Mount Ruin. A dozen gate guards would be child's play.

Still, when we entered the palace and more guards surrounded us, I didn't feel so certain anymore. I knew Kalyll didn't want to hurt his people, and he vowed to do everything in his power not to. He even made the others promise that if a fight broke out, they weren't to kill anyone, only incapacitate.

"What is this all about?" a commanding voice called from a side hall as the commotion built.

Captain Loraerris pressed past the line of guards and came to a stop when he took in his nephew.

"King Kalyll." He pressed a hand to his chest and bowed.

The guards exchanged surprised glances.

From the looks of it, Kalyll's mother was holding her end of the deal. She had come to visit Kalyll in the dungeon and explained what he needed to do in order to keep the throne from Cardian's dark intentions. The instructions had included waiting until the gray smoke of King Beathan's pyre clouded the morning sky.

And now it seemed it also had included getting her brother into the scheme. Was he the only one? Were there others among these guards who would fight for Kalyll if it came to it? I could only hope they understood that allowing Cardian to become king spelled disaster for everyone.

Finally, Kalyll had made the queen promise that she wouldn't hurt a hair on my little head. I was sure she wasn't happy about that one, and I wondered if she would still make me pay for this mess one way or another.

"I am here to see Prince Cardian," Kalyll reiterated.

"Of course, my king. Please, follow this way."

When the guards started to move, Captain Loraerris glared back. "Stay here."

Both relieved and confused, they remained.

We traversed several halls until I felt utterly lost. Finally, we reached a set of grand doors. They stood tall and wide, adorned with intricate carvings and sparkling jewels. They were made of a shimmering, iridescent material that seemed to shift and change colors. The large handles were carved from sparkling crystal. Tall, slender columns flanked either side and seemed to twist and turn as if alive. As we moved closer to the doors, the air itself seemed to thrum with a sense of otherworldly energy.

"These lead to the throne room," Kalyll said, noticing my awed expression.

It was clear the grand doors were not just a means of entrance, but also a symbol of the otherworldly magic and majesty of the Fae.

I shivered.

The huge doors splayed open with a clank as if announcing our presence. Captain Loraerris allowed Kalyll to lead the way, a subtle way to signal his authority. A group of people lounged on the dais at the end of the room, talking loudly and laughing. At first, they appeared unconcerned by our presence, but by degrees, they quieted. Cardian, who was sitting on the throne wearing a too-big jeweled crown, jumped to his feet.

"What is the meaning of this, Captain Loraerris?" he demanded, gesturing to Varamede, who quickly scrambled to his feet from a layer of cushions next to the throne.

The captain ignored the question, and as we stopped several feet from the dais, he moved off to the side, bowing respectfully at Kalyll.

Cardian's face turned red with fury. "You will regret this betrayal, uncle. I see your loyalties lie with the false king."

The captain stood impassive, staring straight ahead, not a hint of concern disturbing his stern features.

"Guards!" Cardian shouted. Steps sounded right and left. Doors flew open and his personal guard poured in, caging us in.

My fingers flexed at my sides, itching like never before. Kryn cracked his neck, a crooked smile slashing his face. He was burning for a fight, while all I could do was pray that this ended without bloodshed.

Kalyll inched his hand to the hilt of his sword. "You make a mockery of father's throne and crown. It seems you never learned they aren't toys."

"The only mockery here is you, an impostor of tainted blood."

For an instant, Kalyll's gaze cut to one side as if he noticed something. "I am no impostor, brother. I'm the legitimate heir to the Seelie throne, but I will forgive your rash behavior, as you don't know all the details."

Cardian laughed and peered down at his brother with pity. "No one here will believe your lies. There are witnesses that—"

Steps echoed from the side, the very spot where Kalyll's gaze had wandered just a moment ago. Queen Eithne appeared. She wore an all-white dress and held her head down as she approached. Her hands were linked, poised below her breasts, her entire demeanor communicating a sense of resignation.

"Mother, what are you doing here?" Cardian demanded.

She continued walking without a word, stopped in front of Kalyll, and placed a hand on his cheek. She smiled benevolently, looking nothing like the conniving woman I'd met. Now, she was the picture of motherly abnegation.

With a sigh, she faced Cardian and approached the dais. Her attention lingered on those lounging on the cushions. Distaste shaped her features.

"I owe everyone an explanation," she said, then climbed one step and turned away from the dais.

Guards and a number of court members had made their way in, driven by curiosity or, perhaps, the queen's insinuation and cunning.

"My husband's untimely death is the only culprit for this unfortunate confusion. He and I had a plan in place for when succession became necessary. We dreamed of retiring together and allowing our eldest son to take his rightful place, but now that has been taken away from us."

Cardian descended the steps and spoke to his mother through clenched teeth. "What are you doing? Whatever it is, it won't work. Your impostor son belongs in a dungeon."

The queen gave him an understanding smile that only made him tremble with rage. "I wish you had talked to me before you acted so rashly, but I understand your desire to protect your father's legacy. It is only our fault for keeping secrets and letting prejudice dictate our actions. Her voice rose as she fully addressed the crowd again. "Beathan was a shadowdrifter."

A gasp rose in the crowd.

"You're lying." Cardian took the queen by the arm and shook her. "You are lying, you cheating whore."

Kalyll wedged himself between his mother and brother, forcing him to let her go. "You now know the truth, brother. There is no need to worry about the Adanorin legacy anymore. That is now my job, and you may step down and resume your . . . customary activities."

"This is ridiculous," Cardian shouted. "There have never been shadowdrifters in the Adanorin line. Never. Our legacy isn't tainted by such foul blood."

The queen looked sad. "This was precisely the type of judgment your father feared. Just the reason he kept it a secret, as many before him did."

"You're crazy if you think the court will swallow such lies and allow this beast," he pointed at Kalyll, "to take the throne and lead them. It would be a disgrace." His head swiveled from side to side, eyes scanning the crowd, practically begging someone to agree with him.

But despite what they might believe about shadowdrifters, no one said anything.

Appearing trapped, Cardian peered sharply over his shoulder.

One of his friends stood from his bed of cushions. He opened his mouth, but when he met Kalyll's deathly glare, he closed it again. Instead, he took several steps back and disappeared behind a heavy curtain. Cardian looked to Varamede next. I halfway expected him to also run away, but he proved to have a stronger spine.

"How convenient for you to wait until King Beathan's body burned in the pyre to come forth," Varamede said.

"Uh, yes, yes," Cardian interjected. "Without his body, we cannot prove he wasn't a shadowdrifter. Indeed, very convenient for you."

"I would *not* make a mockery of my father's funeral, as I knew you would if I showed my face here," Kalyll said. "It is time for you to abandon this little game, Cardian." He leaned forward and whispered his next words. "I know you let Garrik Mythorne in and are responsible for father's death. Consider yourself lucky I'm letting you live."

Cardian's entire face paled. He took several shaky steps back, looking like cornered prey. "Kill him," he shouted, hiding behind Varamede.

The prince's lackey didn't hesitate at the order. In fact, he smiled as if he relished the opportunity.

"No," I cried out.

Acting without thinking, I threw my arms forward, even as Kalyll turned to liquid shadows to avoid the impact.

Power burst from my hands and crashed against Varamede's electric attack, meeting it halfway. People screamed and retreated.

I stared, dumbfounded, at the stream of energy that poured from me. A hint of the yellow light I recognized as my healing magic poured forth, but there was darkness intertwined with it.

The pressure that had lived inside my chest since the day I killed that poor guard in my chamber loosened as the strange force spilled out, steadily driving Varamede's magic back. At last, I understood what I'd been harboring inside me, some sort of twisted life energy that could be turned into an even greater weapon.

Clenching my jaw, I leaned forward and invited whatever had been living in my chest to take its leave. My attack intensified, growing brighter, pushing Varamede's lightning back and causing him to falter. I wanted him dead. I was willing to kill to protect the male I loved.

But Varamede didn't cower. Instead, he redoubled his efforts.

A mass of tittering energy built between us, growing and growing. I squinted as the huge ball of cracking electricity and swirling light and shadows pushed its way to encompass the entire dais.

The pressure in my chest quickly withered to nothing, and my energy faltered. The pulsing mass pushed closer to me, then my strength gave out, and the miasma shattered against my chest.

"No no no!" I heard Kalyll's mournful screams. They stretched away in the distance as I collapsed and lost consciousness.

CHAPTER 41
KALYLL

"No no no!" I fell to my knees in front of her limp body. "A healer. Now," I bellowed.

Arabis was on her knees on the other side, fingers at Daniella's wrist. "She's alive. Hurry, get someone!"

Jeondar was pushing through the guards, yelling, "Where is a damn healer?"

I gently lifted her and cradled her to me. My eyes desperately roved over her face, searching for her vivacity and wit, but her features were blank.

Please. Please. Please, I begged any god that would listen. *Don't take her from me.*

You will mourn her. Deeply.

The Envoy's words roared in my head. But she couldn't die. We had to marry. She had to be my queen.

"Daniella." I lowered my head and pressed a soft kiss to her lips. I stared intently at her lashes. They didn't flutter. Not one bit. "Where is the healer?" My throat went raw as I shouted.

I was dimly aware of the chaos around me. Swords clashed. Some sort of battle, but I didn't care. All I cared about was her.

"Jeondar," Arabis called, her fingers still on Daniella's small wrist. "Hurry up!"

I met Arabis's blue eyes. They were wide, with pinpricks of black in the middle. She understood my question.

"She's slipping away, Kalyll."

"No."

I couldn't allow it. Desperation made me pull out my dagger. I didn't know what drove me, but I cut a wound in my hand and a matching one in hers.

Arabis stared in confusion but said nothing.

The demon energy had saved me in Mount Ruin. It *had* to save her now.

I placed my hand next to hers, urging my power to go into my mate.

Nothing happened. I clasped her hand, our blood energy mingling.

Nothing still.

Arabis shook her head.

I growled in anger, my entire body trembling.

"This way. Hurry up!" Jeondar came pushing through the crowd, a robed healer at his heels.

Thank the gods.

Arabis moved out of the way and the healer took her place. I pulled away too to let him do his job. He noticed the blood and picked up her hand.

"Not that," I snapped. "That's nothing. Lightning hit her. Varamede's lightning."

I would kill him. I would rip his head off with my bare hands for hurting her.

The healer regrouped. Hovering his hands over Daniella's body, he assessed her injuries. The color drained from his face.

"Save her!" I commanded him.

The male placed his hands on her chest and closed his eyes. He shook a little, and I could only guess he was pouring healing energy into her. There was no glow like when Daniella used her powers. He didn't possess her kind of power, a power that seemed to have morphed or grown into something else.

The healer's eyes sprang open, but Daniella's remained closed.

"Why are you stopping?" I demanded.

He shook his head. "There isn't enough life force left in her."

"Don't you dare tell me that. Save. Her."

He closed his eyes again, tried again.

Arabis let out a sob, then pressed a hand to her mouth to trap it in.

"No. no. NO." I was losing her.

The healer hung his head, looking defeated, and I wanted to tear him to pieces for being a fucking failure. My claws unsheathed. I raked them over the marble floor, causing a high-pitched screech. I was on the verge of pouncing when Silver stepped up, directed his hands at Daniella, and sent a stream of freezing energy into her.

The fight went out of me as I stared at her frozen shape, a light sheet of frost laying on her skin.

Arabis looked up. "Silver . . . What did you . . . ?"

"She isn't dead," he said. "She isn't dead."

Daniella lay on a high, narrow bed, her hands crossed over her chest. She was as beautiful as ever, her features just as kind and warm. Except that if I touched her . . . none of that warmth remained.

She was frozen, the small spark of life still left in her suspended. Silver had saved her, if this could be called that. Other healers had been called and none had been able to bring her back. They were all useless. Completely useless.

I'd ordered the tower chamber cleared for her. The windows were open to let daylight in. She would never be a prisoner again. I hated myself for caging her, for bringing her to this end.

Cylea and Arabis came into the room. They placed two large vases full of flowers on pedestals at each side of the bed. They retired quietly to wait for me outside. We were leaving. I hated to be apart from her for even a few hours, but we had a couple of weasels to hunt down.

In the confusion, Cardian and Varamede had scurried away. I had no idea where they'd gone, but I would find them. They'd been at large for two days now, and I couldn't wait any longer, lest the trail go cold. They would die along with Kellam Mythorne, who was already, according to my generals' intelligence, preparing his troops.

My own troops stood in wait for my command. The bastard didn't know what he was doing. The rage they'd unleashed in me would be their doom.

"I will avenge you, melynthi. I promise you." I kissed her forehead and went in search of Cardian and Varamede. When I found them, they would learn the true meaning of pain.

HE NEEDS MY HELP,
BUT HE'LL BE MY DOWNFALL.

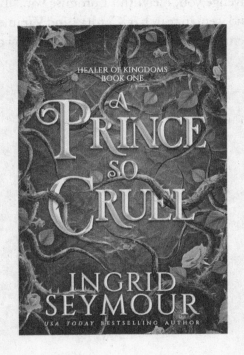

OUT NOW.

HEADLINE
ETERNAL

THE FINAL BATTLE LOOMS,
AND OUR LOVE HANGS IN THE BALANCE.

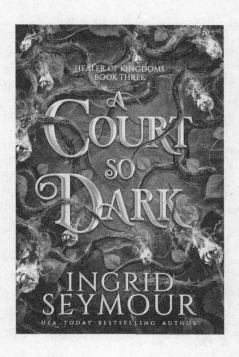

OUT NOW.

HEADLINE
ETERNAL

FIND YOUR HEART'S DESIRE...

VISIT OUR WEBSITE: www.headlineeternal.com
FIND US ON FACEBOOK: facebook.com/eternalromance
CONNECT WITH US ON X: @eternal_books
FOLLOW US ON INSTAGRAM: @headlineeternal
EMAIL US: eternalromance@headline.co.uk